He tottered erect. Snow had gotten under his parka hood. It began to melt, trickling over his ribs in search of a really good place to refreeze. "Great greasy comets," said Flandry, "I might have been sitting in the Everest House with a bucket of champagne, lying to some beautiful wench about my exploits, but no, I had to come here and do 'em!"

Slowly, he dragged himself up the hill, crouched on its brow, and peered through an unnecessarily cold and thorny bush.

And that's when the real fun began . . .
They seemed to rise from weeds and snowdrifts, as if the earth had spewed them. Noiselessly they rushed in, a dozen white scuttering shapes as big as police dogs. . . . A heavy body landed between his shoulders. He went down and felt jaws rip his leather coat. . . . Two of the animals were on him. . . . The Terran drove his knife into a hairy shoulder. The animal writhed free, leaving him weaponless. Now they were piling on him where he lay.

Flandry didn't think it was any fun at all. . . .

ALSO BY POUL ANDERSON:

THE PEREGRINE
THE MAN WHO COUNTS
THE NIGHT FACE
THE LONG WAY HOME
QUESTION AND ANSWER
ENSIGN FLANDRY
AGENT OF THE TERRAN EMPIRE

All from ACE Science Fiction

SF

FLANDRY OF TERRA

Poul Anderson

SF
ace books
A Division of Charter Communications Inc.
A GROSSET & DUNLAP COMPANY
360 Park Avenue South
New York, New York 10010

"A Message in Secret," *Fantastic,* December, 1959. Copyright © 1959 by Ziff-Davis Publications, Inc. Reprinted 1961 by Ace Books, Inc., under the title "Mayday Orbit."

"The Plague of Master," *Fantastic Stories of Imagination,* December, 1960 and January, 1961, under the title "A Plague of Masters." Copyright © 1960 by Ziff-Davis Publications, Inc. Reprinted 1961 by Ace Books, Inc., under the title "Earthman, Go Home!"

"The Game of Glory," *Venture Science Fiction,* March 1958. Copyright © 1957 by Fantasy House, Inc.

An Ace Book
Cover art by Michael Whelan
First Ace printing: July 1979

2 4 6 8 0 9 7 5 3
Manufactured in the United States of America

To
Jack and Norma Vance
—and, by all means, Johnny

CONTENTS

THE GAME OF
GLORY

A murdered man on a winter planet gave Flandry his first clue. Until then, he had only known that a monster fled Conjumar in a poisoned wreck of a spaceship, which might have gone twenty light-years before killing its pilot but could surely never have crossed the Spican marches to refuge.

And the trouble was—even for the Terran Empire, which contained an estimated four million stars—a sphere twenty light-years across held a devil's number of suns.

Flandry went through motions. He sent such few agents as could be spared from other jobs, for they were desperately under-manned in the frontier provinces, to make inquiries on the more likely planets within that range. Of course they drew blanks. Probability was stacked against them. Even if they actually visited whatever world the fugitive had landed on, he would be lying low for a while.

Flandry swore, recalled his men to more urgent tasks, and put the monster under filed-but-not-forgotten. Two years went by. He was sent to Betelgeuse and discovered how to lie to a telepath. He slipped into the Merseian Empire itself, wormed and blackmailed until he found a suit-

able planet (uninhabited, terrestroid, set aside as a
hunting preserve of the aristocrats) and got home
again: whereafter the Terran Navy quietly built an
advanced base there and Flandry wondered if the
same thing had happened on his side of the fence.
He went to Terra on leave, was invited to the
perpetual banquet of the Lyonid family, spent
three epochal months, and was never quite sure
whether he seduced the wrong man's wife or she
him. At any rate, he fought a reluctant duel, gave
up hope of early promotion to rear admiral, and
accepted re-assignment to the Spican province.

Thus it was he found himself on Brae.

This world had been more or less independent
until a few months ago. Then military considera-
tions forced the establishment of a new base in the
region. It did not have to be Brae, but Brae was
asked, by a provincial governor who thought its
people would be delighted at the extra trade and
protection. The Braean High Temple, which had
long watched its old culture and religion sapped
by Terran influence, declined. One does not decline an Imperial invitation. It was repeated. And
again it was refused. The provincial governor insisted. Brae said it would go over his head and
appeal to the Emperor himself. The governor,
who did not want attention drawn to his precise
mode of government, called for local Navy help.

Wherefore Flandry walked through smashed
ruins under a red dwarf sun, with a few
snowflakes falling like blood drops out of great
clotted clouds. He was directing the usual project
in cases like this—search, inquiry, more search,
more interrogation, until the irreconcilables had
been found and exiled, the safely collaboration-
minded plugged into a governmental framework.

But when the blaster crashed, he whirled and ran toward the noise as if to some obscure salvation.

"Sir!" cried the sergeant of his escort. "Sir, not there—snipers, terrorists—*wait!*"

Flandry leaped the stump of a wall, zigzagged across a slushy street, and crouched behind a wrecked flyer. His own handgun was out, weaving around; his eyes flickered in habitual caution. On a small plaza ahead of him stood a squad of Imperial marines. They must have been on routine patrol when someone had fired at them from one of the surrounding houses. They responded with tiger precision. A tracer dart, flipped from a belt almost the moment the shot came, followed the trail of ions to a certain facade. A rover bomb leaped from its shoulder-borne rack, and the entire front wall of the house went up in shards. Before the explosion ended, the squad attacked. Some of the debris struck their helmets as they charged.

Flandry drifted to the plaza. He saw now why the men's reaction was to obliterate: it was an invariable rule when a marine was bushwacked dead.

He stooped over the victim. This was a young fellow, African-descended, with husky shoulders; but his skin had gone gray. He gripped his magnetic rifle in drilled reflex (or was it only a convulsive clutching at his mother's breast, as a dying man's mouth will try to suck again?) and stared through frog-like goggles on a turtle-like helmet. He was not, after all, dead yet. His blood bubbled from a stomach ripped open, losing itself in muddy snow. Under that dim sun, it looked black.

Flandry glanced up. His escort had surrounded

him, though their faces turned wistfully toward the *crump-crump* of blasters and bomb guns. They were marines too.

"Get him to a hospital," said Flandry.

"No use, sir," answered the sergeant. "He'd be dead before we arrived. We've no revival equipment here yet, either, or stuff to keep him functional till they can grow another belly on him."

Flandry nodded and hunkered down by the boy. "Can I help you son?" he asked, as gently as might be.

The wide lips shinned back from shining teeth. "Ah, ah, ah," he gasped. "It's him in Uhunhu that knows." The eyes wallowed in their sockets. "Ai!" 'List nay, they said. Nay let recruiters 'list you . . . damned Empire . . . even to gain warskill, don't 'list . . . shall freedom come from slave-masters, asked he in Uhunhu. He and his 'ull teach what we must know, see you?" The boy's free hand closed wildly on Flandry's. "D'you understand?"

"Yes," said Flandry. "It's all right. Go to sleep."

"Ai, ai, look at her up there, grinning—" Despite himself, Flandry stared skyward. He was crouched by a fountain, which now held merely icicles. A slender column rose from the center, and on top of it the nude statue of a girl. She was not really human, she had legs too long, and a tail and pouch and sleek fur, but Flandry had not often seen such dancing loveliness trapped in metal; she was springtime and a first trembling kiss under windy poplars. The waning marine screamed.

"Leave me 'lone, leave me 'lone, you up there, leave me 'lone! Stop grinning! I 'listed for to learn how to make Nyanza free, you hear up there, don't lap my blood so fast. It's nay my fault I made more slaves. I wanted to be free too! Get your teeth out of me, girl . . . mother, mother, don't eat me, mother—" Presently the boy died.

Captain Sir Dominic Flandry, Intelligence Corps, Imperial Terrestrial Navy, squatted beside him, under the fountain, while the marines blew down another house or two for good measure. A squadron of full-armored infantry did a belt-flit overhead, like jointed faceless dolls. A stringed instrument keened from a window across the square: Flandry did not know the Braean scale, the music might be dirge or defiance or ballad or coded signal.

He asked finally: "Anyone know where this chap was from?"

His escort looked blank. "A colonial, sir, judging from the accent," ventured one of the privates. "We sign on a lot, you know."

"Tell me more," snapped Flandry. He brooded a while longer. "There'll be records, of course."

His task had suddenly shifted. He would have to leave another man in charge here and check the dead boy's home himself, so great was the personnel shortage. Those delirious babblings could mean much or nothing. Most likely nothing, but civilization was spread hideously thin out here, where the stars faded toward barbarism, and the Empire of Merseia beyond, and the great unmapped Galactic night beyond that.

As yet he did not think of the monster, only that he was lonesome among his fellow conquerors and would be glad to get off on a one-man mission. At least a world bearing some Africans might be decently warm.

He shivered and got up and left the square. His

escort trudged around him, their slung rifles pointed at a thin blue sky. Behind them the girl on the fountain smiled.

II

The planet was five parsecs from Brae. It was the third of an otherwise uninteresting F5 dwarf, its official name was Nyanza, it had been colonized some 500 years back during the breakup of the Commonwealth. It had been made an Imperial client about a century ago, a few abortive revolts were crushed, now there was only a resident— which meant a trouble-free but unimportant and little visited world. The population was estimated at 10^7. That was all the microfiles had to say about Nyanza.

Flandry had checked them after identifying the murdered man, who turned out to be Thomas Umbolu, 19, free-born commoner of Jairnovaunt on Nyanza, no dependents, no personal oaths or obligations of fealty, religion "Christian variant," height 1.82 meter, weight 84 kilos, blood type O plus. . . . His service record was clean, though only one year old. A routine pre-induction hypno had shown no serious disaffection; but of course that hadn't meant a damn thing since the techniques of deep conditioning became general knowledge; it was just another bureaucratic ritual.

Flandry took a high-speed flitter and ran from Brae. Even so, the enforced idleness of the trip was long enough to remind him acutely that he had been celibate for weeks. He spent a good deal of the time in calisthenics. It bored him rigid, but a trim body had saved his life more than once and made it easy to get bed partners on softened worlds like Terra.

When the robopilot said they were going into approach, he spent some while dressing himself. An Intelligence officer had wide latitude as regards uniforms, and Flandry took more advantage of it than most. After due consideration, he clad his tall form in peacock-blue tunic, with white cross-belts and as much gold braid as regulations would stand; red sash and matched guns, needler and blaster; iridescent white trousers; soft black boots of authentic Terran beefleather. He hung a scarlet cloak from his shoulders and cocked a winged naval cap on his long sleek head. Surveying himself in the mirror, he saw a lean sunlamp-browned face, gray eyes, seal-brown hair and mustache, straight nose, high cheekbones: yes, he knew his last plasmecosmetic job had made his face too handsome, but somehow never got around to changing it again. He put a cigarette between his lips, adjusted its jaunty angle with care, inhaled it to light, and went to his pilot's seat. Not that he had anything to do with the actual piloting.

Nyanza shone before him, the clearest and most beautiful blue of his life, streaked with white cloud-belts and shuddering with great auroral streamers. He spotted two moons, a smallish one close in and a large one further out. He scowled. Where were the land masses? His robot made radio contact and the screen offered him a caucasoid face above a short-sleeved shirt.

"Captain Sir Dominic Flandry, Imperial Navy Intelligence, requesting permission to land."

Sometimes he wondered what he would do if his polite formula ever met a rude no.

The visage gaped. "Oh . . . oh . . . already?"

"Hm?" said Flandry. He caught himself. "Ah, yes," he said wisely.

"But only today, sir!" babbled the face. "Why, we haven't even thought about sending a courier out yet—it's been such a nightmare—oh, thank God you're here, sir! You'll see for yourself, at once, there isn't a Technician in the City—on Altla—on all Nyanza, who doesn't set loyalty to his Majesty above life itself!"

"I'm sure his Majesty will be very much relieved," said Flandry. "Now, if you please, how about a landing beam?" After a pause, a few clicks, and the beginning downward rush of his ship: "Oh, by the way, Bubbles. Where did you put your continents today?"

"Continents, sir?"

"You know. Large dirty places to stand on."

"Of course I know, sir!" The control man drew himself up. "We're no parochials in the City. I've been to Spica myself."

"Would it be despicable if you had not?" mused Flandry. Most of him was listening to the fellow's accent. The inexhaustible variations on Anglic were a hobby of his.

"But as for the continents, sir, why, I thought you would know. Nyanza has none. Altla is just a medium-sized island. Otherwise there are only rocks and reefs, submerged at double high tide, or even at Loa high."

"Oh, I knew," said Flandry reassuringly. "I just wanted to be sure you knew." He turned off the receiver and sat thinking. Damn those skimpy

pilot's manuals! He'd have had to go to Spica for
detailed information. If only there were a faster-
than-light equivalent of radio. Instant communications unified planets; but the days and weeks
and months between stars let their systems drift
culturally apart—let hell brew for years, unnoticed till it boiled over—made a slow growth of
feudalism, within the Imperial structure itself,
inevitable. Of course, that would give civilization
something to fall back on when the Long Night
finally came.

The spaceport was like ten thousand minor
harbors: little more than a grav-grid, a field, and
some ancillary buildings, well out of town.
Beyond the hangars, to west and south, Flandry
saw a greenness of carefully tended forest. Eastward rose the spires of a small ancient city.
Northward the ground sloped down in harsh
grass and boulders until it met a smothering white
surf and an impossibly blue ocean. The sky above
was a little darker than Terra's—less dust to scat-
ter light—and cloudless; the sun was blindingly
fierce, bluish tinged. It was local summer: Altla
lay at 35° N. latitude on a Terra-sized planet with a
21° axial tilt. The air held an illusion of being
cooler than it was, for it blew briskly and smelled
of salt and the ultraviolet-rich sun gave it a thun-
derous tinge of ozone.

Still, Flandry wished he had not been quite
such a dude. The portmaster, another blond
caucasoid, looked abominably comfortable in
shorts, blouse, and kepi. Flandry took a morose
satisfaction in noting that the comfort was merely
physical.

"Portmaster Heinz von Sonderburg, sir, at your

service. Naturally, we waive quarantine on your behalf; no Imperial knight would—Ah. Your luggage will be seen to, Captain . . . Flandry? Of course. Most honored. I have communicated with her Excellency and am happy to report she can offer you the usual official hospitality. Otherwise we would have had to do our poor best for you in the City—"

"Her Excellency?" asked Flandry when they were airborne.

"Is that not the proper usage?" Von Sonderburg made washing motions with his hands. "Oh, dear, I am so sorry. This is such an isolated planet—the occasion so seldom arises—Believe me, sir, we are uncouth only in manner. The City, at least, has an enlightened forward-looking spirit of absolute loyalty to the Imperium which—"

"It's just that I thought, in a case like this, where the only Terrans on the planet are the resident and family, they'd have appointed a man." Flandry looked down toward the city. It was old, haphazardly raised out of native stone, with steep narrow streets, teeming pedestrians, very few cars or flyers.

But the docks were big, sleekly modern and aswarm with ships. He made out everything from plastic pirogues to giant submarines. There was a majority of sailing craft, which implied an unhurried esthetic-minded culture; but they were built along radical hydrodynamic lines, which meant that the culture also appreciated efficiency. A powered tug was leaving the bay with a long tail of loaded barges, and air transport was extensively in use.

Elsewhere Flandry recognized a set of large

sea-water processing units and their attached factories, where a thousand dissolved substances were shaped into usefulness. A twin-hulled freighter was unloading bales of . . . sea weed? . . . at the dock of an obvious plastics plant. So, he thought, most of Nyanza fished, hunted, and ranched the planet-wide ocean; this one island took the raw materials and gave back metal, chemical fuel, synthetic timbers and resins and glassites and fibers, engines. He was familiar enough with pelagic technics—most overpopulated worlds turned back at last to Mother Ocean. But here they had begun as sailors, from the very first. It should make for an interesting society. . . .

Von Sonderburg's voice jerked back his attention. "But of course, poor Freeman Bannerji was a man. I am merely referring to his, ah, his relict, poor Lady Varvara. She is an Ayres by birth, you know, the Ayres of Antarctica. She has borne her loss with the true fortitude of Imperial aristocratic blood, yes, we can be very proud to have been directed by the late husband of Lady Varvara Ayres Bannerji."

Flandry constructed his sentence to preserve the illusion: "Do you know the precise time he died?"

"Alas, no, sir. You can speak to the City constabulary, but I fear even they would have no exact information. Sometime last night, after he retired. You understand, sir, we have not your advanced police methods here. A harpoon gun—oh, what a way to meet one's final rest!" Von Sonderburg shuddered delicately.

"The weapon has not been found?" asked Flandry impassively.

"No, I do not believe so, sir. The killer took it with him, portable, you know. He must have crept up the wall with vacsoles, or used a flung grapnel to catch the windowsill and—His Excellency was a sound sleeper and his lady, ah, preferred separate quarters. Ah . . . you can take it for granted, sir, I am certain, that the murderer did not go through the house to reach Freeman Bannerji's retiring chamber. The servants are all of Technician birth, and no Technician would dream of—"

The resident's mansion hove into view. It was probably 75 years old, but its metal and tinted plastic remained a blatant, arrogant leap in formal gardens, amidst a shrill huddle of tenements. As the aircar set down, Flandry noticed that the City population was mostly caucasoid, not even very dark-skinned. They were crowded together in child-pullulating streets, blowsy women waved excited arms and shouted their hagglings, such of the men as did not work in industry kept grimy little shops. A pair of native constables in helmet and breastplate stood guard at the mansion gates. Those were tall Africans, who used stepped-down shockbeams with a sort of casual contempt to prevent loitering.

Lady Varvara was caucasoid herself, though the Chinese strain in the Ayres pedigree showed in dark hair and small-boned body. She posed, exquisite in a simple white mourning gown, beside a full-length stereo of her late husband. Hurri Chundra Bannerji had been a little brown middle-aged Terran with wistful eyes: doubtless the typical fussy, rule-bound, conscientious civil servant whose dreams of a knighthood die slowly over the decades. And now he was murdered.

Flandry bowed over Lady Varvara's frail hand. "Your Ladyship," he said, "accept my most heartfelt sympathy, and grant me forgiveness that I must intrude at a moment of such loss."

"I am glad you came," she whispered. "So very glad."

It had a shaken sincerity that almost upset Flandry's court manners. He backed off with another ritual bow. "You must not trouble yourself further, your Ladyship. Let me deal with the authorities."

"Authorities!" The word was a bitter explosion among her few thin pieces of Terran crystal. Otherwise the room was dominated by the conch-whorls of an art that had not seen Earth in centuries. "What authorities? Did you bring a regiment with you?"

"No." Flandry glanced around the long low-ceilinged room. A noiseless City-bred butler had just placed decanter and glasses by the trellis-wall which opened on the garden. When he left, there did not seem to be anyone else in earshot. Flandry took out his cigarets and raised his brows inquiringly at the woman. He saw she was younger than himself.

Her colorless lips bent into a smile. "Thank you," she said, so low he could almost not hear it.

"Eh? For what, your Ladyship? I'm afraid it's a frosty comfort to have me here."

"Oh, no," she said. She moved closer. Her reactions were not wholly natural: too calm and frank for a new-made widow, then suddenly and briefly too wild. A heavy dose of mysticine, he guessed. It was quite the thing for upper-class Imperials to erect chemical walls against grief or fear or—

What do you do when the walls come down? he thought.

"Oh, no," repeated Lady Varvara. Her words flowed quick and high-pitched. "Perhaps you do not understand, Captain. You are the first Terran I have seen, besides my husband, for . . . how long? Something like three Nyanzan years, and that's about four Terran. And then it was just a red-faced military legate making a routine check. Otherwise, who did we see? The City Warden and his officers paid a few courtesy calls every year. The sea chiefs had to visit us too when they happened to be on Altla . . . not for our sake, you understand, not to curry favor, only because it was beneath their dignity not to observe the formalities. *Their* dignity!" Her cheeks flamed. She stood close to him now, glaring upward; her fists drew the skin tight over bird-like knuckles. "As you would feel obliged to notice the existence of an unwelcome guest!"

"So the Empire is not popular here?" murmured Flandry.

"I don't know," she said pallidly, relaxing. "I don't know. All I know is—the only people we ever saw, with any regularity—our only friends, God help us, friends!—were the Lubbers."

"The what, my lady?"

"City people. Technicians. Pinkskins. Whatever you want to call them. Like that fat little von Sonderburg." She was shrill again. "Do you know what it's like, Captain, to associate with no one but an inferior class? It rubs off on you. Your soul gets greasy. Von Sonderburg now . . . always toadying up to Hurri Chundra . . . he would never light a cigar in my presence without asking me, in the most heavy way—exactly the same words, I have heard them a million times, till I could scream—'Does my lady object if I have a little smoke?' ''

Varvara whirled from him. Her bare shoulders shuddered. "Does my lady object? Does my lady object? And then you come, Captain—your lungs still full of Earth air, I swear—you come and take out a cigaret case and raise your eyebrows. Like that. No more. A gesture we all used at Home, a ritual, an assumption that I have eyes to see what you're doing and intelligence to know what you want—Oh, be welcome, Captain Flandry, be welcome!" She gripped the trellis with both hands and stared out into the garden. "You're from Terra," she whispered. "I'll come to you tonight, any time, right now if you want, just to repay you for being a Terran."

Flandry tapped a cigaret on his thumbnail, put it to his lips at half mast, and drew deeply. He glanced at the sad brown eyes of Hurri Chundra Bannerji and said without words: *Sorry, old chap. I'm not a ghoul, and I'll do what I can to avoid this, but my job demands I be tactful. For the Empire and the Race!*

"I'm sorry to intrude when you're overwrought, your Ladyship," he said. "Of course, I'll arrange for your passage to provincial headquarters, and if you want to return Home from there—"

"After all these years," she mumbled, "who would I know?"

"Uh . . . may I suggest my lady, that you rest for a while—?"

An intercom chime saved both of them. Varvara said a shaky "Accept" and the connection closed.

The butler's voice came: "Beg pardon, madame, but I have just received word of a distinguished native person who has arrived. Shall I ask postponement of the formal visit?"

"Oh . . . I don't know." Varvara's tone was dead. She did not look at Flandry. "Who is it?"

"Lady Tessa Hoorn, madame, Lightmistress of Little Skua in Jairnovaunt."

III

When they reached the Zurian Current, the water, which had been a Homeric blue, turned deep purple, streaked with foam that flashed like crystallized snow. "This bends to north beyond Iron Shoals and carries on past the Reefs of Sorrow," remarked Tessa Hoorn. "Gains us a few knots speed. Though we've naught to hurry for, have we?"

Flandry blinked through dark contact lenses at the incredible horizon. Sunlight flimmered off the multitudinous laughter of small waves. "I suppose the color is due to plankton," he said.

"Plankton-like organisms," corrected Tessa. "We're nay on Earth, Captain. But aye, off this feed the oilfish, and off them the decapus, both of use to us." She pointed. "Yonder flags bear Dilolo stripes, quartered on Saleth green: the fishing boats of the Prince of Aquant."

Flandry's dazzled eyes could hardly even see the vessels, in that merciless illumination. Since the wind dropped, the Hoorn ship had been running on its auxiliary engine and now there was no shade from the great sails. An awning was spread amidships and some superbly muscled deckhands sprawled under it, clapping time to an eerie chant-pipe, like young gods carved in oiled ebony. The Terran would have given much for some of that shadow. But since Tessa Hoorn stood here in the bows, he must submit. It was an endurance contest, he recognized, with all the advantages on her side.

"Does your nation fish this current too?" he asked.

"A little," she nodded. "But mostly we in Jairnovaunt sail west and north, with harpoons for the kraken—ha, it's a pale life never to have speared fast to a beast with more of bulk than your own ship!—and smaller game. Then T'chaka Kruger farms a great patch of beanweed in the Lesser Sargasso. And in sooth I confess, not alone the commons but some captains born will scrape the low-tide reefs for shells or dive after sporyx. Then there are carpenters, weavers, engineers, medics, machinists, all trades that must be plied: and mummers and mimes, though most such sport is given by wandering boats of actors, masterless madcap folk who come by as fancy strikes 'em." She shrugged broad shoulders. "The Commander can list you all professions in his realm if you wish it, Imperial."

Flandry regarded her with more care than pleasure. He had not yet understood her attitude. Was it contempt, or merely hatred?

The sea people of Nyanza were almost entirely African by descent, which meant that perhaps three-fourths of their ancestors had been negroid, back when more or less "pure" stocks still existed. In a world of light, more actinic than anything on Earth, reflected off water, there had been a nearly absolute selection for dark coloring: not a Nyanzan outside the city on Altla was any whiter than the ace of spades. Otherwise genes swapped around pretty freely—kinky hair, broad noses, and full lips were the rule, but with plenty of exceptions. Tessa's hair formed a soft, tightly curled coif around her ears; her nostrils flared, in a wide arch-browed face, but the bridge was aquiline. Without her look of inbred haughtiness, it would have been a wholly beautiful face. The rest of her was even more stunning, almost as tall as Flandry, full-breasted, slim-waisted, and muscled like a Siamese cat. She wore merely a gold medallion of rank on her forehead, a belt with a knife, and the inevitable aqualung on her back . . . which left plenty on view to admire. But even in plumes and gown and rainbow cloak, she had been a walking shout as she entered the resident's mansion.

However, thought Dominic Flandry, *that word "stunning" can be taken two ways. I am not about to make a pass at the Lightmistress of Little Skua.*

He asked cautiously: "Where are the Technicians from?"

"Oh, those." A faint sneer flickered on her red mouth. "Well, see you, the firstcomers here settled on Altla, but then as more folk came in, space was lacking, so they began to range the sea. That proved so much better a life that erelong few cared to work on land. So sith the positions stood open, ai-hai!—it swarmed in with dirt-loving men and their shes. Most came from Deutschwelt, as it happened. When we had enough of yon ilk, and knew they'd breed, we closed the sluice, for they dare nay work as sailors, they get skin sicknesses, and Altla has little room."

"I should think they'd be powerful on the planet, what with the essential refineries and—"

"Nay, Captain. Altla and all thereon is owned in common by the *true* Nyanzan nations. The Technicians are but hirelings. Though in sooth, they've a sticky way with money and larger bank accounts than many a skipper. That's why we bar them from owning ships."

Flandry glanced down at himself. He had avoided the quasi-uniform of the despised class and had packed outfits of blouse, slacks, zori, and sash for himself; the winged cap sat on his head bearing the sunburst of Empire. But he could not evade the obvious fact, that his own culture was more Lubberly than pelagic. And an Imperial agent was often hated, but must not ever allow himself to be despised. Hence Flandry cocked a brow (*Sardonic Expression* 22-C, he thought) and drawled:

"I see. You're afraid that, being more intelligent, they'd end up owning every ship on the planet."

He could not see if she flushed, under the smooth black sweat-gleaming skin, but her lips drew back and one hand clapped to her knife. He thought that the sea bottom was no further away than a signal to her crew. Finally she exclaimed, "Is it the new fashion on Terra to insult a hostess? Well you know it's nay a matter of inborn brain, but of skill. The Lubbers are reared from birth to handle monies. But how many of 'em can handle a rigging—or even name the lines? Can you?"

Flandry's unfairness had been calculated. So was his refusal to meet her reply squarely. "Well," he said, "the Empire tries to respect local law and custom. Only the most uncivilized practices are not tolerated."

It stung her, she bridled. Most colonials were violently sensitive to their isolation from the Galactic mainstream. They did not see that their own societies were not backward on that account—were often healthier—and the answer to that lay buried somewhere in the depths of human unreasonableness. But the fact could be used.

Having angered her enough, Flandry finished coldly: "And, of course, the Empire cannot tolerate treasonable conspiracies."

Tessa Hoorn answered him in a strained voice, "Captain, there's nay conspiring here. Free-born folk are honest with foemen, too. It's you who put on slyness. For see you, I happened by Altla homebound from The Kraal, and visited yon mansion for courtoisie sake. When you asked passage to Jairnovaunt, I granted it, sith such is nay refused among ocean people. But well I knew you fared with me, liefer than fly the way in an hour or two, so you could draw me out and spy on me. And you've nay been frank as to your reasons for guesting my country." Her deep tones became a growl. "That's Lubber ways! You'll nay get far 'long your mission, speaking for a planet of Lubbers and Lubberlovers!"

She drew her knife, looked at it, and clashed it back into the sheath. Down on the quarterdeck, the crewmen stirred, a ripple of panther bodies. It grew so quiet that Flandry heard the steady snore of the bow through murmurous waves, and the lap-lap on the hull, and the creak of spars up in the sky.

He leaned back against a blistering bulwark and said with care: "I'm going to Jairnovaunt because a boy died holding my hand. I want to find his parents. . . ." He offered her a cigaret, and helped himself when she shook her head. "But I'm not going just to extend my personal sympathies. Imperial expense accounts are not quite that elastic. For that matter, while we're being honest, I admit I'd hardly invite Bubbles or Flutters to my own house."

He blew smoke; it was almost invisible in the flooding light. "Maybe you wouldn't conspire behind anyone's back, m' lady. Come to think of it, who would conspire in front of anyone's face? But somebody on Nyanza is hatching a very nasty egg. That kid didn't sign up when the Imperial recruiter stopped by for glory or money: he enlisted to learn modern militechnics, with the idea of turning them against the Empire. And he died in trampled snow, sniped by a local patriot he was chasing. Who lured that young fellow out to die Lightmistress? And who sneaked up a wall and harpooned a harmless little lonely bureaucrat in his sleep? Rather more to the point, who sent that murderer-by-stealth, and why? Really, this is a pretty slimy business all around. I should think you'd appreciate my efforts to clean it off your planet."

Tessa bit her lip. At last, not meeting his shielded gaze, she said, "I'm nay wise of any such plots, Captain. I won't speak 'loud 'gainst your Empire—my thoughts are my own, but it's true we've nay suffered much more than a resident and some taxes—"

"Which were doubtless higher when every nation maintained its own defenses," said Flandry. "Yes, we settle for a single man on worlds like this. We'd actually like to have more, because enough police could smell out trouble before it's grown too big, and could stop the grosser barbarities left over from independent days—"

Again she bristled. He said in a hurry: "No, please, for once that's not meant to irritate. By and large, Nyanza looks as if it's always been quite a humane place. If you don't use all the latest technological gimcrackery, it's because it's nonfunctional in this culture, not because you've forgotten what your ancestors knew. I'm just enough of a jackleg engineer to see that these weird-looking sails of yours are aerodynamic marvels; I'm certain that paraboloidal jib uses the Venturi effect with malice aforethought. Your language is grammatically archaic but semantically efficient. I can envision some of the bucolic poets at court going into raptures over your way of life. And getting seasick if they tried it, but that's another story. . . . Therefore," he finished soberly, "I'm afraid I'm a little more sympathetic to Hurri Chundra Bannerji, who fussed about and established extrasystemic employment contacts for your more ambitious young men and built breakwaters and ordered vaccines and was never admitted to your clubs, than I am sorry for you."

She looked over the side, into curling white and purple water, and said very low, "The Empire was nay asked here."

"Neither was anyone else. The Terran Empire

established itself in this region first. The Merseian Empire would be a rather more demanding master—if only because it's still vigorous, expansive, virtuous, and generally uncorrupted, while Terra is the easygoing opposite." That brought her up sharply in astonishment, as he had expected. "Since the Empire must protect its frontiers, lest Terra herself be clobbered out of the sky, we're going to stay. It would not be advisable for some young Nyanzan firebrains to try harpooning space dreadnaughts. Anyone who provokes such gallant idiocy is an enemy of yours as well as mine."

Her eyes were moody upon his. After a long time she asked him, "Captain, have you ever swum undersea?"

"I've done a little skindiving for fun," he said, taken aback. He had spoken half honestly and half meretriciously, never quite sure which sentence was one or another, and thought he had touched the proper keys. But this surprised him.

"Nay more? And you stand all 'lone on a world that's aloof of you where it doesn't, perchance, scheme murder? Captain, I repent me what I said 'bout your folk being Lubbers."

The relief was like a wave of weakness. Flandry sucked in his cheeks around his cigaret and answered lightly: "They cannot do worse than shoot me, which would distress only my tailor and my vintner. Have you ever heard that the coward dies a thousand deaths, the hero dies but once?"

"Aye."

"Well, after the 857th death I got bored with it."

She laughed and he continued a line of banter,

so habitual by now that most of him thought on
other affairs. Not that he seriously expected the
Lightmistress of Little Skua to become bodily ac-
cessible to him; he had gathered an impression of
a chaste folk. But the several days' voyage to Jairnovaunt could be made very pleasant by a small
shipboard flirtation, and he would learn a great
deal more than if his fellow voyagers were hostile.
For instance, whether the imported wine he had
noticed in the galley was preferable to native sea-
berry gin. He had not been truthful in claiming
indifference whether he lived or died: not while a
supple young woman stood clad in sunlight, and
blooded horses stamped on the ringing plains of
Ilion, and smoke curled fragrant about coffee and
cognac on Terra. But half the pleasure came from
these things being staked against darkness.

IV

A tide was flowing when they reached Jairnovaunt, and all the rocks, and the housings upon
them, were meters under the surface. The Hoorn
ship steered a way between pennant-gay buoys to
one of the anchored floating docks. There
swarmed the sea people, snorting like porpoises
among moored hulls or up like squirrels in tall
masts. Fish were being unloaded and sails re-
paired and engines overhauled, somewhere a
flute and a drum underlay a hundred deep voices
chanting *Way-o* as bare feet stamped out a riga-
doon. Flandry noticed how silence spread
ripple-fashion from the sight of him. But he followed Tessa overboard as soon as her vessel was
secured.

No Nyanzan was ever far from his aqualung. They seemed to have developed a more advanced model here than any Flandry had seen elsewhere: a transparent helmet and a small capacitance-battery device worn on the back, which electrolyzed oxygen directly from the water and added enough helium from a high-compression tank to dilute. By regulating the partial pressures of the gases, one could go quite deep.

This was only a short swim, as casual as a Terran's stroll across the bridgeway. Slanting through clear greenish coolth, Flandry saw that Jairnovaunt was large—sunken domes and towers gleamed farther than his vision reached. Work went on: a cargo submarine, with a score of human midges flitting about it, discharged kelpite bales into a warehouse tube. But there were also children darting among the eerie spires and grottos of a coraloid park, an old man scattered seeds for a school of brilliant-striped little fish, a boy and a girl swam hand in hand through voiceless wonder.

When he reached the long white hall of the Commander, Jairnovaunt's hereditary chief executive, Flandry was still so bemused by the waving, fronded formal gardens that he scarcely noticed how graceful the portico was. Even the airlock which admitted him blended into the over-all pattern, a curiously disturbing one to the Terran mind, for it contrasted delicate traceries and brutal masses as if it were the ocean itself.

When the water had been pumped out, an airblast dried them, Flandry's shimmerite clothes as well as Tessa's sleek skin. They stepped into a hallway muraled with heroic abstractions.

Beyond two guards bearing the ubiquitous harpoon rifles, and beyond an emergency bulkhead, the passage opened on a great circular chamber lined with malachite pillars under a clear dome. Some twoscore Nyanzans stood about. Their ages seemed to range upward from 20 or so; some wore only a 'lung, others a light-colored shirt and kilt; all bore dignity like a mantle. Quite a few were women, gowned and plumed if they were clothed at all, but otherwise as free and proud as their men.

Tessa stepped forward and saluted crisply. "The Lightmistress of Little Skua, returning from The Kraal as ordered, sir."

Commander Inyanduma III was a powerfully built, heavy-faced man with graying woolly hair: his medallion of rank was tattooed, a golden Pole Star bright on his brows. "Be welcome," he said, "and likewise your guest. He is now ours. I call his name holy."

The Terran flourished a bow. "An honor, sir. I am Captain Dominic Flandry, Imperial Navy. Lightmistress Hoorn was gracious enough to conduct me here."

He met the Commander's eyes steadily, but placed himself so he could watch Tessa on his edge of vision. Inyanduma tipped an almost imperceptible inquiring gesture toward her. She nodded, ever so faintly, and made a short-lived O with thumb and forefinger. *I'd already wormed out that she went to The Kraal on official business,* remembered Flandry, *but she wouldn't say what and only now will she even admit it succeeded. Too secret to mention on her ship's radiophone! As human beings, we enjoyed each*

*other's company, traveling here. But as agents of
our kings—?*

Inyanduma swept a sailor's muscular hand
about the room. "You see our legislative leaders,
Captain. When the Lightmistress 'phoned you
were hither-bound, we supposed it was because
of his Excellency's slaying, which had been
broadcast 'round the globe. It's a grave matter, so I
gathered our chiefs of council, from both the
House of Men and the Congress of Women."

A rustling and murmuring went about the
green columns, under the green sea. There was
withdrawal in it, and a sullen waiting. These were
not professional politicians as Terra knew the
breed. These were the worthies of Jairnovaunt:
aristocrats and shipowners, holding seats ex *of-
ficio*, and a proportion of ships' officers elected
by the commons. Even the nobles were
functional—Tessa Hoorn had inherited not the
right but the duty to maintain lightships and
communications about the reefs called Little
Skua. They had all faced more storms and under-
water teeth than they had debate.

Flandry said evenly: "My visit concerns worse
than a murder, sir and gentles. A resident might
be killed by any disgruntled individual, that's an
occupational hazard. But I don't think one living
soul hated Bannerji personally. And that's what's
damnable!"

"Are you implying treason, sir?" rumbled Inyanduma.

"I am, sir. With more lines of evidence than one.
Could anybody direct me to a family named Umbolu?"

It stirred and hissed among the councillors of

Jairnovaunt. And then a young man trod forth—a huge young man with a lion's gait, cragged features and a scar on one cheek. "Aye," he said so it rang in the hall. "I hight Derek Umbolu, captain of the kraken-chaser *Bloemfortein*. Tessa, why brought you a damned Impy hither?"

"Belay!" rapped Inyanduma. "We'll show courtoisie here."

Tessa exclaimed to the giant: "Derek, Derek, he could have flown to us in an hour! And we meditate nay rebellion—" Her voice trailed off; she stepped back from his smoldering gaze, her own eyes widening and a hand stealing to her mouth. The unspoken question shivered, *Do we?*

"Let 'em keep 'way from us!" growled Derek Umbolu. "We'll pay the tribute and hold to the bloody Pax if they'll leave us and our old ways 'lone. But they don't!"

Flandry stepped into collective horror. "I'm not offended," he said. "But neither do I make policy. Your complaints against the local administration should be taken to the provincial governor—"

"Yon murdering quog!" spat Derek. "I've heard about Brae, and more."

Since Flandry considered the description admirable (he assumed a quog was not a nice animal) he said hastily: "I must warn you against *lèse majesté*. And now let's get to my task. It's not very pleasant for me either. Captain Umbolu, are you related to an Imperial marine named Thomas?"

"Aye. I've a younger brother who 'listed for a five-year hitch."

Flandry's tones gentled. "I'm sorry. It didn't strike me you might be so closely—Thomas Umbolu was killed in action on Brae."

Derek closed his eyes. One great hand clamped

on the hilt of his sheath knife till blood trickled from beneath the nails. He looked again at the world and said thickly: "You came here swifter than the official news, Captain."

"I saw him die," said Flandry. "He went like a brave man."

"You've nay crossed space just to tell a colonial that much."

"No," said Flandry. "I would like to speak alone with you sometime soon. And with his other kin."

The broad black chest pumped air, the hard fingers curved into claws. Derek Umbolu rasped forth: "You'll nay torment my father with your devilments, nor throw shame on us with your secrecy. Ask it out here, 'fore 'em all."

Flandry's shoulder muscles tightened, as if expecting a bullet. He looked to the Commander. Inyanduma's starred face was like obsidian. Flandry said: "I have reason to believe Thomas Umbolu was implicated in a treasonable conspiracy. Of course, I could be wrong, in which case I'll apologize. But I must first put a great many questions. I am certainly not going to perform before an audience. I'll see you later."

"You'll leave my father be or I'll kill you!"

"Belay!" cried Inyanduma. "I said he was a guest." More softly: "Go, Derek, and tell Old John what you must."

The giant saluted, wheeled, and stalked from the room. Flandry saw tears glimmer in Tessa's eyes. The Commander bowed ponderously at him. "Crave your pardon, sir. He's a stout heart . . . surely you'll find nay treason in his folk . . . but the news you bore was harsh."

Flandry made some reply. The gathering became decorous, the Lightmasters and Coast-watchers offered him polite conversation. He felt reasonably sure that few of them knew about any plottings: revolutions didn't start that way.

Eventually he found himself in a small but tastefully furnished bedroom. One wall was a planetary map. He studied it, looking for a place called Uhunhu. He found it near the Sheikhdom of Rossala, which lay north of here; if he read the symbols aright, it was a permanently submerged area.

A memory snapped into his consciousness. He swore for two unrepeating minutes before starting a chain of cigarets. If that was the answer—

V

The inner moon, though smaller, raised the largest tides, up to nine times a Terrestrial high; but it moved so fast, five orbits in two of Nyanza's 30-hour days, that the ebb was spectacularly rapid. Flandry heard a roar through his wall, switched on the transparency, and saw water tumbling white from dark rough rock. It was close to sunset, he had sat in his thoughts for hours. A glance at the electric ephemeris over his bunk told him that Loa, the outer satellite, would not dunk the hall till midnight. And that was a much weaker flow, without the whirlpool effects which were dangerous for a lower-case lubber like himself.

He stubbed out his cigaret and sighed. *Might as well get the nasty part over with.* Rising, he shucked all clothes but a pair of trunks and a 'lung; he put on the swimshoes given him and buckled his guns—they were safely waterproof— into their holsters. A directory-map of the immediate region showed him where Captain John Umbolu lived. He recorded a message that business called him out and his host should not wait dinner: he felt sure Inyanduma would be more relieved than offended. Then he stepped through the airlock. It closed automatically after him.

Sunset blazed across violet waters. The white spume of the breakers was turned an incredible gold; tide pools on the naked black skerry were like molten copper. The sky was deep blue in the east, still pale overhead, shading to a clear cloudless green where the sun drowned. Through the surf's huge hollow crashing and grinding, Flandry heard bells from one of the many rose-red spires . . . or did a ship's bell ring among raking spars, or was it something he had heard in a dream once? Beneath all the noise, it was unutterably peaceful.

No one bothered with boats for such short distances. Flandry entered the water at a sheltered spot, unfolded the web feet in his shoes, and struck out between the scattered dome-and-towered reefs. Other heads bobbed in the little warm waves, but none paid him attention. He was glad of that. Steering a course by marked buoys, he found old Umbolu's house after a few energetic minutes.

It was on a long thin rock, surrounded by lesser stones on which a murderous fury exploded. The Terran paddled carefully around, in search of a safe approach. He found it, two natural breakwaters formed by gaunt rusty coraloid pinnacles, with a path that led upward through gardens now sodden heaps until it struck the little hemisphere. Twilight was closing in, slow and deeply blue; an evening planet came to white life in the west.

Flandry stepped onto the beach under the crags. It was dark there. He did not know what reflex of deadly years saved him. A man glided from behind one of the high spires and fired a harpoon. Flandry dropped on his stomach before he had seen more than a metallic glitter. The killing missile hissed where he had been.

"*If* you please!" He rolled over, yanking for his sleepy-needle gun. A night-black panther shape sprang toward him. His pistol was only half un-limbered when the hard body fell upon his. One chopping, wrist-numbing karate blow sent the weapon a-clatter from his grasp. He saw a bearded, hating face behind a knife.

Flandry blocked the stab with his left arm. The assassin pulled his blade back. Before it could return, Flandry's thumb went after the nearest eye. His opponent should have ignored that distraction for the few necessary moments of slicing time—but, instead, grabbed the Terran's wrist with his own free hand. Flandry's right hand was still weak, but he delivered a rabbit punch of sorts with it and took his left out of hock by jerking past his enemy's thumb. Laying both hands and a knee against the man's knife arm, he set about breaking same.

The fellow screeched, writhed, and wriggled free somehow. Both bounced to their feet. The dagger lay between them. The Nyanzan dove after it. Flandry put his foot on the blade. "Finders keepers," he said. He kicked the scrabbling man behind the ear and drew his blaster.

The Nyanzan did not stay kicked. Huddled at Flandry's knees, he threw a sudden shoulder block. The Terran went over on his backside. He glimpsed the lean form as it rose and leaped; it was in the water before he had fired.

After the thunder-crash had echoed to naught and no body had emerged, Flandry retrieved his needler. Slowly, his breathing and pulse eased. "That," he confessed aloud, "was as ludicrous a case of mutual ineptitude as the gods of slapstick ever engineered. We both deserve to be tickled to death by small green centipedes. Well . . . if you keep quiet about it, I will."

He squinted through the dusk at the assassin's knife. It was an ordinary rustproof blade, but the bone hilt carried an unfamiliar inlaid design. And had he ever before seen a Nyanzan with a respectable growth of beard?

He went on up the path and pressed the house bell. The airlock opened for him and he entered.

The place had a ship's neatness, and it was full of models, scrimshaw, stuffed fish, all the sailor souvenirs. But emptiness housed in it. One old man sat alone with his dead; there was no one else.

John Umbolu looked up through dim eyes and nodded. "Aye," he said, "I 'waited you, Captain. Be welcome and be seated."

Flandry lowered himself to a couch covered with the softscaled hide of some giant swimming thing John Umbolu had once hunted down. The leather was worn shabby. The old man limped to him with a decanter of imported rum. When they had both been helped, he sat himself in a massive armchair and their goblets clinked together. "Your honor and good health, sir," said John Umbolu.

Flandry looked into the wrinkled face and said quietly: "Your son Derek must have told you my news."

"I've had the tidings," nodded Umbolu. He took a pipe from its rack and began to fill it with slow careful motions. "You saw him die, sir?"

"He held my hand. His squad was ambushed on a combat mission on Brae. He . . . it was soon over."

"Drowning is the single decent death," whispered the Nyanzan. "My other children, all but Derek, had that much luck." He lit his pipe and blew smoke for a while. "I'm sorry Tom had to go yon way. But it is kind of you to come tell me of it."

"He'll be buried with full military honors," said Flandry awkwardly. *If they don't have so many corpses they just bulldoze them under.* "Or if you wish, instead of the battle-casualty bonus you can have his ashes returned here."

"Nay," said Umbolu. His white head wove back and forth. "What use is that? Let me have the money, to build a reef beacon in his name." He thought for a while longer, then said timidly: "Perchance I could call further on your kindness. Would you know if . . . you're 'ware, sir, soldiers on leave and the girls they meet . . . it's possible Tom left a child somewhere . . ."

"I'm sorry, I wouldn't know how to find out about that."

"Well, well, I expected nay more. Derek must be wed soon then, if the name's to live."

Flandry drew hard on a cigaret, taken from a waterproof case. He got out: "I have to tell you what your son said as he lay dying."

"Aye. Say forth, and fear me nay. Shall the fish blame the hook if it hurts him a little?"

Flandry related it. At the end, the old man's eyes closed, just as Derek's had done, and he let the empty glass slip from his fingers.

Finally: "I know naught of this. Will you believe that, Captain?"

"Yes, sir," Flandry answered.

"You fear Derek may be caught in the same net?"

"I hope not."

"I too. I'd nay have any son of mine in a scheme that works by midnight murder—whatever they may think of your Empire. Tom . . . Tom was young and didn't understand what was involved. Will you believe that too?" asked John Umbolu anxiously. Flandry nodded. The Nyanzan dropped his head and cupped his hands about the pipe bowl, as if for warmth. "But Derek . . . why, Derek's in the Council. Derek would have open eyes—Let it nay be so!"

Flandry left him with himself for a time, then: "Where might any young man . . . first have encountered the agents of such a conspiracy?"

"Who knows, sir? 'Fore his growth is gained, an Umbolu boy has shipped to all ports of the planet. Or there are always sailors from every nation on Nyanza, right here in Jairnovaunt."

Flandry held out the knife he had taken. "This

belongs to a bearded man," he said. "Can you tell me anything about it?"

The faded eyes peered close. "Rossala work." It was an instant recognition, spoken in a lifeless voice. "And the Rossala men flaunt whiskers."

"As I came ashore here," said Flandry, "a bearded person with this knife tried to kill me. He got away, but—"

He stopped. The old sea captain had risen. Flandry looked up at an incandescent mask of fury, and suddenly he realized that John Umbolu was a very big man.

Gigantic fists clenched over the Terran's head. The voice roared like thunder, one majestic oath after the next, until rage at last found meaningful words. "Sneak assassins on my very ground! 'Gainst my guest! By the blazing bones of Almighty God, sir, you'll let me question every Rossalan in Jairnovaunt and flay yon one 'live!"

Flandry rose too. An upsurging eagerness tingled in him, a newborn plot. And at the same time—*Warily, child, warily! You'll not get cooperation at this counter without some of the most weasel-like arguments and shameless emotional buttonpushing in hell's three-volume thesaurus.*

Well, he thought, *that's what I get paid for.*

VI

Hours had gone when he left the house. He had eaten there, but sheer weariness dragged at him. He swam quite slowly back to the Commander's rock. When he stood on it, he rested for a while, looking over the sea.

Loa was up, Luna-sized, nearly full, but with

several times the albedo of Earth's moon. High in a clear blackness, it drowned most of the alien constellations. The marker lights about every rock, color-coded for depth so that all Jairnovaunt was one great jewelbox, grew pallid in the moon-dazzle off the ocean.

Flandry took out a cigaret. It was enough to be alone with that light: at least, it helped. Imperial agents ought to have some kind of conscience-ectomy performed. . . . He drew smoke into his lungs.

"Can you nay rest, Captain?"

The low woman-voice brought him bounding around. When he saw the moonlight gleam off Tessa Hoorn, he put back his gun, sheepishly.

"You seem a wee bit wakeful yourself," he answered. "Unless you are sleep-walking, or sleep-diving or whatever people do here. But no, surely I am the one asleep. Don't rouse me."

The moon turned her into darknesses and lithe witcheries, with great marching waters to swirl beneath her feet. She had been swimming—Loa glistened off a million cool drops, her only garment. He remembered how they had talked and laughed and traded songs and recollections and even hopes, under tall skies or moonlit sails. His heart stumbled, and glibness died.

"Aye. My net would nay hold fast to sleep this night." She stood before him, eyes lowered. It was the first time she had not met his gaze. In the streaming unreal light, he saw how a pulse fluttered in her throat. "So I wended from my bunk and—" The tones faded.

"Why did you come here again?" he asked.

"Oh . . . it was a place to steer for. Or perchance. . . . Nay!" Her lips tried to smile, but were not quite steady. "Where were you this evening, sith we are so curious?"

"I spoke to Old John," he said, because so far truth would serve his purpose. "It wasn't easy."

"Aye. I wouldn't give your work to an enemy, Dominic. Why do you do it?"

He shrugged. "It's all I really know how to do."

"Nay!" she protested. "To aid a brute of a governor or a null of a resident—you're too much a man. You could come . . . here, even—Nay, the sun wouldn't allow it for long. . . ."

"It's not quite for nothing," he said. "The Empire is—" he grinned forlornly—"less perfect than myself. True. But what would replace it is a great deal worse."

"Are you so sure, Dominic?"

"No," he said in bitterness.

"You could dwell on a frontier world and do work you are sure is worth yourself. I . . . even I have thought, there is more in this universe than Nyanza . . . if such a planet had oceans, I could—"

Flandry said frantically: "Didn't you mention having a child, Tessa?"

"Aye, a Commander-child, but sith I'm unwed as yet the boy was adopted out." He looked his puzzlement and she explained, as glad as he to be impersonal: "The Commander must not wed, but lies with whom he will. It's a high honor, and if she be husbandless the woman gets a great dowry from him. The offspring of these unions are raised by the mothers' kin; when they are all old enough, the councillors elect the best-seeming son heir apparent."

Somewhere in his rocking brain, Flandry thought that the Terran Emperors could learn a good deal from Nyanza. He forced a chuckle and said: "Why, that makes you the perfect catch, Tessa—titled, rich, and the mother of a potential chieftain. How did you escape so far?"

"There was nay the right man," she whispered. "Inyanduma himself is so much a man, see you, for all his years. Only Derek Umbolu—how you unlock me, Terran!—and him too proud to wed 'bove his station." She caught her breath and blurted desperately: "But I'm nay more a maid, and I will nay wait until Full Entropy to be again a woman."

Flandry could have mumbled something and gotten the devil out of there. But he remembered through a brawling in his blood that he was an Imperial agent and that something had been done by this girl in southern waters which they kept secret from him.

He kissed her.

She responded shyly at first, and then with a hunger that tore at him. They sat for a long while under the moon, needing no words, until Flandry felt with dim surprise that the tide was licking his feet.

Tessa rose. "Come to my house," she said.

It was the moment when he must be a reptile-blooded scoundrel . . . or perhaps a parfait gentil knight, he was desolately uncertain which. He remained seated, looking up at her, where she stood crowned with stars, and said:

"I'm sorry. It wouldn't do."

"Fear me naught," she said with a small catch of laughter, very close to a sob. "You can leave when you will. I'd nay have a man who wouldn't stay freely. But I'll do my best to keep you, Dominic, dearest."

He fumbled after another cigaret. "Do you think I'd like anything better?" he said. "But there's a monster loose on this planet, I'm all but sure of it. I will not give you just a few hours with half my mind on my work. Afterward—" He left it unfinished.

She stood quiet for a time that stretched.

"It's for Nyanza too," he pleaded. "If this goes on unreined, it could be the end of your people."

"Aye," she said in a flat tone.

"You could help me. When this mission is finished—"

"Well . . . what would you know?" She twisted her face away from his eyes.

He got the cigaret lighted and squinted through the smoke. "What were you doing in The Kraal?"

"I'm nay so sure now that I do love you, Dominic."

"Will you tell me, so I'll know what I have to face?"

She sighed. "Rossala is arming. They are making warcraft, guns, torpedoes—none nuclear, sith we have nay facilities for it, but more than the Terran law allows us. I don't know why, though rumor speaks of sunken Uhunhu. The Sheikh guards his secrets. But there are whispers of freedom. It may or may not be sooth. We'll nay make trouble with the Imperium for fellow Nyanzans, but . . . we arm ourselves, too, in case Rossala should start again the old wars. I arranged an alliance with The Kraal."

"And if Rossala should not attack you, but revolt against Terra?" asked Flandry. "What would your own re-armed alliance do?"

"I know naught 'bout that. I am but one Nyanzan. Have you nay gained enough?"

She slammed down her 'lung helmet and dove off the edge. He did not see her come up again.

VII

With a whole planetful of exotic sea foods to choose from, the Commander hospitably breakfasted his guest on imported beefsteak. Flandry walked out among morning tide pools, through a gusty salt wind, and waited in grimness and disgruntlement for events to start moving.

He was a conspicuous figure in his iridescent white garments, standing alone on a jut of rock with the surf leaping at his feet. A harpoon gunner could have fired upward from the water and disappeared. Flandry did not take his eyes off the blue and green whitecaps beyond the breakers. His mind dwelt glumly on Tessa Hoorn . . . God damn it, he would go home by way of Morvan and spend a week in its pleasure city and put it all on the expense account. What was the use of this struggle to keep a decaying civilization from being eaten alive, if you never got a chance at any of the decadence yourself?

A black shape crossed his field of vision. He poised, warily. The man swam like a seal, but straight into the surf. There were sharp rocks in that cauldron—hold it!—Derek Umbolu beat his way through, grasped the wet stone edge Flandry stood on, and chinned himself up. He pushed back his helmet with a crash audible over the sea-thunder and loomed above Flandry like a basalt cliff. His eyes went downward 30 centimeters to lock with the Terran's, and he snarled:

"What have you done to her?"

"My lady Hoorn?" Flandry asked. "Unfortunately, nothing."

A fist cocked. "You lie, Lubber! I know the lass. I saw her this dawn and she had been weeping."

Flandry smiled lop-sided. "And I am necessarily to blame? Don't you flatter me a bit? She spoke rather well of you, Captain."

A shiver went through the huge body. Derek stepped back one pace; teeth caught at his lip. "Say nay more," he muttered.

"I'd have come looking for you today," said Flandry. "We still have a lot to talk about. Such as the man who tried to kill me last night."

Derek spat. "A pity he didn't succeed!"

"Your father thought otherwise, seeing the attempt was made on his own rock. He was quite indignant."

Derek's eyes narrowed. His nostrils stirred, like an angry bull's, and his head slanted forward. "So you spoke to my father after all, did you, now? I warned you, Impy—"

"We had a friendly sort of talk," said Flandry. "*He* doesn't believe anything can be gained by shooting men in their sleep."

"I suppose all your own works would stand being refereed?"

Since they would certainly not, Flandry donned a frown and continued: "I'd keep an eye on your father, though. I've seen these dirty little fanaticisms before. Among the first people to be butchered are the native-born who keep enough native sense and honor to treat the Imperial like a fellow-being. You see, such people are too likely to understand that the revolution is really organized by some rival imperialism, and that you can't win a war where your own home is the battleground."

"Arrgh!" A hoarse animal noise, for no words were scornful enough.

"And my would-be assassin is still in business," continued Flandry. "He knows I did talk to your father. Hate me as much as you like, Captain Umbolu, but keep a guard over the old gentleman. Or at least speak to a certain Rossalan whom I don't accuse you of knowing."

For a moment longer the brown eyes blazed against the glacial gray blandness of the Terran's. Then Derek clashed his helmet down and returned to the water.

Flandry sighed. He really should start the formal machinery of investigation, but—He went back to the house with an idea of borrowing some fishing tackle.

Inyanduma, seated at a desk among the inevitable documents of government, gave him a troubled look. "Are you certain that there is a real conspiracy on Nyanza?" he asked. "We've ever had our hotheads, like all others . . . aye, I've seen other planets, I 'listed for the space Navy in my day and hold a reserve commission."

Flandry sat down and looked at his fingernails. "Then why haven't you reported what you know about Rossala?" he asked softly.

Inyanduma started. "Are you a telepath?"

"No. It'd make things too dull." Flandry lit a fresh cigaret. "I know Rossala is arming, and that your nation is alarmed enough about it to prepare defensive weapons and alliances. Since the Empire would protect you, you must expect the Empire to be kicked off Nyanza."

"Nay," whispered Inyanduma. "We've nay certainty of aught. It's but . . . we won't bring a horde of detectives, belike a Terran military force, by denouncing our fellow nation . . . on so little proof. . . . And yet we must keep some freedom of action, in case—"

"*Especially* in case Rossala calls on you to join in cutting the Terran apron strings?"

"Nay, nay—"

"Under such circumstances, it would be pathetic." Flandry shook his tongue-clicking head. "It's so amateurishly done that I feel grossly overpaid for my time here. But whoever engineered the conspiracy in the first place is no amateur. He used your parochial loyalties with skill. And he must expect to move soon, before a pre-occupied Imperium can find out enough about his arrangements to justify sending in the marines. The resident's assassination is obviously a key action. It was chance I got here the very day that had happened, but someone like me would surely have arrived not many days later, and not been a great deal longer about learning as much as I've done. Of course, if they can kill me it will delay matters for a while, which will be helpful to them; but they don't seem to expect they'll need much time."

Flandry paused, nodded to himself, and carried on. "Ergo, if this affair is not stopped, we can expect Rossala to revolt within a few weeks at the very latest. Rossala will call on the other Nyanzan nations to help—and they've been cleverly maneuvered into arming themselves and setting up a skeleton military organization. If the expert I suspect is behind the revolution, those leaders such as yourself, who demur at the idea, will die and be replaced by more gullible ones. Of course, Nyanza will have been promised outside help: I don't imagine even Derek Umbolu thinks one planet can stand off all Terra's power. Merseia is not too far away. If everything goes smoothly, we'll end up with a nominally independent Nyanza which is actually a Merseian puppet—deep within Terran space. If the attempt fails, well, what's one more radioactive wreck of a world to Merseia?"

There was a stillness.

In the end Inyanduma said grayly: "I don't know but what the hazard you speak of will be better than to call in the Terrans; for in sooth all our nations have broken your law in that we have gathered weapons as you say. The Imperials would nay leave us what self-government we now have."

"They might not be necessary," said Flandry. "Since you do have those weapons, and the City constabulary is a legally armed native force with some nuclear equipment . . . you could do your own housecleaning. I could supervise the operation, make sure it was thorough, stamp my report to headquarters Fantastically Secret, and that would be the close of the affair."

He stood up. "Think it over," he said.

It was peaceful out on the rock. Flandry's reel hummed, the lure flashed through brilliant air, the surf kittened gigantically with his hook. It did not seem to matter greatly that he got never a nibble. The tide began to rise again, he'd have to go inside or exchange his rod for a trident. . . .

A kayak came over drowned skerries like something alive. Derek Umbolu brought it to Flandry's feet and looked up. His face was sea-wet, which was merciful; Flandry did not want to know whether the giant was crying.

"Blood," croaked Derek. "Blood, and the chairs broken, I could see in the blood how he was dragged out and thrown to the fish."

Hollowness lay in Dominic Flandry's heart. He felt his shoulders slump. "I'm sorry," he said. "Oh, God, I'm sorry."

Words ripped out, flat, hurried, under the ramping tidal noise:

"They center in Rossala, but someone in Uhunhu captains it. I was to seize control here when they rise, if Inyanduma will nay let us help the revolution. I hated the killing of old Bannerji, but it was needful. For now there will be nay effective space traffic control, till they replace him, and in two weeks there will come ships from Merseia with heavy nuclear war-weapons such as we can't make on this planet. The same man who gaffed Bannerji tried for you. He was the only trained assassin in Jairnovaunt—and a neighbor gave you alibi—so I believe none of his whinings that he'd nay touched my father. His name was Mamoud Shufi. Cursed be it till the sun is cold clinkers!"

One great black hand unzipped the kayak cover. The other hand swooped down, pulled out something which dripped, and flung it at the Terran's feet so hard that one dead eye burst from the lopped-off head.

VIII

Elsewhere on Nyanza it growled battle, men speared and shot each other, ships went to the bottom and buildings cracked open like rotten fruit. Where Flandry stood was only turquoise and lace. Perhaps some of the high white clouds banked in the west had a smoky tinge.

A crewman with a portable sonic fathometer nodded. "We're over Uhunhu shoals now, sir."

"Stop the music," said Flandry. The skipper transmitted several orders, he felt the pulse of engines die, the submarine lay quiet. Looking down gray decks past the shark's fin of a conning tower, Flandry saw crewmen gathering in a puzzled, almost resentful way. They had expected to join the fighting, till this Terran directed the ship eastward.

"And now," said Derek Umbolu grimly, "will you have the kindness to say why we steered clear of Rossala?"

Flandry cocked an eyebrow. "Why are you so anxious to kill other men?" he countered.

Derek bristled. "I'm nay afraid to hazard my skin, Impy . . . like someone I could name!"

"There's more to it than that," said Flandry. He was not sure why he prattled cheap psychology when a monster crouched under his feet. Postponing the moment? He glanced at Tessa Hoorn, who had insisted on coming. "Do you see what I mean, Lightmistress? Do you know why he itches so to loose his harpoon?"

Some of the chill she had shown him in the past week thawed. "Aye," she said. "Belike I do. It's blood guilt enough that we're party to a war

'gainst our own planetmen, without being safe
into the bargain."

He wondered how many shared her feelings.
Probably no large number. After he and Inyanduma flew to the City and got the Warden to
mobilize his constables, a call had gone out for
volunteers. The Nyanzan public had only been
informed that a dangerous conspiracy had been
discovered, centered in Rossala, that the Sheikh
had refused the police right of entry, and that
therefore a large force would be needed to seize
that nation over the resistance of its misguided
citizens and occupy it while the Warden's
specialists sniffed out the actual plotters. And
men had come by the many thousands, from all
over the planet.

It was worse, though, for those who knew what
really lay behind this police operation.

Flandry mused aloud, "I wonder if you'll ever
start feeling that way about your fellowmen,
wherever they happen to live?"

"Enough!" rapped Derek Umbolu. "Say why
you brought us hither and be done!"

Flandry kindled a cigaret and stared over the
rail, into chuckling sun-glittering waves so clear
that he could see how the darkness grew with
every meter of depth. He said:

"Down there, if he hasn't been warned somehow that I know about him, is the enemy."

"Ai-a!" Tessa Hoorn dropped a hand to her
gun; but Flandry saw with an odd little pain how
she moved all unthinkingly closer to Derek. "But
who would lair in drowned Uhunhu?"

"The name I know him by is A'u," said Flandry.
"He isn't human. He can breathe water as well as

air—I suppose his home planet must be pretty wet, though I don't know where it is. But it's somewhere in the Merseian Empire, and he, like me, belongs to the second oldest profession. We've played games before now. I flushed him on Conjumar two Earth-years ago: my boys cleaned up his headquarters, and his personal spaceship took a near miss that left it lame and radioactive. But he got away. Not home, his ship wasn't in that good a condition, but away."

Flandry trickled smoke sensuously through his nostrils. It might be the last time. "On the basis of what I've seen here, I'm now certain that friend A'u made for Nyanza, ditched, contacted some of your malcontents, and started cooking revolution. The whole business has his signature, with flourishes. If nothing else, a Nyanzan uprising and Merseian intervention would get him passage home; and he might have inflicted a major defeat on Terra in the process."

A mumbling went through the crewfolk, wrath which was half terror. "Sic semper local patriots," finished Flandry. "I want to be ruddy damn sure of getting A'u, and he has a whole ocean bottom to hide on if he's alarmed, and we'll be too busy setting traps for the Merseian gunrunners due next week to play tag for very long. Otherwise I'd certainly have waited till we could bring a larger force."

"Thirty men 'gainst one poor hunted creature?" scoffed Tessa.

"He's a kind of big creature," said Flandry quietly to her.

He looked at his followers, beautiful and black in the sunlight, with a thousand hues of blue at their backs, a low little wind touching bare skins, and the clean male shapes of weapons. It was too fair a world to gamble down in dead Uhunhu. Flandry knew with wry precision why he was leading this chase—not for courage, nor glory, nor even one more exploit to embroider for some high-prowed yellow-haired bit of Terran fluff. He went because he was an Imperial and if he stayed behind the colonials would laugh at him.

Therefore he took one more drag of smoke, flipped his cigaret parabolically overboard, and murmured: "Be good, Tessa, and I'll bring you back a lollipop. Let's go chilluns."

And snapped down his helmet and dove cleanly over the side.

The water became a world. Overhead was an area of sundazzle, too bright to look on; elsewhere lay cool dusk fading downward into night. The submarine was a basking whale shape . . . too bad he couldn't just take it down and torpedo A'u, but an unpleasant session with a man arrested in Altla had told him better—A'u expected to be approached only by swimming men. . . . The roof of sunlight grew smaller as he drove himself toward the bottom, until it was a tiny blinding star and then nothing. There was a silken sense of his own steadily rippling muscles and the sea that slid past them, the growing chill stirred his blood in its million channels, a glance behind showed his bubble-stream like a trail of argent planets, his followers were black lightning bolts through an utterly quiet green twilight. O God, to be a seal!

Dimly now, the weed-grown steeps of Uhunhu rose beneath him, monstrous gray dolmens and menhirs raised by no human hands, sunken a million years ago . . . A centuries-drowned ship, the embryo of a new reef ten millennia hence, with a few skulls strewn for fish to nest in, was shockingly raw and new under the leaning walls. Flandry passed it in the silence of a dream.

He did not break that quietude, though his helmet bore voice apparatus. If A'u was still here, A'u must not be alarmed by orders to fan out in a search pattern. Flandry soared close enough to Derek to nod, and the giant waved hands and feet in signals understood by the men. Presently Flandry and Derek were alone in what might once have been a street or perhaps a corridor.

They glided among toppling enormities; now and then one of denser shadow, but it was only a rock or a decapus or a jawbone the size of a portal. Flandry began to feel the cold, deeper than his skin, almost deeper than the silence.

A hand clamped bruisingly on his wrist. He churned to a halt and hung there, head cocked, until the sound that Derek had dimly caught was borne past vibrator and ocean and receiver to his own ears. It was the screaming of a man being killed, but so far and faint it might have been the death agony of a gnat.

Flandry blasphemed eighteen separate gods, kicked himself into motion, and went like a hunting eel through Uhunhu. But Derek passed him and he was almost the last man to reach the fight.

"A'u," he said aloud, uselessly, through the bawl of men and the roil of bloodied waters. He remembered the harpoon rifle slung across his shoulders, unlimbered it, checked the magazine, and wriggled close. Thirty men—no, twenty-nine at the most—a corpse bobbed past, wildly staring through a helmet cracked open—twenty-eight men swirled about one monster. Flandry did not want to hit any of them.

He swam upward, until he looked down on A'u. The great black shape had torpedoed from a dolmen. Fifteen meters long, the wrinkled leather skin of some Arctic golem, the gape of a whale and the boneless arms of an elephant . . . but with hands, with hands . . . A'u raged among his hunters. Flandry saw how the legs which served him on land gripped two men in the talons and plucked their limbs off. There was no sound made by the monster's throat, but the puny human jabber was smashed by each flat concussion of the flukes, as if bombs burst.

Flandry nestled the rifle to his shoulder and fired. Recoil sent him backward, end over end. He did not know if his harpoon had joined the score in A'u's tormented flanks. It had to be this way, he thought, explosives would kill the men too under sea pressure and . . . Blood spurted from a transfixed huge hand. A'u got his back against a monolith, arched his tail, and shot toward the surface. Men sprayed from him like bow water.

Flandry snapped his legs and streaked to meet the thing. The white belly turned toward him, a cliff, a cloud, a dream. He fired once and saw his harpoon bite. Once more! A'u bent double in anguish, spoke blood, somehow sensed the man and plunged at him. Flandry looked down a cave of horrible teeth. He looked into the eyes behind; they were blind with despair. He tried to scramble aside. A'u changed course with a snake's ease. Flandry had a moment to wonder if A'u knew him again.

A man flew from the blood-fog. He fired a harpoon, holding himself steady against its back-thrust. Instead of letting the line trail, to tangle the beast, he grabbed it, was pulled up almost to the side. The gills snapped at him like mouths. He followed the monster, turn for turn through cold deeps, as he sought aim. Finally he shot. An eye went out. A brain was cloven. A'u turned over and died.

Flandry gasped after breath. His helmet rang and buzzed, it was stifling him, he must snatch it off before he choked. . . . Hands caught him. He looked into the victory which was Derek Umbolu's face. "Wait there, wait, Terra man," said a remote godlike calm. "All is done now."

"I, I, I, thanks!" rattled Flandry.

His wind came back to him. He counted the men that gathered, while they rose with all due slowness toward the sun. Six were dead. Cheap enough to get rid of A'u.

If I had been cast away, alone, on the entire world of a hideous race . . . I wonder if I would have had the courage to survive this long.

I wonder if there are some small cubs, on a water planet deep among the Merseian stars, who can't understand why father hasn't come home.

He climbed on deck at last, threw back his helmet and sat down under Tessa Hoorn's anxious gaze. "Give me a cigaret," he said harshly. "And break out something alcoholic."

She wrestled herself to steadiness. "Caught you the monster?" she asked.

"Aye," said Derek.

"We close to didn't," said Flandry. "Our boy Umbolu gets the credit."

"Small enough vengeance for my father," said the flat voice of sorrow.

The submarine's captain saluted the pale man who sat hugging his knees, shivering and drinking smoke. "Word just came in from Rossala, sir," he reported. "The Sheikh has yielded, though he swears he'll protest the outrage to the next Imperial resident. But he'll let the constables occupy his realm and search as they wish."

Search for a number of earnest, well-intentioned young patriots, who'll never again see morning over broad waters. Well—I suppose it all serves the larger good. It must. Our noble homosexual Emperor says so himself.

"Excellent," said Flandry. His glance sought Derek. "Since you saved my life, you've got a reward coming. Your father."

"Hoy?" The big young man trod backward a step.

"He isn't dead," said Flandry. "I talked him into helping me. We faked an assassination. He's probably at home this minute, suffering from an acute case of conscience."

"*What?*" The roar was like hell's gates breaking down.

Flandry winced. "Pianissimo, please." He waved the snarling, fist-clenching bulk back with his cigaret. "All right, I played a trick on you."

"A trick I could have 'waited from a filthy Impy!" Tessa Hoorn spat at his feet.

"Touch me, brother Umbolu, and I'll arrest you for treason," said Flandry. "Otherwise I'll exercise my discretionary powers and put you on lifetime probation in the custody of some responsible citizen." He grinned wearily. "I think the Lightmistress of Little Skua qualifies."

Derek and Tessa stared at him, and at each other.

Flandry stood up. "Probation is conditional on your getting married," he went on. "I recommend that in choosing a suitable female you look past that noble self-righteousness, stop considering the trivium that she can give you some money, and consider all that you might give her." He glanced at them, saw that their hands were suddenly linked together, and had a brief, private, profane conversation with the Norn of his personal destiny. "That includes heirs," he finished. "I'd like to have Nyanza well populated. When the Long Night comes for Terra, somebody will have to carry on. It might as well be you."

He walked past them, into the cabin, to get away from all the dark young eyes.

A MESSAGE
IN SECRET

A MESSAGE IN
SECRET

Seen on approach, against crystal darkness and stars crowded into foreign constellations, Altai was beautiful. More than half the northern hemisphere, somewhat less in the south, was polar cap. Snowfields were tinged rosy by the sun Krasna; naked ice shimmered blue and cold green. The tropical belt, steppe and tundra, which covered the remainder, shaded from bronze to tarnished gold, here and there the quicksilver flash of a big lake. Altai was ringed like Saturn, a tawny hoop with subtle rainbow iridescence flung spinning around the equator, three radii out in space. And beyond were two copper-coin moons.

Captain Sir Dominic Flandry, field agent, Naval Intelligence Corps of the Terrestrial Empire, pulled his gaze reluctantly back to the spaceship's bridge. "I see where its name came from," he remarked. *Altai* meant *Golden* in the language of the planet's human colonists; or so the Betelgeusean trader who passed on his knowledge electronically to Flandry had insisted. "But Krasna is a misnomer for the sun. It isn't really red to the human eye. Not nearly as much as your star, for instance. More of an orange-yellow, I'd say."

The blue visage of Zalat, skipper of the battered merchant vessel, twisted into the grimace which was his race's equivalent of a shrug. He was moderately humanoid, though only half as tall as a man, stout, hairless, clad in a metal mesh tunic. "I zuppoze it was de, you zay, contrazt." He spoke Terrestrial Anglic with a thick accent, as if to show that the independence of the Betelgeusean System—buffer state between the hostile realms of Terra and Merseia—did not mean isolation from the mainstream of interstellar culture.

Flandry would rather have practiced his Altaian, especially since Zalat's Anglic vocabulary was so small so to limit conversation to platitudes. But he deferred. As the sole passenger on this ship, of alien species at that, with correspondingly special requirements in diet, he depended on the captain's good will. Also, the Betelgeuseans took him at face value. Officially, he was only being sent to re-establish contact between Altai and the rest of mankind. Officially, his mission was so minor that Terra didn't even give him a ship of his own, but left him to negotiate passage as best he might. . . . So, let Zalat chatter.

"After all," continued the master, "Altai was firzt colonized more dan zeven hoondert Terra-years a-pazt: in de verry dawn, you say, of interztellar travel. Little was known about w'at to eggzpect. Krazna muzt have been deprezzingly cold and red, after Zol. Now-to-days, we have more aztronautical zophizticatzion."

Flandry looked to the blaze of space, stars and stars and stars. He thought that an estimated four million of them, included in that vague sphere called the Terrestrial Empire, was an insignificant portion of this one spiral arm of this one commonplace galaxy. Even if you added the other empires, the sovereign suns like Betelgeuse, the reports of a few explorers who had gone extremely far in the old days, that part of the universe known to man was terrifyingly small. And it would always remain so.

"Just how often do you come here?" he asked, largely to drown out silence.

"About onze a Terra-year," answered Zalat. "However, dere is ot'er merchantz on dis route. I have de fur trade, but Altai alzo produzes gemz, mineralz, hides, variouz organic productz, even dried meatz, w'ich are in zome demand at home. Zo dere is usually a Betelgeusean zhip or two at Ulan Baligh."

"Will you be here long?"

"I hope not. It iz a tediouz plaze for a nonhuman. One pleasure houze for uz haz been eztablizhed, but—" Zalat made another face. "Wid de dizturbanzez going on, fur trapping and caravanz have been much hampered. Lazt time I had to wait a ztandard mont' for a full cargo. Diz time may be worze."

Oh-oh, thought Flandry. But he merely asked aloud: "Since the metals and machinery you bring in exchange are so valuable, I wonder why some Altaians don't acquire spaceships of their own and start trading."

"Dey have not dat kind of zivilization," Zalat replied. "Remember, our people have been coming here for lezz dan a zentury. Before den Altai was izolated, onze de original zhipz had been worn out. Dere was never zo great an interezt among dem in re-eztablizhing galactic contact az would overcome de handicap of poverty in metalz w'ich would have made zpazezship building eggzpenzive for dem. By now, might-be, zome of de younger Altaian malez have zome wizh for zuch an enterprize. But lately de Kha Khan has forbidden any of his zubjectz from leaving de planet, eggzept zome truzted and verry clozemout' perzonal reprezentatives in de Betelgeuzean Zyztem. Dis prohibition is might-be one reazon for de inzurrectionz."

"Yeh." Flandry gave the ice fields a hard look. "If it were my planet, I think I'd look around for an enemy to sell it to."

And still I'm going there, he thought. *Talk about your unsung heroes—! Though I suppose, the more the Empire cracks and crumbles, the more frantically a few of us have to scurry around patching it. Or else the Long Night could come in our own sacrosanct lifetimes.*

And in this particular instance, his mind ran on, *I have reason to believe that an enemy is trying to buy the planet.*

II

Where the Zeya and the Talyma, broad shallow rivers winding southward over the steppes from polar snows, met at Ozero Rurik, the city named Ulan Baligh was long ago founded. It had never been large, and now the only permanent human settlement on Altai had perhaps 20,000 residents. But there was always a ring of encampments around it, tribesmen come to trade or confer or hold rites in the Prophet's Tower. Their tents and trunks walled the landward side of Ulan Baligh, spilled around the primitive spaceport, and raised campfire smoke for many kilometers along the indigo lakeshore.

As the spaceship descended, Captain Flandry was more interested in something less picturesque. Through a magnifying viewport in the after turret, to which he had bribed his way, he saw that monorail tracks encircled the city like spider strands; that unmistakable launchers for heavy missiles squatted on them; that some highly efficient modern military aircraft lazed on grav repulsors in the sky; that barracks and emplacements for an armored brigade were under construction to the west, numerous tanks and beetlecars already prowling on guard; that a squat building in the center of town must house a negagrav generator powerful enough to shield the entire urban area.

That all of this was new.

That none of it came from any factories controlled by Terra.

"But quite probably from our little green chums," he murmured to himself. "A Merseian base here, in the buffer region, outflanking us at Catawrayannis. . . . Well, it wouldn't be decisive in itself, but it would strengthen their hand quite a bit. And eventually, when their hand looks strong enough, they're going to fight."

He suppressed a tinge of bitterness at his own people, too rich to spend treasure in an open attack on the menace—most of them, even, denying that any menace existed, for what would dare break the Pax Terrestria? After all, he thought wryly, he enjoyed his furloughs Home precisely because Terra was decadent.

But for now, there was work at hand. Intelligence had collected hints in the Betelgeuse region: traders spoke of curious goings-on at some place named Altai; the archives mentioned a colony far off the regular space lanes, not so much lost as overlooked; inquiry produced little more than this, for Betelgeusean civilians like Zalat had no interest in Altaian affairs beyond the current price of angora pelts.

A proper investigation would have required some hundreds of men and several months. Being spread horribly thin over far too many stars, Intelligence was able to ship just one man to Betelgeuse. At the Terran Embassy, Flandry received a slim dossier, a stingy expense account, and orders to find what the devil was behind all this. After which, overworked men and machines forgot about him. They would remember when he reported back, or if he died in some spectacular fashion; otherwise, Altai might well lie obscure for another decade.

Which could be a trifle too long, Flandry thought.

He strolled with elaborate casualness from the turret to his cabin. It must not be suspected on Altai what he had already seen: or, if that information leaked out, it must absolutely not be suspected that *he* suspected these new installations involved more than suppressing a local rebellion. The Khan had been careless about hiding the evidence, presumably not expecting a Terran investigator. He would certainly not be so careless as to let the investigator take significant information home again.

At his cabin, Flandry dressed with his usual care. According to report, the Altaians were people after his own heart: they liked color on their clothes, in great gobs. He chose a shimmerite blouse, green embroidered vest, purple trousers with gold stripe tucked into tooled-leather half boots, crimson sash and cloak, black beret slanted rakishly over his sleek seal-brown hair. He himself was a tall well-muscled man; his long face bore high cheekbones and straight nose, gray eyes, neat mustache. But then, he patronized Terra's best cosmetic biosculptor.

The spaceship landed at one end of the concrete field. Another Betelgeusean vessel towered opposite, confirming Zalat's claims about the trade. Not precisely brisk—maybe a score of ships per standard year—but continuous, and doubtless by now important to the planet's economy.

As he stepped out the debarkation lock, Flandry felt the exhilaration of a gravity only three-fourths that of Home. But it was quickly lost when the air stung him. Ulan Baligh lay at eleven degrees north latitude. With an axial tilt about like Terra's, a wan dwarf sun, no oceans to moderate the climate, Altai knew seasons almost to the equator. The northern hemisphere was approaching winter. A wind streaking off the pole sheathed Flandry in chill, hooted around his ears, and snatched the beret from his head.

He grabbed it back, swore, and confronted the portmaster with less dignity than he had planned. "Greeting," he said as instructed; "may peace dwell in your yurt. This person is named Dominic Flandry, and ranges Terra, the Empire."

The Altaian blinked narrow black eyes, but otherwise kept his face a mask. It was a wide, rather flat countenance, but not purely mongoloid: hook nose, thick close-cropped beard, light skin bespoke caucasoid admixture as much as the hybrid language. He was short, heavy-set, a wide-brimmed fur hat was tied in place, his leather jacket was lacquered in an intricate design, his pants were of thick felt and his boots fleece-lined. An old-style machine pistol was holstered at his left side, a broad-bladed knife on the right.

"We have not had such visitors—" He paused, collected himself, and bowed. "Be welcome, all guests who come with honest words," he said ritually. "This person is named Pyotr Gutchluk, of the Kha Khan's sworn men." He turned to Zalat. "You and your crew may proceed directly to the yamen. We can handle the formalities later. I must personally conduct so distinguished a . . . a guest to the palace."

He clapped his hands. A couple of servants appeared, men of his own race, similarly dressed and similarly armed. Their eyes glittered, seldom leaving the Terran; the woodenness of their faces must cover an excitement which seethed. Flandry's luggage was loaded on a small electro-truck of antique design. Pyotr Gutchluk said, half inquiringly, "Of course so great an orluk as yourself would prefer a varyak to a tulyak."

"Of course," said Flandry, wishing his education had included those terms.

He discovered that a varyak was a native-made motorcycle. At least, that was the closest Terran word. It was a massive thing on two wheels, smoothly powered from a bank of energy capacitors, a baggage rack aft and a machine-gun mount forward. It was steered with the knees, which touched a crossbar. Other controls were on a manual panel behind the windscreen. An outrigger wheel could be lowered for support when the vehicle was stationary or moving slowly. Pyotr Gutchluk offered a goggled crash helmet from a saddlebag and took off at 200 kilometers an hour.

Flandry, accelerating his own varyak, felt the wind come around the screen, slash his face and nearly drag him from the saddle. He started to slow down. But—*Come now, old chap. Imperial prestige, stiff upper lip, and so on drearily.* Somehow he managed to stay on Gutchluk's tail as they roared into the city.

Ulan Baligh formed a crescent, where the waters of Ozero Rurik cut a bay into the flat shore. Overhead was a deep-blue sky, and the rings. Pale by day, they made a frosty halo above the orange sun. In such a light, the steeply upcurving red tile roofs took on the color of fresh blood. Even the ancient gray stone walls beneath were tinged faint crimson. All the buildings were large, residences holding several families each, commercial ones jammed with tiny shops. The streets were wide, clean-swept, full of nomads and the wind. Gutchluk took an overhead road, suspended from pylons cast like dragons holding the cables in their teeth. It seemed an official passageway, nearly empty save for an occasional varyak patrol.

It also gave a clear view of the palace, standing in walled gardens: a giant version of the other houses but gaudily painted and colonnaded with wooden dragons. The royal residence was, however, overshadowed by the Prophet's Tower. So was everything else.

Flandry understood from vague Betelgeusean descriptions that most of Altai professed a sort of Moslem-Buddhist synthesis, codified centuries ago by the Prophet Subotai. The religion had only this one temple, but that was enough. A sheer two kilometers it reared up into the thin hurried air, as if it would spear a moon. Basically a pagoda, blinding red, it had one blank wall facing north. No, not blank either, but a single flat tablet on which, in a contorted Sino-Cyrillic alphabet, the words of the Prophet stood holy forever. Even Flandry, with scant reverence in his heart, knew a moment's awe. A stupendous will had raised that spire above these plains.

The elevated road swooped downward again. Gutchluk's varyak slammed to a halt outside the palace. Flandry, taller than any man of Altai, was having trouble with his steering bar. He almost crashed into the wrought-bronze gate. He untangled his legs and veered in bare time, a swerve that nearly threw him. Up on the wall, a guard leaned on his portable rocket launcher and laughed. Flandry heard him and swore. He continued the curve, steered a ring around Gutchluk so tight that it could easily have killed them both, slapped down the third wheel and let the cycle slow itself to a halt while he leaped from the saddle and took a bow.

"By the Ice People!" exclaimed Gutchluk. Sweat shone on his face. He wiped it off with a shaky hand. "They breed reckless men on Terra!"

"Oh, no," said Flandry, wishing he dared mop his own wet skin. "A bit demonstrative, perhaps, but never reckless."

Once again he had occasion to thank loathed

hours of calisthenics and judo practice for a re-
sponsive body. As the gates opened—Gutchluk
had used his panel radio to call ahead—Flandry
jumped back on his varyak and putt-putted
through under the guard's awed gaze.

The garden was rocks, arched bridges, dwarf
trees, and mutant lichen. Little that was Terran
would grow on Altai. Flandry began to feel the
dryness of his own nose and throat. This air
snatched moisture from him as greedily as it did
heat. He was more grateful for the warmth inside
the palace than he wished to admit.

A white-bearded man in a fur-trimmed robe
made a deep bow. "The Kha Khan himself bids
you welcome, Orluk Flandry," he said. "He will
see you at once."

"But the gifts I brought—"

"No matter now, my lord." The chamberlain
bowed again, turned and led the way down
arched corridors hung with tapestries. It was very
silent: servants scurried about whispering,
guards with modern blasters stood rigid in
dragon-faced leather tunics and goggled helmets,
tripods fumed bitter incense. The entire sprawl
ing house seemed to crouch, watchful.

I imagine I have upset them somewhat, thought
Flandry. *Here they have some cozy little
conspiracy—with beings sworn to lay all Terra
waste, I suspect—and suddenly a Terran officer
drops in, for the first time in five or six hundred
years. Yes-s-s.*

So what do they do next? It's their move.

III

Oleg Yesukai, Kha Khan of All the Tribes, was bigger than most Altaians, with a long sharp face and a stiff reddish beard. He wore gold rings, a robe thickly embroidered, silver trim on his fur cap, but all with an air of impatient concession to tedious custom. The hand which Flandry, kneeling, touched to his brow, was hard and muscular; the gun at the royal waist had seen use. This private audience chamber was curtained in red, its furniture inlaid and grotesquely carved; but it also held an ultramodern Betelgeusean graphone and a desk buried under official papers.

"Be seated," said the Khan. He himself took a low-legged chair and opened a carved-bone cigar box. A smile of sorts bent his mouth. "Now that we've gotten rid of all my damned fool courtiers, we need no longer act as if you were a vassal." He took a crooked purple stogie from the box. "I would offer you one of these, but it might make you ill. In thirty-odd generations, eating Altaian food, we have probably changed our metabolism a bit."

"Your majesty is most gracious." Flandry inhaled a cigaret of his own and relaxed as much as the straightbacked furniture permitted.

Oleg Khan spoke a stockbreeder's pungent obscenity. "Gracious? My father was an outlaw on the tundra at fifteen." (He meant local years, a third again as long as Terra's. Altai was about one A.U. distant from Krasna, but the sun was less massive than Sol.) "At thirty he had seized Ulan Baligh with 50,000 warriors and deposited old

Tuli Khan naked on the artic snows: so as not to shed royal blood, you understand. But he never would live here, and all his sons grew up in the ordu, the encampment, as he had done, practiced war against the Tebtengri as he had known war, and mastered reading, writing, and science to boot. Let us not bother with graciousness, Orluk Flandry. I never had time to learn any."

The Terran waited passive. It seemed to disconcert Oleg, who smoked for a minute in short ferocious drags, then leaned forward and said, "Well, why does your government finally deign to notice us?"

"I had the impression, your majesty," said Flandry in a mild voice, "that the colonists of Altai came this far from Sol in order to escape notice."

"True. True. Don't believe that rat crud in the hero songs. Our ancestors came here because they were weak, not strong. Planets where men could settle at all were rare enough to make each one a prize, and there was little law in those days. By going far and picking a wretched icy desert, a few shiploads of Central Asians avoided having to fight for their home. Nor did they plan to become herdsmen. They tried to farm, but it proved impossible. Too cold and dry, among other things. They could not build an industrial, food-synthesizing society either: not enough heavy metals, fossil fuels, fissionables. This is a low-density planet, you know. Step by step, over generations, with only dim traditions to guide them, they were forced to evolve a nomadic life. And that was suited to Altai; that worked, and their numbers increased. Of course, legends have grown up. Most of my people still believe Terra is some kind of lost utopia and our ancestors were hardy warriors." Oleg's rust-colored eyes narrowed upon Flandry. He stroked his beard. "I've read enough, thought enough, to have a fair idea of what your Empire is and what it can do. So—why this visit, at this exact moment?"

"We are no longer interested in conquest for its own sake, your majesty," said Flandry. True, as far as it went. "And our merchants have avoided this sector for several reasons. It lies far from heartland stars; the Betelgeuseans, close to their own home, can compete on unequal terms; the risk of meeting some prowling warship of our Merseian enemies is unattractive. There has, in short, been no occasion, military or civilian, to search out Altai." He slipped smoothly into prevarication gear. "However, it is not the Emperor's wish that any members of the human family be cut off. At the very least, I bring you his brotherly greetings." (That was subversive. It should have been "fatherly." But Oleg Khan would not take kindly to being patronized.) "At most, if Altai wished to rejoin us, for mutual protection and other benefits, there are many possibilities which could be discussed. An Imperial resident, say, to offer help and advice—"

He let the proposal trail off, since in point of fact a resident's advice tended to be, "I suggest you do thus and so lest I call in the Marines."

The Altaian king surprised him by not getting huffy about sovereign status. Instead, amiable as a tiger, Oleg Yesukai answered: "If you are distressed about our internal difficulties, pray do not be. Nomadism necessarily means tribalism, which usually means feud and war. I already spoke of my father's clan seizing planetary leadership from the Nuro Bator. We in turn have rebellious gurkhans. As you will hear in court, that alliance called the Tebtengri Shamanate is giving us trouble. But such is nothing new in Altain history. Indeed, I have a firmer hold over more of the planet than any Kha Khan since the Prophet's day. In a little while more I shall bring every last clan to heel."

"With the help of imported armament?" Flandry elevated his brows a millimeter. Risky though it was to admit having seen the evidence, it might be still more suspicious not to. And indeed the other man seemed unruffled. Flandry continued, "The Imperium would gladly send a technical mission."

"I do not doubt it." Oleg's response was dry.

"May I respectfully ask what planet supplies the assistance your majesty is now receiving?"

"Your question is impertinent, as well you know. I do not take offense, but I decline to answer." Confidentially: "The old mercantile treaties with Betelgeuse guarantee monopolies in certain exports to their traders. This other race is taking payment in the same articles. I am not bound by oaths sworn by the Nuro Bator dynasty, but at present it would be inexpedient that Betelgeuse discover the facts."

It was a good spur-of-the-moment lie: so good that Flandry hoped Oleg would believe he had fallen for it. He assumed a fatuous Look-Mom-I'm-a-man-of-the-world smirk. "I understand, great Khan. You may rely on Terrestrial discretion."

"I hope so," said Oleg humorously. "Our traditional punishment for spies involves a method to keep them alive for days after they have been flayed."

Flandry's gulp was calculated, but not altogether faked. "It is best to remind your majesty," he said, "just in case some of your less well-educated citizens should act impulsively, that the Imperial Navy is under standing orders to redress any wrong suffered by any Terran national anywhere in the universe."

"Very rightly," said Oleg. His tone made clear his knowledge that that famous rule had become a dead letter, except as an occasional excuse for bombarding some obstreperous world unable to fight back. Between the traders, his own study missions sent to Betelgeuse, and whoever was arming him—the Kha Khan had become as unmercifully well-informed about galactic politics as any Terran aristocrat.

Or Merseian. The realization was chilling. Flandry had perforce gone blind into his assignment. Only now, piece by piece, did he see how big and dangerous it was.

"A sound policy," continued Oleg. "But let us be perfectly frank, Orluk. If you should suffer, let us say, accidental harm in my dominions—and *if* your masters should misinterpret the circumstances, though of course they would not—I should be forced to invoke assistance which is quite readily available."

Merseia isn't far, thought Flandry, and Intelligence knows they've massed naval units at their closest base. If I want to hoist Terran vintages again, I'd better start acting the fool as never before in a gloriously misspent life.

Aloud, a hint of bluster: "Betelgeuse has treaties with the Imperium, your majesty. They would not interfere in a purely interhuman dispute!" And then, as if appalled at himself: "But surely there won't be any. The, uh, conversation has, uh, taken an undesirable turn. Most unfortunate, your majesty! I was ah, am interested in, er, unusual human colonies, and it was suggested to me by an archivist that—"

And so on and so on.

Oleg Yesukai grinned.

IV

Altai rotated once in 35 hours. The settlers had adapted, and Flandry was used to postponing sleep. He spent the afternoon being guided around Ulan Baligh, asking silly questions which he felt sure his guides would relay to the Khan. The practice of four or five meals during the long day—his were offered in the town houses of chieftains belonging to Clan Yesukai—gave him a chance to build up the role of a young Terran fop who had wangled this assignment from an uninterested Imperium, simply for a lark. A visit to one of the joyhouses, operated for transient nomads, helped reinforce the impression. Also, it was fun.

Emerging after sunset, he saw the Prophet's Tower turned luminous, so that it stood like a bloody lance over brawling, flicker-lit streets. The tablet wall was white, the words thereon in jet: two kilometers of precepts for a stern and bitter way of life. "I say," he exclaimed, "we haven't toured that yet. Let's go."

The chief guide, a burly gray warrior leathered by decades of wind and frost, looked uneasy. "We must hasten back to the palace, Orluk," he said. "A banquet is being prepared."

"Oh, fine. Fine! Though I don't know how much of an orgy I'm in any shape for after this bout. Eh, what?" Flandry nudged the man's ribs with an indecent thumb. "Still, a peek inside, really I must. It's unbelievable, that skyscraper, don't you know."

"We must first cleanse ourselves."

A young man added bluntly: "In no case could it be allowed. You are not an initiate, and there is no holier spot in all the stars."

"Oh, well, in that case—Mind if I photograph it tomorrow?"

"Yes," said the young man. "It is not forbidden, perhaps, but we could not be responsible for what the ordinary tribesman who saw you with your camera might do. None but the Tebtengri would look on the Tower with anything but reverent eyes."

"Teb—"

"Rebels and heathen, up in the north." The older man touched brow and lips, a sign against evil. "Magic-workers at Tengri Nor, traffickers with the Ice People. It is not well to speak of them, only to exterminate them. Now we must hasten, Orluk."

"Oh, yes. Yes. To be sure. Yes, indeed." Flandry scrambled into the tulyak, an open motor carriage with a dragon figurehead.

As he was driven to the palace, he weighed what he knew in an uncomforting balance. Something was going on, much bigger than a local war. Oleg Khan had no intention Terra should hear about it. A Terran agent who actually learned a bit of truth would not go home alive; only a well-born idiot could safely be allowed return passage. Whether or not Flandry could convince the Altaians he was that idiot, remained to be seen. It wouldn't be easy, for certainly he must probe deeper.

Furthermore, my lad, if somehow you do manage to swirl your cloak, twiddle your mustache, and gallop off to call an Imperial task force, Oleg may summon his friends. They are obviously not a private gun-selling concern, as he wants me to think; all Altai couldn't produce enough trade goods to pay for that stuff. So, if the friends get here first and decide to protect this military investment of theirs, there's going to be a fight. And with them dug in on the surface, as well as cruising local space, they'll have all the advantages. The Navy won't thank you, lad, if you drag them into a losing campaign.

He kindled a fresh cigaret and wondered miserably why he hadn't told HQ he was down with Twonk's Disease.

The valet assigned to him, at his guest suite in the palace, was a little puzzled by Terran garments. Flandry spent half an hour choosing his own ensemble. At last, much soothed, he followed an honor guard, who carried bared daggers in their hands, to the banquet hall, where he was placed at the Khan's right.

There was no table. A great stone trough stretched the length of the hall, a hundred men sitting cross-legged on either side. Broth, reminiscent of won-ton soup but with a sharp taste, was poured into it from wheeled kettles. When next the Khan signaled, the soup was drained through traps, spigots flushed the trough clean, and even less identifiable solid dishes were shoveled in. Meanwhile cups of hot, powerfully alcoholic herb tea were kept filled, a small orchestra caterwauled on pipes and drums, and there were some fairly spectacular performances by varyak riders, knife dancers, acrobats, and marksmen. At the meal's end, an old tribal bard stood up and chanted lays; a plump and merry little man was summoned from the bazaars downtown to tell his original stories; gifts from the Khan were given every man present; and the affair broke up. Not a word of conversation had been spoken.

Oh, well, I'm sure everyone else had a hilarious time, Flandry grumbled to himself.

Not quite sober, he followed his guards back to his apartment. The valet bade him goodnight and closed the thick fur drapes which served for internal doors.

There was a radiant globe illuminating the room, but it seemed feeble next to the light filling a glazed balcony window. Flandry opened this and looked out in wonder.

Beneath him lay the darkened city. Past twinkling red campfires, Ozero Rurik stretched in blackness and multiple moonshivers, out to an unseen horizon. On his left the Prophet's Tower leaped up, a perpetual flame crowned with unwinking winter-brilliant stars. Both moons were near the full, ruddy discs six and eight times as broad to the eye as Luna, haloed by ice crystals. Their light drenched the plains, turned the Zeya and Talyma into ribbons of mercury. But the rings dominated all else, bridging the southern sky with pale rainbows. Second by second, thin fire-streaks crossed heaven up there, as meteoric particles from that huge double band hurtled into the atmosphere.

Flandry was not much for gaping at landscapes. But this time it took minutes for him to realize how frigid the air was.

He turned back to the comparative warmth of his suite. As he closed the window, a woman entered from the bedroom.

Flandry had expected some such hospitality. He saw that she was taller than most Altaians, with long blue-black hair and lustrous tilted eyes of a greenish hue rare on this planet. Otherwise a veil and a gold-stiffened cloak hid her. She advanced quickly, till she was very near him, and he waited for some token of submission.

Instead, she stood watching him for close to a minute. It grew so still in the room that he heard the wind on the lake. Shadows were thick in the corners, and the dragons and warriors on the tapestries appeared to stir.

Finally, in a low uneven voice, she said: "Orluk, are you indeed a spy from the Mother of Men?"

"Spy?" Flandry thought, horrified, about *agents provocateurs.* "Good cosmos, no! I mean, that is to say, nothing of the sort!"

She laid a hand on his wrist. The fingers were cold, and clasped him with frantic strength. Her other hand slipped the veil aside. He looked upon a broad fair-skinned face, delicately arched nose, full mouth, and firm chin: handsome rather than pretty. She whispered, so fast and fiercely he had trouble following:

"Whatever you are, you must listen! If you are no warrior, then give the word when you go home to those who are. I am Bourtai Ivanskaya of the Tumurji folk, who belonged to the Tebtengri Shamanate. Surely you have heard speak of them, enemies of Oleg, driven into the north but still at war with him. My father was a noyon, a division commander, well known to Juchi Ilyak. He fell at the battle of Rivers Meet, last year, where the Yesukai men took our whole ordu. I was brought here alive, partly as a hostage—" A flare of haughtiness: "As if that could influence my people!— and partly for the Kha Khan's harem. Since then I have gained a little of his confidence. More important, I have my own connection now, the harem is always a center of intrigue, nothing is secret from it for very long, but much which is secret begins there—"

"I know," said Flandry. He was stunned, almost overwhelmed, but could not help adding: "Bedfellows make strange politics."

She blinked incomprehension and plunged on: "I heard today that a Terran envoy was landed. I thought perhaps, perhaps he was come, knowing a little of what Oleg Yesukai readies against the Mother of Men. Or if he does not, he must be told! I found what woman would be lent him, and arranged the substitution of myself. Ask me not how! I have wormed secrets which give me power over more than one harem guard—it is not enough to load them with antisex hormone on such a tour of duty! I had the right. Oleg Khan is my enemy and the enemy of my dead father, all means of revenge are lawful to me. But more, worse, Holy Terra lies in danger. Listen, Terra man—"

Flandry awoke. For those few seconds, it had been so fantastic he couldn't react. Like a bad stereodrama, the most ludicrous clichés, he was confronted with a girl (it would be a girl, too, and not simply a disgruntled man!) who babbled her autobiography as prologue to some improbable revelation. Now suddenly he understood that this was real: that melodrama does happen once in a while. And if he got caught playing the hero, any role except comic relief, he was dead.

He drew himself up, fended Bourtai off, and said in haste: "My dear young lady, I have not the slightest competence in these matters. Furthermore, I've heard far more plausible stories from far too many colonial girls hoping for a free ride to Terra. Which, I assure you, is actually not a nice place at all for a little colonial girl without funds. I do not wish to offend local pride, but the idea that a single backward planet could offer any threat to the Imperium would be funny if it were not so yawnworthy. I beg you, spare me."

Bourtai stepped back. The cloak fell open. She wore a translucent gown which revealed a figure somewhat stocky for Terran taste but nonetheless full and supple. He would have enjoyed watching that, except for the uncomprehending pain on her face.

"But, my lord Orluk," she stammered, "I swear to you by the Mother of us both—"

You poor romantic, it cried in him, what do you think I am, a god? If you're such a yokel you never heard of planting microphones in a guest room, Oleg Khan is not. Shut up before you kill us both!

Aloud, he got out a delighted guffaw. "Well, by

Sirius, I do call this thoughtful. Furnishing me with a beautiful spy atop everything else! But honestly, darling, you can drop the pretense now. Let's play some more adult games, eh, what?''

He reached out for her. She writhed free, ran across the room, dodged his pursuit and almost shouted through swift tears: "No, you fool, you blind brainless cackler, you will listen! You will listen if I must knock you to the floor and tie you up—and tell them, tell when you come home, ask them only to send a real spy and learn for themselves!''

Flandry cornered her. He grabbed both flailing wrists and tried to stop her mouth with a kiss. She brought her forehead hard against his nose. He staggered back, half blind with the pain, and heard her yelling: "It is the Merseians, great greenskinned monsters with long tails, the Merseians, I tell you, who come in secret from a secret landing field. I have seen them myself, walking these halls after dark, I have heard from a girl to whom a drunken orkhon babbled, I have crept like a rat in the walls and listened myself. They are called Merseians, the most terrible enemy your race and mine have yet known, and—''

Flandry sat down on a couch, wiped blood off his mustache, and said weakly: "Never mind that for now. How do we get out of here? Before the guards come to shoot us down, I mean.''

V

Bourtai fell silent, and he realized he had spoken in Anglic. He realized further that they wouldn't be shot, except to prevent escape. They would be questioned, gruesomely.

He didn't know if there were lenses as well as microphones in the walls. Nor did he know if the bugs passed information on to some watchful human, or only recorded data for study in the morning. He dared assume nothing but the former.

Springing to his feet, he reached Bourtai in one bound. She reacted with feline speed. A hand, edge on, cracked toward his larynx. He had already dropped his head, and took the blow on the hard top of his skull. His own hands gripped the borders of her cloak and crossed forearms at her throat. Before she could jab him in the solar plexus, he yanked her too close to him. She reached up thumbs, to scoop out his eyeballs. He rolled his head and was merely scratched on the nose. After the last buffet, that hurt. He yipped, but didn't let go. A second later, she went limp in his strangle.

He whirled her around, got an arm lock, and let her sag against him. She stirred. So brief an oxygen starvation had brought no more than a moment's unconsciousness. He buried his face in her dark flowing hair, as if he were a lover. It had a warm, somehow summery smell. He found an ear and breathed softly:

"You little gristlehead, did it ever occur to you that the Khan is suspicious of me? That there must be listeners? Now our forlorn chance is to get out of here. Steal a Betelgeusean spaceship, maybe. First, though, I must pretend I am arresting you, so they won't come here with too much haste and alertness for us. Understand? Can you play the part?

She grew rigid. He felt her almost invisible nod. The hard young body leaning on him eased into a smoothness of controlled nerve and muscle. He had seldom known a woman this competent in a physical emergency. Unquestionably, Bourtai Ivanskaya had military training.

She was going to need it.

Aloud, Flandry huffed: "Well, I've certainly never heard anything more ridiculous! There aren't any Merseians around here. I checked very carefully before setting out. Wouldn't want to come across them, don't you know, and spend maybe a year in some dreary Merseian jail while the pater negotiated my release. Eh, what? Really now, it's perfect rot, every word." He hemmed and hawed a bit. "I think I'd better turn you in, madam. Come along, now, no tricks!"

He marched her out the door, into a pillared corridor. One end opened on a window, twenty meters above a night-frozen fishpond. The other stretched into dusk, lit by infrequent bracketed lamps. Flandry hustled Bourtai down that side. Presently they came to a downward-sweeping staircase. A pair of sentries, in helmets, leather jackets, guns and knives, stood posted there. One of them aimed and barked: "Halt! What would you?"

"This girl, don't you know," panted Flandry. He nudged Bourtai, who gave some realistic squirmings. "Started to babble all sorts of wild nonsense. Who's in charge here? She thought I'd help her against the Kha Khan. Imagine!"

"What?" A guardsman trod close.

"The Tebtengri will avenge me!" snarled Bourtai. "The Ice People will house in the ruin of this palace!"

Flandry thought she was overacting, but the guards both looked shocked. The nearer one sheathed his blaster. "I shall hold her, Orluk," he said. "Boris, run for the commander."

As he stepped close, Flandry let the girl go. With steel on his pate and stiff leather on his torso, the sentry wasn't very vulnerable. Except— Flandry's right hand rocketed upward. The heel of it struck the guard under the nose. He lurched backward, caromed off the balustrade, and flopped dead on the stairs. The other, half-turned to go, spun about on one booted heel. He snatched for his weapon. Bourtai put a leg behind his ankles and pushed. Down he went, Flandry pounced. They rolled over, clawing for a grip. The guard yelped. Flandry saw Bourtai over his opponent's shoulder. She had taken the belt off the first warrior and circled about with the leather in her hands. Flandry let his enemy get on top. Bourtai put the belt around the man's neck, a knee between his shoulder-blades, and heaved.

Flandry scrambled from below. "Get their blasters," he gasped. "Here, give me one. Quick! We've made more racket than I hoped. Do you know the best way to escape? Lead on, then!"

Bourtai raced barefoot down the steps. Her goldcloth cloak and frail gown streamed behind her, insanely, unfitting for the occasion. Flandry came behind, one flight, two flights.

Boots clattered on marble. Rounding yet another spiral curve, Flandry met a squad of soldiers quick-stepping upward. The leader hailed him: "Do you have the evil woman, Orluk?"

So there had been a continuous listener. Of course, even surrendering Bourtai, Flandry could not save his own skin. Harmless fop or no, he had heard too much.

The squad's eyes registered the girl's blaster

even as their chief spoke. Someone yelled. Bourtai fired into the thick of them. Ionic lightning crashed. Flandry dropped. A bolt sizzled where he had been. He fired, wide-beam, the energy too diluted to kill even at this range but scorching four men at once. As their screams lifted, he bounced back to his feet, overleaped the fallen front line, stiff-armed a warrior beyond, and hit the landing.

From here, a bannister curled grandly to the ground floor. Flandry whooped, seated himself, and slid. At the bottom was a sort of lobby, with glass doors opening on the garden. The moons and rings were so bright that no headlights shone from the half-dozen varyaks roaring toward this entrance. Mounted guardsmen, attracted by the noise of the fight—Flandry stared around. Arched windows flanked the doors, two meters up. He gestured to Bourtai, crouched beneath one and made a stirrup of his hands. She nodded, soared to the sill, broke glass with her gun butt, and fired into the troop. Flandry took shelter behind a column and blasted loose at the remnant of the infantry squad, stumbling down the stairs in pursuit. Their position hopelessly exposed to him, they retreated from sight.

A varyak leaped through the doors. The arms of the soldier aboard it shielded his face against flying glass. Flandry shot before the man had uncovered himself. The varyak, sensitively controlled, veered and went down across the doorway. The next one hurtled over it. The rider balanced himself with a trained body, blazing away at the Terran. Bourtai dropped him from above.

She sprang down unassisted. "I got two more

outside," she said. "Another pair are lurking, calling for help—"

"We'll have to chance them. Where are the nearest gates?"

"They will be closed! We cannot burn through the lock before—"

"I'll find a means. Quick, up on this saddle. Slowly, now, out the door behind me. Right the putt-putts of those two men you killed and stand by." Flandry had already dragged a corpse from one varyak (not without an instant's compassionate wondering what the man had been like alive) and set the machine back on its wheels. He sprang to the seat and went full speed out the shattered door.

So far, energy weapons had fulfilled their traditional military function, giving more value to purposeful speed of action than mere numbers. But there was a limit: two people couldn't stave off hundreds for very long. He had to get clear.

Flame sought him. He lacked skill to evade such fire by tricky riding. Instead, he plunged straight down the path, crouched low and hoping he wouldn't be pierced. A bolt burned one leg, slightly but with savage pain. He reached the gloomy, high-arched bridge he wanted. His cycle snorted up and over. Just beyond the hump, he dropped off, relaxing muscles and cushioning himself with an arm in judoka style. Even so, he bumped his nose. For a moment, tears blinded him, and he used bad words. Then the two enemy varyaks followed each other across the bridge. He sprang up on the railing, unseen, and shot both men as they went by.

Vaguely, he heard an uproar elsewhere. One by

one, the palace windows lit, until scores of dragon eyes glared into night. Flandry slid down the bridge, disentangled the heaped varyaks, and hailed Bourtai. "Bring the other machines!" She came, riding one and leading two more by tethers to the guide bars. He had felt reasonably sure that would be standard equipment; if these things were commonly used by nomads, there'd be times when a string of pack vehicles was required.

"We take two," he muttered. Here, beneath an overleaning rock, they were a pair of shadows. Moonlight beyond made the garden one fog of coppery light. The outer wall cut that off, brutally black, with merlons raised against Altai's rings like teeth. "The rest, we use to ram down the gates. Can do?"

"Must do!" she said, and set the varyak control panels. "Here. Extra helmets and clothing are always kept in the saddlebags. Put on the helmet, at least. The clothes we can don later."

"We won't need them for a short dash—"

"Do you think the spaceport is not now a-crawl with Yesukai men?"

"Oh, hell," said Flandry.

He buckled on the headgear, snapped down the goggles, and mounted anew. Bourtai ran along the varyak line, flipping main switches. The riderless machines took off. Gravel spurted from their wheels into Flandry's abused face. He followed the girl.

A pair of warriors raced down a cross path briefly stark under the moons and then eaten again by murk. They had not seen their quarry. The household troops must be in one classic confusion, Flandry thought. He had to escape before hysteria faded and systematic hunting was organized.

The palace gates loomed before him, heavy bars screening off a plaza that was death-white in the moon radiance. Flandry saw his varyaks only as meteoric gleams. Sentries atop the wall had a better view. Blasters thundered, machine guns raved, but there were no riders to drop from those saddles.

The first varyak hit with a doomsday clangor. It rebounded in four pieces. Flandry sensed a chunk of red-hot metal buzz past his ear. The next one crashed, and the bars buckled. The third smote and collapsed across a narrow opening. The fourth flung the gates wide. *"Now!"*

At 200 KPH, Bourtai and Flandry made for the gateway. They had a few seconds without fire from the demoralized men above them. Bourtai hit the toppled machines. Her own climbed that pile, took off, and soared halfway across the plaza. Flandry saw her balance herself, precise as a bird, land on two wheels and vanish in an alley beyond the square. Then it was his turn. He wondered fleetingly what the chances of surviving a broken neck were, and hoped he would not. Not with the Khan's interrogation chambers waiting. Whoops, bang, here we go! He knew he couldn't match Bourtai's performance. He slammed down the third wheel in midair. He hit ground with less violence than expected: first-class shock absorbers on this cycle. An instant he teetered, almost rolling over. He came down on his outrigger. Fire spattered off stone behind him. He retracted the extra wheel and gunned his motor.

A glance north, past the Tower toward the

spaceport, showed him grav-beam air-boats aloft, a hornet swarm. He had no prayer of hijacking a Betelgeusean ship. Nor was it any use to flee to Zalat in the yamen. Where, then, beneath these unmerciful autumnal stars?

Bourtai was a glimpse in moonlight, half a kilometer ahead of him down a narrow nighted street. He let her take the lead, concentrated grimly on avoiding accidents. It seemed like an eyeblink, and it seemed like forever, before they were out of the city and onto the open steppe.

VI

Wind lulled in long grasses, the whispering ran for kilometers, on and on beyond the world's edge, pale yellow-green in a thousand subtle hues rippled by the wind's footsteps. Here and there the spiky red of some frost-nipped bush thrust up; the grasses swirled about it like a sea. High and high overhead, incredibly high, an infinite vault full of wind and deepblue chill, the sky reached. Krasna burned low in the west, dull orange, painting the steppe with ruddy light and fugitive shadows. The rings were an ice bridge to the south; northward the sky had a bleak greenish shimmer which Bourtai said was reflection off an early snowfall.

Flandry crouched in grasses as tall as himself. When he ventured a peek, he saw the airboat that hunted them. It spiraled lazy, but the mathematics guiding it and its cohorts wove a net around this planet. To his eyes, even through binoculars taken from a saddlebag, the boat was so far as to be a mere metallic flash; but he knew it probed for him with telescopes, ferrous detectors, infrared amplifiers.

He would not have believed he could escape the Khan's hundreds of searching craft this long. Two Altaian days, was it? Memory had faded. He knew only a fever dream of bounding north on furious wheels, his skin dried and bleeding from the air; sleeping a few seconds at a time, in the saddle, eating jerked meat from the varyak supplies as he rode, stopping to refill canteens at a waterhole Bourtai had found by signs invisible to him. He knew only how he ached, to the nucleus of his inmost cell, and how his brain was gritty from weariness.

But the plain was unbelievably huge, almost twice the land area of all Terra. The grass was often as high as this, veiling prey from sky-borne eyes. They had driven through several big herds, to break their trail; they had dodged and woven under Bourtai's guidance, and she had a hunter's knowledge of how to confuse pursuit.

Now, though, the chase seemed near its end.

Flandry glanced at the girl. She sat cross-legged, impassive, showing her own exhaustion just by the darkening under her eyes. In stolen leather clothes, hair braided under the crash helmet, she might have been a boy. But the grease smeared on her face for protection had not much affected its haughty good looks. The man hefted his gun. "Think he'll spot us?" he asked. He didn't speak low, but the blowing immensities around reduced all voices to nothing.

"Not yet," she answered. "He is at the extreme detector range, and cannot swoop down at every dubious flicker of instrument readings."

"So . . . ignore him and he'll go away?"

"I fear not." She grew troubled. "They are no fools, the Khan's troopers. I know that search pattern. He and his fellows will circle about, patrolling much the same territory until nightfall. Then, as you know, if we try to ride further, we must turn on the heaters of our varyaks or freeze to death. And that will make us a flame to the infrared spotters."

Flandry rubbed his smooth chin. Altaian garments were ridiculously short on him, so thank all elegant gods for antibeard enzyme! He wished he dared smoke. "What can we do?" he said.

She shrugged. "Stay here. There are well-insulated sleeping bags, which ought to keep us alive if we share a single one. But if the local temperature drops far enough below zero, our own breath and body radiation may betray us."

"How close are we to your friends?"

Bourtai rubbed tired hazel eyes. "I cannot say. They move about, under the Khrebet and along the Kara Gobi fringe. At this time of year they will be drifting southward, so we are not so terribly far from one or another ordu, I suppose. Still, distances are never small on the steppe." After a moment: "If we live the night, we can still not drive to find them. The varyaks' energy cells are nigh exhausted. We shall have to walk."

Flandry glanced at the vehicles, now battered and dusty beyond recognition. Wonderfully durable gadgets, he thought in a vague way. Largely handmade, of course, using small power tools and the care possible in a nonmercantile economy. The radios, though, were short range. . . . No use getting wistful. The first call for Tebtengri help would bring that aircraft overhead down like a swooping falcon.

He eased himself to his back and let his muscles throb. The ground was cold under him. After a moment, Bourtai followed suit, snuggling close in somehow childlike trustfulness.

"If we do not escape, well, such is the space-time pattern," she said, more clamly than he could have managed. "But if we do, what then is your plan, Orluk?"

"Get word to Terra, I suppose. Don't ask me how."

"Will not your friends come avenging when you fail to return?"

"No. The Khan need only tell the Betelgeuseans that I, regrettably, died in some accident or riot or whatever, and will be cremated with full honors. It would not be difficult to fake: a blaster-charred corpse about my size, perhaps, for one human looks much like another to the untrained non-human. Word will reach my organization, and naturally some will suspect, but they have so much else to do that the suspicion will not appear strong enough to act on. The most they will do is send another agent like myself. And this time, expecting him, the Khan can fool him: camouflage the new installations, make sure our man talks only to the right people and sees only the right things. What can one man do against a planet?"

"You have done somewhat already."

"But I told you, I caught Oleg by surprise."

"You will do more," she continued serenely.

"Can you not, for instance, smuggle a letter out through some Betelgeusean? We can get agents into Ulan Baligh."

"I imagine the same thought has occurred to the Khan. He will make sure no one he is not certain of has any contact with any Betelgeusean, and will search all export material with care."

"Write a letter in the Terran language."

"He can read that himself, if no one else."

"Oh, no." Bourtai raised herself on one elbow. "There is not a human on all Altai except yourself who reads the—what do you call it?—the Anglic. Some Betelgeuseans do, of course, but no Altaian has ever learned; there seemed no pressing reason. Oleg himself reads only Altaian and the principal Betelgeusean language. I know; he mentioned it to me one night recently." She spoke quite cooly of her past year. Flandry gathered that in this culture it was no disgrace to have been a harem slave: fortunes of war.

"Even worse," he said. "I can just see Oleg's agents permitting a document in an unknown alphabet to get out. In fact, from now until whenever they have me dead, I doubt if they will let anything they are not absolutely sure about come near a spaceship, or a spacefarer."

Bourtai sat up straight. Sudden, startling tears blurred her gaze. "But you cannot be helpless!" she cried. "You are from Terra!"

He didn't want to disillusion her. "We'll see." Hastily plucking a stalk of grass and chewing it: "This tastes almost like home. Remarkable similarity."

"Oh, but it is of Terran origin." Bourtai's dismay changed mercurially to simple astonishment that he should not know what was so everyday to her. "The first colonists here found the steppe a virtual desert—only sparse plant forms, poison-ous to man. All other native life had retreated into the Arctic and Antarctic. Our ancestors mutated what seeds and small animals they had along, created suitable strains, and released them. Ter-restroid ecology soon took over the whole unfro-zen belt."

Flandry noticed once more that Bourtai's nomadic life had not made her a simple barbarian. Hm, it would be most interesting to see what a true civilization on wheels was like . . . if he survived, which was dubious. . . . He was too tired to concentrate. His thoughts drifted off along a pattern of fact and deduction, mostly things he knew already.

Krasna was obviously an old sun, middle Popu-lation Two, drifted from the galactic nucleus into this spiral arm. As such, it—and its planets—were poor in the heavier elements, which are formed within the stars, scattered by novae and super-novae, and accumulated in the next stellar gener-ation. Being smaller than Sol, Krasna had ma-tured slowly, a red dwarf through most of its long existence.

Initially, for the first billion years or so, internal heat had made Altai more or less Terrestroid in temperature. Protoplasmic life had evolved in shallow seas, and probably the first crude land forms. But when moltenness and most radioactiv-ity were used up, only the dull sun furnished heat. Altai froze. It happened slowly enough for life to adapt during the long period of change.

And then, while who knew how many

megacenturies passed, Altai was ice-bound from pole to pole. An old, old world, so old that one moon had finally spiraled close and shattered to make the rings: so old, indeed, that its sun had completed the first stage of hydrogen burning and moved into the next. From now on, for the next several million years, Krasna would get hotter and brighter. At last Altai's seas, liquid again, would boil; beyond that, the planet itself would boil, as Krasna became nova; and beyond that the star would be a white dwarf, sinking toward ultimate darkness.

But as yet the process was only begun. Only the tropics had reached a temperature men could endure. Most of the water fled thence and snowed down on the still frigid polar quarters, leaving dry plains where a few plants struggled to re-adapt . . . and were destroyed by this invading green grass. . . .

Flandry's mind touched the remote future of his own planet, and recoiled. A gelid breeze slid around him. He grew aware how stiff and chilly he was. And the sun not even set!

He groaned back to a sitting position. Bourtai sat calm in her fatalism. Flandry envied her. But it was not in him, to accept the chance of freezing— to walk, if he survived this night, over hundreds of parched kilometers, through cold strengthening hour by autumn hour.

His mind scuttered about, a trapped weasel seeking any bolthole. Fire, fire, my chance of immortality for a fire—*Hoy, there!*

He sprang to his feet, remembered the aircraft, and hit dirt again so fast that he bumped his bruised nose. The girl listened wide-eyed to his streaming, sputtering Anglic. When he had finished, she sketched a reverent sign. "I too pray the Spirit of the Mother that She guide us," said Bourtai.

Flandry skinned his teeth in a grin. "I, uh, wasn't precisely praying, my dear. No, I think I've a plan. Wild, but—now, listen—"

VII

Arghun Tiliksky thrust his face out of that shadow which blurred the ring of cross-legged men, into the scant sunlight trickling through a small window of the kibitka. "It was evil," he declared sharply. "Nothing is more dreaded than a grass fire. And you set one! No luck can come from such a deed."

Flandry studied him. The noyon of the Mangu Tuman was quite young, even for these times when few men of Tebtengri reached great age; and a dashing, gallant warrior, as everyone said and as he had proved in the rescue. But to some extent, Arghun was the local equivalent of a prude.

"The fire was soon put out, wasn't it?" asked the Terran mildly. "I heard from your scout, the Kha Khan's aircraft swarmed there and tossed foam bombs down till the flames were smothered. Not many hectares were burned over."

"In such tasks," said Toghrul Vavilov, Gur-Khan of the tribe, "all Altaians are one." He stroked his beard and traded bland smiles with Flandry: a kindred hypocrite. "Our scout needed but to carry a few foam bombs himself, and no enemy vessel would molest him. He observed them and returned here in peace."

One of the visiting chieftains exclaimed: "Your noyon verges on blasphemy himself, Toghrul. Sir Dominic is from Terra! If a lord of Terra wishes to set a blaze, who dares deny him?"

Flandry felt he ought to blush, but decided not to. "Be that as it may," he said, "I couldn't think of any better plan. Not all the tribal leaders who have come to this—what do you call the meeting?— this kurultai, have heard just what happened. The girl Bourtai and myself were trapped with little power left in our varyaks, and the probability of freezing or starving in a few more days if we were not detected by infra-red that same night. So, soon after dark, I scurried about on foot, setting fires which quickly coalesced into one. The wind swept the flames from us—but the radiation of our varyak heaters was still undetectable against such a background! Since we could not be extremely far as negagrav flight goes from some ordu of the Shamanate, it seemed likely that at least one aerial scout would come near to investigate the fire. Therefore, after a while, we broke radio silence to call for help. Then we ducked and dodged, hunted by the gathering vessels of Oleg, somewhat screened by the heat and smoke . . . until a flying war party from the Mangu Tuman arrived, beat off the foe, and escaped with us before more of the enemy should arrive."

"And so this council has been called," added Toghrul Vavilov. "The chiefs of all our allied tribes must understand what we now face."

"But the fire—" mumbled Arghun.

Eyes went through gloom to an old man seated under the window. Furs covered frail Juchi Ilyak so thickly that his bald parchment-skinned head looked disembodied. The Shaman stroked a wisp of white beard, blinked eyes that were still sharp, and murmured with a dry little smile: "This is not the time to dispute whether the rights of a man from Holy Terra override the Yassa by which Altai lives. The question seems rather, how shall we all survive in order to raise such legal quibbles at another date?"

Arghun tossed his reddish-black hair and snorted: "Oleg's father, and the whole Nuru Bator dynasty before him, tried to beat down the Tebtengri. But still we hold the northlands. I do not think this will change overnight."

"Oh, but it will," said Flandry in his softest voice. "Unless something is done, it will."

He treated himself to one of the few remaining cigarets and leaned forward so the light would pick out his features, exotic on this planet. He said: "Throughout your history, you have waged war, as you have driven your machines, with chemical power and stored solar energy. A few small, stationary nuclear generators at Ulan Baligh and the mines are all that your way of life demanded. Your economy would not have supported atomic war, even if feuds and boundary disputes were worth it. So you Tebtengri have remained strong enough to hold these subarctic pastures, though all other tribes were to ally against you. Am I right?"

They nodded. He continued: "But now Oleg Khan is getting help from outside. Some of his new toys I have seen with my own eyes. Craft which can fly flourishes around yours, or go beyond the atmosphere to swoop down again; battlecars whose armor your strongest chemical explosives cannot pierce; missiles to devastate so wide an area that no dispersal can save you. As yet, he has not much modern equipment. But more will arrive during the next several months, until he has enough to crush you. And, still worse, he will have allies that are not human."

They stirred uneasily, some of them making signs against witchcraft. Only Juchi the Shaman remained quiet, watching Flandry with impassive eyes. A clay pipe in his hand sent bitter incense toward the roof. "Who are these creatures?" he asked calmly.

"Merseians," said Flandry. "Another imperial race than man—and man stands in the path of their ambitions. For long now we have been locked with them, nominally at peace, actually probing for weaknesses, subverting, assassinating, skirmishing. They have decided Altai would make a useful naval base. Outright invasion would be expensive, especially if Terra noticed and interfered: and we probably would notice, since we watch them so closely. But if the Merseians supply Oleg with just enough help so that he can conquer the whole planet for them—do you see? Once he has done that, the Merseian engineers will arrive; Altaians will dig and die to build fortresses; this entire world will be one impregnable net of strongholds . . . and then Terra is welcome to learn what has been going on!"

"Does Oleg himself know this?" snapped Toghrul.

Flandry shrugged. "Insufficiently well, I imagine. Like many another puppet ruler, he will live to see the strings his masters have tied on him. But that will be too late. I've watched this sort of thing happen elsewhere.

"In fact," he added, "I've helped bring it about now and then—on Terra's behalf!"

Toghrul entwined nervous fingers. "I believe you," he said.

"We have all had glimpses, heard rumors. . . . What is to be done? Can we summon the Terrans?"

"Aye—aye—call the Terrans, warn the Mother of Men—" Flandry felt how passion flared up in the scarred warriors around him. He had gathered that the Tebtengri had no use for Subotai the Prophet but built their own religion around a hard-boiled sort of humanistic pantheism. It grew on him how strong a symbol the ancestral planet was to them.

He didn't want to tell them what Terra was actually like these days. (Or perhaps had always been. He suspected men are only saints and heroes in retrospect.) Indeed, he dare not speak of sottish Emperors, venal nobles, faithless wives, servile commons, to this armed and burning reverence. But luckily, there's a practical problem at hand.

"Terra is farther from here than Merseia," he said. "Even our nearest base is more distant than theirs. I don't believe any Merseians are on Altai at this moment, but surely Oleg has at least one swift spaceship at his disposal, to inform his masters if anything should go wrong. Let us get word to Terra, and let Oleg learn this has happened, what do you think he'll do?" Flandry nodded, owlish. "Right, on the first guess! Oleg will send to that nearest Merseian base, where I know a heavy naval force is currently stationed. I doubt very much if the Merseians will write off their investment tamely. No, they will dispatch their ships at once, occupy various points, blast the Tebtengri lands with nuclear bombs, and dig in. It will not be as smooth and thorough a job as they now plan, but it will be effective. By the time a Terran fleet of reasonable size can get here, the Merseians will be fairly well entrenched. The most difficult task in space warfare is to get a strong enemy off a planet firmly held. It may prove impossible. But even if, thanks to our precipitating matters, the Terrans do blast the Merseians loose, Altai will have been made into a radioactive desert."

Silence clapped down. Men stared at each other, and back to Flandry, with a horror he had seen before and which was one of the few things it still hurt him to watch. He went on quickly:

"So the one decent objective for us is to get a secret message out. If Oleg and the Merseians don't suspect Terra knows, they won't hasten their program. It can be Terra, instead, which suddenly arrives in strength, seizes Ulan Baligh, establishes ground emplacements and orbital forts. I know Merseian strategy well enough to predict that, under those circumstances, they won't fight. It isn't worth it, since Altai cannot be used as an aggressive base against them." He should have said *will not*; but let these people make the heartbreaking discovery for themselves, that Terra's only real interest was to preserve a fat status quo.

Arghun sprang to his feet. As he crouched

under the low ceiling, primness dropped from him. His young leonine face became a sun, he cried: "And Terra will have us! We will be restored to humankind!"

While the Tebtengri whooped and wept at that understanding, Flandry smoked his cigaret with care. After all, he thought, it needn't corrupt them. Not too much. There would be a small naval base, an Imperial governor, an enforced peace between all tribes. Otherwise they could live as they chose. It wasn't worth Terra's while to proselytize. What freedom the Altaians lost here at home, their young men would regain simply by having access to the stars. Wasn't that so? Wasn't it?

VIII

Juchi the Shaman, who bound together all these chiefs, spoke in a whisper that pierced: "Let us have silence. We must weigh how this may be done."

Flandry waited till the men had seated themselves. Then he gave them a rueful smile. "That's a good question," he said. "Next question, please."

"The Betelgeuseans—" rumbled Toghrul.

"I doubt that," said another gur-khan. "If I were Oleg the Damned, I would put a guard around every individual Betelgeusean, as well as every spaceship, until all danger has passed. I would inspect every trade article, every fur or hide or smokegem, before it was loaded."

"Or send to Merseia at once," shivered someone else.

"No," said Flandry. "Not that. We can be sure Merseia is not going to take such hazardous action without being fairly sure that Terra has heard of their project. They have too many commitments elsewhere."

"Besides," said Juchi, "Oleg Yesukai will not make himself a laughing stock before them—screaming for help because one fugitive is loose in the Khrebet."

"Anyhow," put in Toghrul, "he knows how impossible it is to smuggle such an appeal out. Those tribes not of the Shamanate may dislike the Yesukai tyranny, but they are still more suspicious of us, who traffic with the Ice Dwellers and scoff at that stupid Prophet. Even supposing one of them *would* agree to brand a hide for us, or slip a letter into a bale of pelts, and even supposing that did get past Oleg's inspectors, the cargo might wait months to be loaded, months more in some Betelgeusean warehouse."

"And we don't have so many months, I suppose, before Oleg overruns you and the Merseians arrive as planned," finished Flandry.

He sat for a while listening to their desperate chewing of impractical schemes. It was hot and stuffy in here. All at once he could take no more. He rose. "I need fresh air, and a chance to think," he said.

Juchi nodded grave dismissal. Arghun jumped up again. "I come too," he said.

"If the Terran desires your company," said Toghrul.

"Indeed, indeed." Flandry's agreement was absent-minded.

He went out the door and down a short ladder.
The kibitka where the chiefs met was a large,
covered truck, its box fitted out as austere living
quarters. On top of it, as on all the bigger, slower
vehicles, the flat black plates of a solar-energy
collector were tilted to face Krasna and charge an
accumulator bank. Such roofs made this wandering town, dispersed across the hills, seem like a
flock of futuristic turtles.

The Khrebet was not a high range. Gullied
slopes ran up, gray-green with thornbush and yellow with sere grass, to a glacial cap in the north.
Downward swept a cold wind, whining about
Flandry; he shivered and drew the coat, hastily
sewn to his measure, tighter about him. The sky
was pale today, the rings low and wan in the
south, where the hills emptied into steppe.

As far as Flandry could see, the herds of the
Mangu Tuman spread out under care of varyak-
mounted boys. They were not cattle. Terra's
higher mammals were hard to raise on other
planets; rodents are tougher and more adaptable.
The first colonists had brought rabbits along,
which they mutated and cross-bred systemati-
cally. That ancestor could hardly be recognized in
the cow-sized grazing beasts of today, more like
giant dun guinea pigs than anything else. There
were also separate flocks of bio-engineered ostriches.

Arghun gestured with pride.

"Yonder is the library," he said, "and those
children seated nearby are being instructed."

Flandry looked at that kibitka. Of course, given
microprint, you could carry thousands of vol-

umes along on your travels; illiterates could never
have operated these ground vehicles or the negagrav aircraft watchful overhead. Certain other
trucks—including some trains of them—must
house arsenals, sickbay, machine tools, small factories for textiles and ceramics. Poorer families
might live crowded in a single yurt, a round felt
tent on a motor cart; but no one looked hungry or
ragged. And it was not an impoverished nation
which carried such gleaming missiles on flatbed
cars, or operated such a flock of light tanks, or
armed every adult. Considering Bourtai, Flandry
decided that the entire tribe, male and female,
must be a military as well as a social and
economic unit. Everybody worked, and everybody fought, and in their system the proceeds
were more evenly shared than on Terra.

"Where does your metal come from?" he inquired.

"The grazing lands of every tribe include some
mines," said Arghun. "We plan our yearly round
so as to spend time there, digging and smelting—
just as elsewhere we reap grain planted on the last
visit, or tap crude oil from our wells and refine it.
What we cannot produce ourselves, we trade with
others to get."

"It sounds like a virtuous life," said Flandry.

His slight shudder did not escape Arghun, who
hastened to say: "Oh, we have our pleasures, too,
feasts, games and sports, the arts, the great fair at
Kievka Hill each third year—" He broke off.

Bourtai came walking past a campfire. Flandry
could sense her loneliness. Women in this culture
were not much inferior to men; she was free to go
where she would, and was a heroine for having

brought the Terran here. But her family were slain and she was not even given work to do.

She saw the men and ran toward them. "Oh . . . what has been decided?"

"Nothing yet." Flandry caught her hands. By all hot stars, she was a good-looking wench! His face crinkled its best smile. "I couldn't see going in circles with a lot of men, hairy however well-intentioned, when I might be going in circles with you. So I came out here. And my hopes were granted."

A flush crept up her high flat cheeks. She wasn't used to glibness. Her gaze fluttered downward. "I do not know what to say," she whispered.

"You need say nothing. Only be," he leered.

"No—I am no one. The daughter of a dead man . . . my dowry long ago plundered. . . . And you are a Terran! It is not right!"

"Do you think your dowry matters?" said Arghun. His voice cracked.

Flandry threw him a surprised glance. At once the warrior's mask was restored. But for an instant, Flandry had seen why Arghun Tiliksky didn't like him.

He sighed. "Come, we had better return to the kurultai," he said.

He didn't release Bourtai, but tucked her arm under his. She followed mutely along. He could feel her tremble a little, through the heavy garments. The wind off the glacier ruffled a stray lock of dark hair.

As they neared the kibitka of the council, its door opened. Juchi Ilyak stood there, bent beneath his years. The wizened lips opened, and somehow the breath carried across meters of blustering air: "Terran, perhaps there is a way for us. Dare you come with me to the Ice Folk?"

IX

Tengri Nor, the Ghost Lake, lay so far north that Altai's rings were only a pale glimmer, half seen by night on the southern horizon. When Flandry and Juchi stepped from their airboat, it was still day. Krasna was an ember, tinging the snowfields red. But it toppled swiftly, purple shadows glided from drift to drift so fast a man could see them.

Flandry had not often met such quietness. Even in space, there was always the low noise of the machinery that kept you alive. Here, the air seemed to freeze all sound; the tiniest wind blew up fine ice crystals, whirling and glistening above diamond-like snowbanks, and it rippled the waters of Tengri Nor, but he could not hear it. He had no immediate sense of cold on his fur-muffled body, even on his thickly greased face—not in this dry atmosphere—but breathing was a sharpness in his nostrils. He thought he could smell the lake, a chemical pungency, but he wasn't sure. None of his Terran senses were quite to be trusted in this winter place.

He said, and the unexpected loudness was like a gunshot, shocking, so that his question ended in a whisper: "Do they know we are here?"

"Oh, yes. They have their ways. They will meet us soon." Juchi looked northward, past the lake shore to the mountainous ruins. Snow had drifted halfway up those marble walls, white on white, with the final sunlight bleeding across shattered colonnades. Frost from the Shaman's breath began to stiffen his beard.

"I suppose they recognize the markings—know this is a friendly craft—but what if the Kha Khan sent a disguised vessel?"

"That was tried once or twice, years ago. The boats were destroyed by some means, far south of here. The Dwellers have their awareness." Juchi raised his arms and started swaying on his feet. A high-pitched chant came from his lips, he threw back his head and closed his eyes.

Flandry had no idea whether the Shaman was indulging superstition, practicing formal ritual, or doing what was actually necessary to summon the glacier folk. He had been in too many strange places to dogmatize. He waited, his eyes ranging the scene.

Beyond the ruins, westward along the northern lake shore, a forest grew. White slender trees with intricate, oddly geometric branches flashed like icicles, like jewels. Their thin bluish leaves vibrated, it seemed they should tinkle, that all this forest was glass, but Flandry had never been near a wilderness so quiet. Low gray plants carpeted the snow between the gleaming boles. Where a rock thrust up here and there, it was almost buried under such lichenoid growth. In some place less cold and hushed, Flandry would have thought of tropical richness.

The lake itself reached out of sight, pale blue between snowbanks. As evening swept across the waters, Flandry could see against shadow that mists hovered above.

Juchi had told him, quite matter-of-factly, that the protoplasmic life native to Altai had adapted to low temperatures in past ages by synthesizing methanol. A fifty-fifty mixture of this and water remained fluid below minus forty degrees. When it finally must freeze, it did not expand into cell-disrupting ice crystals, but became gradually more slushy. Lower life forms remained functional till about seventy below, Celsius; after that they went dormant. The higher animals, being homeothermic, need not suspend animation till the air reached minus a hundred degrees.

Biological accumulation of alcohol kept the polar lakes and rivers fluid till midwinter. The chief problem of all species was to find minerals, in a world largely glaciated. Bacteria brought up some from below; animals traveled far to lick exposed rock, returned to their forests and contributed heavy atoms when they died. But in general, the Altaian ecology made do without. It had never evolved bones for instance, but had elaborated chitinous and cartilaginous materials beyond anything seen on Terra.

The account had sounded plausible and interesting, in a warm kibitka on a grassy slope, with microtexts at hand to give details. When he stood on million-year-old snow, and watching night creep up like smoke through crystal trees and cyclopean ruins, hearing Juchi chant under a huge green sunset sky, Flandry discovered that scientific explanations were but little of the truth.

One of the moons was up. Flandry saw something drift across its copper shield. The objects neared, a flock of white spheres, ranging in diameter from a few centimeters to a giant bigger than the airboat. Tentacles streamed downward from them. Juchi broke off. "Ah," he said. "Aeromedusae. The Dwellers cannot be far."

"What?" Flandry hugged himself. The cold was beginning to be felt now, as it gnawed through fur and leather toward flesh.

"Our name for them. They look primitive, but are actually well evolved, with sense organs and brains. They electrolyze hydrogen metabolically to inflate themselves, breathe backward for propulsion, feed on small game which they shock insensible. The Ice Folk have domesticated them."

Flandry stole a glance at a jagged wall, rearing above gloom to catch a sunbeam and flush rose. "They did more than that, once," he said with pity.

Juchi nodded, oddly little impressed. "I daresay intelligence grew up on Altai in response to worsening conditions—the warming sun." His tone was detached. "It built a high civilization, but the shortage of metals was a handicap, and the steady shrinking of the snow area may have led to a cultural collapse. Yet that is not what the Dwellers themselves claim. They have no sense of loss about their past." He squinted slant eyes in a frown, seeking words. "As nearly as I can understand them, which is not much, they . . . abandoned something unsuitable . . . they found better methods."

Two beings came from the forest.

At first glance they were like dwarfish white-furred men. Then you saw details of squat build and rubbery limbs. The feet were long and webbed, expandable to broad snowshoes or foldable to short skis. The hands had three fingers opposing a thumb set in the middle of the wrist. The ears were feathery tufts; fine tendrils waved above each round black eye; sad gray monkey faces peered from a ruff of hair. Their breath did not steam like the humans': their body temperature was well below the Celsius zero. One of them bore a stone lamp in which an alcohol flame wavered. The other had an intricately carved white staff; in an undefinable way, the circling medusa flock seemed to be guided by it.

They came near, halted, and waited. Nothing moved but the low wind, ruffling their fur and streaming the flame. Juchi stood as quiet. Flandry made himself conform, though his teeth wanted to clap in his jaws. He had seen many kinds of life, on worlds more foreign than this. But there was a strangeness here which got under his skin and crawled.

The sun went down. Thin dustless air gave no twilight. Stars blazed forth, pyrotechnic in a sudden blackness. The edge of the rings painted a remote arc. The moon threw cuprous radiance over the snow, shadows into the forest.

A meteor split the sky with noiseless lightning. Juchi seemed to take that as a signal. He began talking. His voice was like ice, toning as it contracted in midnight cold: not altogether a human voice. Flandry began to understand what a Shaman was, and why he presided over the northland tribes. Few men were able to master the Dwellers' language and deal with them. Yet trade and alliance—metal given for organic fuel and curious plastic substances; mutual defense against the Kha Khan's sky raiders—was a large part of the Tebtengri strength.

One of the beings made answer. Juchi turned to Flandry. "I have said who you are and whence you come. They are not surprised. Before I spoke your need, he said their—I do not know just what the word means, but it has something to do with communication—he said they could reach Terra itself, as far as mere distance was concerned, but only through . . . dreams?"

Flandry stiffened. It could be. It could be. How long had men been hunting for some faster-than-light equivalent of radio? A handful of centuries. What was that, compared to the age of the universe? Or even the age of Altai? He realized, not simply intellectually but with his whole organism, how old this planet was. In all that time—

"Telepathy?" he blurted. "I've never heard of telepathy with so great a range!"

"No. Not that, or they would have warned us of this Merseian situation before now. It is nothing that I quite understand." Juchi spoke with care: "He said to me, all the powers they possess look useless in this situation."

Flandry sighed. "I might have known it. That would have been too easy. No chance for heroics."

"They have found means to live, less cumbersome than all those buildings and engines were," said Juchi. "They have been free to think for I know not how many ages. But they have therefore grown weak in sheerly material ways. They help us withstand the aggressions from Ulan Baligh; they can do nothing against the might of Merseia."

Half seen in red moonlight, one of the autochthones spoke.

Juchi: "They do not fear racial death. They

know all things must end, and yet nothing ever really ends. However, it would be desirable that their lesser brethren in the ice forests have a few more million years to live, so that they may also evolve toward truth."

Which is a fine, resounding ploy, thought Flandry, *provided it be not the simple fact.*

Juchi: "They, like us, are willing to become clients of the Terrestrial Empire. To them, it means nothing; they will never have enough in common with men to be troubled by any human governors. They know Terra will not gratuitously harm them—whereas Merseia would, if only by provoking that planet-wide battle of space fleets you describe. Therefore, the Cold People will assist us in any way they can, though they know of none at present."

"Do these two speak for their whole race?" asked Flandry dubiously.

"And for the forests and the lakes," said Juchi.

Flandry thought of a life which was all one great organism, and nodded. "If you say so, I'll accept it. But if they can't help—"

Juchi gave an old man's sigh, like wind over the acrid waters. "I had hoped they could. But now—Have you no plan of your own?"

Flandry stood a long time, feeling the chill creep inward. At last he said: "If the only spaceships are at Ulan Baligh, then it seems we must get into the city somehow, to deliver our message. Have these folk any means of secretly contacting a Betelgeusean?"

Juchi inquired. "No," he translated the answer. "Not if the traders are closely guarded, and their awareness tells them that is so."

One of the natives stooped forward a little, above the dull blue fire, so that his face was illuminated. Could as human an emotion as sorrow really be read into those eyes? Words droned. Juchi listened.

"They can get us into the city, undetected, if it be a cold enough night," he said. "The medusae can carry us through the air, actually seeing radar beams and eluding them. And, of course, a medusa is invisible to metal detectors as well as infra-red scopes." The Shaman paused. "But what use is that, Terra man? We ourselves can walk disguised into Ulan Baligh.

"But could we fly—?" Flandry's voice trailed off.

"Not without being stopped by traffic control officers and investigated."

"S-s-so." Flandry raised his face to the glittering sky. He took the moonlight full in his eyes and was briefly dazzled. Tension tingled along his nerves.

"We've debated trying to radio a Betelgeusean ship as it takes off, before it goes into secondary drive," He spoke aloud, slowly, to get the hammering within himself under control. "But you said the Tebtengri have no set powerful enough to broadcast that far, thousands of kilometers. And, of course, we couldn't beamcast, since we couldn't pinpoint the ship at any instant."

"True. In any event, the Khan's aerial patrols would detect our transmission and pounce."

"Suppose a ship, a friendly spaceship, came near this planet without actually landing . . . could the Ice Dwellers communicate with it?"

Juchi asked; Flandry did not need the translated

answer: "No. They have no radio sets at all. Even if they did, their 'casting would be as liable to detection as ours. And did you not say yourself, Orluk, all our messages must be kept secret, right to the moment that the Terran fleet arrives in strength? That Oleg Khan must not even suspect a message has been sent?"

"Well, no harm in asking." Flandry's gaze continued to search upward, till he found Betelgeuse like a torch among the constellations. "Could we *know* there was such a ship in the neighborhood?"

"I daresay it would radio as it approached . . . notify Ulan Baligh spaceport—" Juchi conferred with the nonhumans. "Yes. We could have men, borne by medusae, stationed unnoticeably far above the city. They could carry receivers. There would be enough beam leakage for them to listen to any conversation between the spaceship and the portmaster. Would that serve?"

Flandry breathed out in a great freezing gust. "It might."

Suddenly, and joyously, he laughed. Perhaps no such sound had ever rung across Tengri Nor. The Dwellers started back, like frightened small animals. Juchi stood in shadow. For that instant, only Captain Dominic Flandry of Imperial Terra had light upon him. He stood with his head raised into the copper moonlight, and laughed like a boy.

"By Heaven," he shouted, "we're going to do it!"

X

An autumn gale came down off the pole. It gathered snow on its way across the steppe, and struck Ulan Baligh near midnight. In minutes, the steep red roofs were lost to sight. Close by a lighted window, a man saw horizontal white streaks, whirling out of darkness and back into darkness. If he went a few meters away, pushing through drifts already knee-high, the light was gone. He stood blind, buffeted by the storm, and heard it rave.

Flandry descended from the upper atmosphere. Its cold had smitten so deep he thought he might never be warm again. In spite of an oxygen tank, his lungs were starving. He saw the blizzard from above as a moon-dappled black blot, the early ice floes on Ozero Rurik dashed to and fro along its southern fringe. A cabling of tentacles meshed him, he sat under a giant balloon rushing downward through the sky. Behind him trailed a flock of other medusae, twisting along air currents he could not feel to avoid radar booms he could not see. Ahead of him was only one, bearing a Dweller huddled against a cake of ice; for what lay below was hell's own sulfurous wind to the native.

Even Flandry felt how much warmer it was, when the snowstorm enclosed him. He crouched forward, squinting into a nothingness that yelled. Once his numbed feet, dangling down, struck a rooftree. The blow came as if from far away. Palely at first, strengthening as he neared, the Prophet's Tower thrust its luminous shaft up and out of sight.

Flandry groped for the nozzle at his shoulder. His destination gave just enough light for him to see through the driven flakes. Another medusa crowded close, bearing a pressure tank of paint. Somehow, Flandry reached across the air between and made the hose fast.

Now, Arctic intelligence, do you understand what I want to do? Can you guide this horse of mine for me?

The wind yammered in his ears. He heard other noises like blasting, the powerful breaths by which his medusa moved itself. Almost, he was battered against the tablet wall. His carrier wobbled in midair, fighting to maintain position. An inlaid letter, big as a house, loomed before him, black against shining white. He aimed his hose and squirted.

Damn! The green jet was flung aside in a flaw of wind. He corrected his aim and saw the paint strike. It remained liquid even at this temperature . . . no matter, it was sticky enough. . . . The first tank was quickly used up. Flandry coupled to another. Blue this time. All the Tebtengri had contributed all the squirtable paint they had, every hue in God's rainbow. Flandry could but hope there would be enough.

There was, though he came near fainting from chill and exhaustion before the end of the job. He could not remember ever having so brutal a task. Even so, when the last huge stroke was done, he could not resist adding an exclamation point at the very bottom—three centimeters high.

"Let's go," he whispered. Somehow, the mute Dweller understood and pointed his staff. The medusa flock sprang through the clouds.

Flandry had a moment's glimpse of a military airboat. It had detached itself from the flock hovering above the spaceport, perhaps going off duty. As the medusae broke from the storm into clear moonlight and ringlight, the craft veered. Flandry saw its guns stab energy bolts into the flock, and reached for his own futile blaster. His fingers were wooden, they didn't close. . . .

The medusae, all but his and the Dweller's whipped about. They surrounded the patrol boat, laid tentacles fast and clung. It was nearly buried under them. Electric fires crawled, sparks dripped, these creatures could break hydrogen from water. Flandry recalled in a dull part of his mind that a metallic fuselage was a Faraday cage, immune to lightning. But when concentrated electric discharges burned holes, spotwelded control circuits—the boat staggered in midair. The medusae detached themselves. The boat plummeted.

Flandry relaxed and let his creature bear him northward.

XI

The town seethed. There had been rioting in the Street of Gunsmiths, and blood still dappled the new-fallen snow. Armed men tramped around palace and spaceport; mobs hooted beyond them. From the lake shore encampments came war music, pipes squealed, gongs crashed, the young men rode their varyaks in breakneck circles and cursed.

Oleg Khan looked out the palace window. "It

shall be made good to you," he muttered. "Oh, yes, my people, you shall have satisfaction."

Turning to the Betelgeusean, who had just been fetched, he glared into the blue face. "You have seen?"

"Yes, your majesty." Zalat's Altaian, usually fluent and little accented, grew thick. He was a badly shaken being. Only the quick arrival of the royal guards had saved his ship from destruction by a thousand shrieking fanatics. "I swear, I, my crew, we had nothing to do with . . . we are innocent as—"

"Of course! Of course!" Oleg Yesukai brought one palm down in an angry slicing motion. "I am not one of those ignorant rodent herders. Every Betelgeusean has been under supervision, every moment since—" He checked himself.

"I have still not understood why," faltered Zalat.

"Was my reason not made clear to you? You know the Terran visitor was killed by Tebtengri operatives, the very day he arrived. It bears out what I have long suspected, those tribes have become religiously xenophobic. Since they doubtless have other agents in the city, who will try to murder your people in turn, it is best all of you be closely guarded, have contact only with men we know are loyal, until I have full control of the situation."

His own words calmed Oleg somewhat. He sat down, stroked his beard and watched Zalat from narrowed eyes. "Your difficulties this morning are regrettable," he continued smoothly. "Because you are outworlders, and the defiling symbols are not in the Altaian alphabet, many people leaped to the conclusion that it was some dirty word in your language. I, of course, know better. I also know from the exact manner in which a patrol craft was lost last night, how this outrage was done: unquestionably by Tebtengri, with the help of the Arctic devil-folk. Such a vile deed would not trouble them in the least; they are not followers of the Prophet. But what puzzles me—I admit this frankly, though confidentially—*why?* A daring, gruelling task . . . merely for a wanton insult?"

He glanced back toward the window. From this angle, the crimson Tower looked itself. You had to be on the north to see what had been done: the tablet wall disfigured by more than a kilometer of splashed paint. But from that side, the fantastic desecration was visible across entire horizons.

The Kha Khan doubled a fist. "It shall be repaid them," he said. "This has rallied the orthodox tribes behind me as no other thing imaginable. When their children are boiled before their eyes, the Tebtengri will realize what they have done."

Zalat hesitated. "Your majesty "

"Yes?" Oleg snarled, as he must at something.

"Those symbols are letters of the Terran alphabet."

"*What?*"

"I know the Anglic language somewhat," said Zalat. "Many Betelgeuseans do. But how could those Tebtengri ever have learned—"

Oleg, who knew the answer to that, interrupted by seizing the captain's tunic and shaking him. "What does it say?" he cried.

"That's the strangest part, your majesty," stammered Zalat. "It doesn't mean anything. Not that makes sense."

"Well, what sound does it spell, then? Speak before I have your teeth pulled!"

"Mayday," choked Zalat. "Just Mayday, your majesty."

Oleg let him go. For a while there was silence. At last the Khan said: "Is that a Terran word?"

"Well . . . it could be. I mean, well, May is the name of a month in the Terran calendar, and Day means 'diurnal period.' " Zalat rubbed his yellow eyes, searching for logic. "I suppose Mayday could mean the first day of May."

Oleg nodded slowly. "That sounds reasonable. The Altaian calendar, which is modified from the ancient Terran, has a similar name for a month of what is locally springtime. Mayday—spring festival day? Perhaps."

He returned to the window and brooded across the city. "It's long until May," he said. "If that was an incitement to . . . anything . . . it's foredoomed. We are going to break the Tebtengri this very winter. By next spring—" He cleared his throat and finished curtly: "Certain other projects will be well under way."

"How could it be an incitement, anyhow, your majesty?" argued Zalat, emboldened. "Who in Ulan Baligh could read it?"

"True. I can only conjecture, some wild act of defiance—or superstition, magical ritual—" The Khan turned on his heel. "You are leaving shortly, are you not?"

"Yes, your majesty."

"You shall convey a message. No other traders

are to come here for a standard year. We will have troubles enough, suppressing the Tebtengri and their aboriginal allies." Oleg shrugged. "In any event, it would be useless for merchants to visit us. War will disrupt the caravans. Afterward—perhaps."

Privately, he doubted it. By summer, the Merseians would have returned and started work on their base. A year from now, Altai would be firmly in their empire, and, under them, the Kha Khan would lead his warriors to battles in the stars, more glorious than any of the hero songs had ever told.

XII

Winter came early to the northlands. Flandry, following the Mangu Tuman in their migratory cycle, saw snow endless across the plains, under a sky like blued steel. The tribe, wagons and herds and people, were a hatful of dust strewn on immensity: here a moving black blot, there a thin smoke-streak vertical in windless air. Krasna hung low in the southeast, a frosty rod-gold wheel.

Three folk glided from the main ordu. They were on skis, rifles slung behind their parkas, hands holding tethers which led to a small negagrav tow unit. It flew quickly, so that the skis sang on the thin crisp snow.

Arghun Tiliksky said hard-voiced: "I can appreciate that you and Juchi keep secret the reason for that Tower escapade of yours, five weeks ago. What none of us know, none can reveal if captured. Yet you seem quite blithe about the con-

sequences. Our scouts tell us that infuriated warriors flock to Oleg Khan, that he has pledged to
annihilate us this very year. In consequence, all
the Tebtengri must remain close together, not
spread along the whole Arctic Circle as before—
and hereabouts, there is not enough forage under
the snow for that many herds. I say to you, the
Khan need only wait, and by the end of the season
famine will have done half his work for him!''

"Let's hope he plans on that," said Flandry.
"Less strenuous than fighting, isn't it?"

Arghun's angry young face turned toward him.
The noyon clipped: "I do not share this awe of all
things Terran. You are as human as I. In this
environment, where you are untrained, you are
much more fallible. I warn you plainly, unless
you give me good reason to do otherwise, I shall
request a kurultai. And at it I will argue that we
strike now at Ulan Baligh, try for a decision while
we can still count on full bellies."

Bourtai cried aloud, "No! That would be asking
for ruin. They outnumber us down there, three or
four to one. And I have seen some of the new
engines the Merseians brought. It would be
butchery!"

"It would be quick." Arghun glared at Flandry.
"Well?"

The Terran sighed. He might have expected it.
Bourtai was always near him, and Arghun was
always near Bourtai, and the officer had spoken
surly words before now. He might have known
that this invitation to hunt a flock of sataru—
mutant ostriches escaped from the herds and gone
wild—masked something else. At least it was decent of Arghun to warn him.

"If you don't trust me," he said, "though Lord knows I've fought and bled and frostbitten my nose in your cause—can't you trust Juchi Ilyak? He and the Dwellers know my little scheme; they'll assure you it depends on our hanging back and avoiding battle."

"Juchi grows old," said Arghun. "His mind is feeble as—Hoy, there!"

He yanked a guide line. The negagrav unit purred to a stop and hung in air, halfway up a long slope. His politics dropped from Arghun, he pointed at the snow with a hunting dog's eagerness. "Spoor," he hissed. "We go by muscle power now, to sneak close. The birds can outrun this motor if they hear it. Do you go straight up this hill, Orluk Flandry; Bourtai and I will come around on opposite sides of it—"

The Altaians had slipped their reins and skied noiselessly from him before Flandry quite understood what had happened. Looking down, the Terran saw big splay tracks: a pair of sataru. He started after them. How the deuce did you manage these foot-sticks, anyway? Waddling across the slope, he tripped himself and went down. His nose clipped a boulder. He sat up, swearing in eighteen languages and Old Martian phonoglyphs.

"This they call fun?" He tottered erect. Snow had gotten under his parka hood. It began to melt, trickling over his ribs in search of a really good place to refreeze. "Great greasy comets," said Flandry, "I might have been sitting in the Everest House with a bucket of champagne, lying to some beautiful wench about my exploits . . . but no, I had to come out here and do 'em!"

Slowly, he dragged himself up the hill, crouched on its brow, and peered through an unnecessarily cold and thorny bush. No two-legged birds, only a steep slant back down to the plain . . . wait!

He saw blood and the dismembered avian shapes an instant before the beasts attacked him.

They seemed to rise from weeds and snowdrifts, as if the earth had spewed them. Noiselessly they rushed in, a dozen white scuttering forms big as police dogs. Flandry glimpsed long sharp noses, alert black eyes that hated him, high backs and hairless tails. He yanked his rifle loose and fired. The slug bowled the nearest animal over. It rolled halfway downhill, lay a while, and crawled back to fight some more.

Flandry didn't see it. The next was upon him. He shot it point black. One of its fellows crouched to tear the flesh. But the rest ran on. Flandry took aim at a third. A heavy body landed between his shoulders. He went down, and felt jaws rip his leather coat.

He rolled over, somehow, shielding his face with one arm. His rifle had been torn from him: a beast fumbled it in forepaws almost like hands. He groped for the dagger at his belt. Two of the animals were on him, slashing with chisel teeth. He managed to kick one in the nose. It squealed, bounced away, sprang back with a couple of new arrivals to help.

Someone yelled. It sounded very far off, drowned by Flandry's own heartbeat. The Terran drove his knife into a hairy shoulder. The beast writhed free, leaving him weaponless. Now they were piling on him where he lay. He fought with boots and knees, fists and elbows, in a cloud of kicked-up snow. An animal jumped in the air, came down on his midriff. The wind whooffed out of him. His face-defending arm dropped, and the creature went for his throat.

Arghun came up behind. The Altaian seized the animal by the neck. His free hand flashed steel, he disemboweled it and flung it toward the pack in one expert movement. Several of them fell on the still snarling shape and fed. Arghun booted another exactly behind the ear. It dropped as if poleaxed. One jumped from the rear, to get on his back. He stooped, his right hand made a judo heave, and as the beast soared over his head he ripped its stomach with his knife.

"Up, man!" He hoisted Flandry. The Terran stumbled beside him, while the pack chattered around. Now its outliers began to fall dead: Bourtai had regained the hillcrest and was sniping. The largest of the animals whistled. At that signal, the survivors bounded off. They were lost to view in seconds.

When they had reached Bourtai, Arghun sank down gasping. The girl flew to Flandry. "Are you hurt?" she sobbed.

"Only in my pride—I guess—" He looked past her to the noyon. "Thanks," he said inadequately.

"You are a guest," grunted Arghun. After a moment: "They grow bolder each year. I had never expected to be attacked this near an ordu. Something must be done about them, if we live through the winter."

"What are they?" Flandry shuddered toward relaxation.

"Gurchaku. They range in packs over all the

steppes, up into the Khrebet. They will eat anything but prefer meat. Chiefly sataru and other
feral animals, but they raid our herds, have killed
people—" Arghun looked grim. "They were not
as large in my grandfather's day, nor as cunning."

Flandry nodded. "Rats. Which is not an exclamation."

"I know what rats are," said Bourtai. "But the
gurchaku—"

"A new genus. Similar things have happened
on other colonized planets." Flandry wished for a
cigaret. He wished so hard that Bourtai had to
remind him before he continued: "Oh, yes. Some
of the stowaway rats on your ancestors' ships
must have gone into the wilds, as these began to
be Terrestrialized. Size was advantageous: helped
them keep warm, enabled them to prey on the big
animals you were developing. Selection pressure,
short generations, genetic drift within a small
original population. . . . Nature is quite capable
of forced-draft evolution on her own hook."

He managed a tired grin at Bourtai. "After all,"
he said, "if a frontier planet has beautiful girls,
tradition requires that it have monsters as well."

Her blush was like fire.

They returned to camp in silence. Flandry entered the yurt given him, washed and changed
clothes, lay down on his bunk and stared at the
ceiling. He reflected bitterly on all the Terran
romancing he had ever heard, the High Frontier in
general and the dashing adventures of the Intelligence Corps in particular. So what did it amount
to? A few nasty moments with men or giant rats
that wanted to kill you; stinking leather clothes,
wet feet, chilblains and frostbite, unseasoned

food, creaking wheels exchanged for squealing runners; temperance, chastity, early rising, weighty speech with tribal elders, not a book he could enjoy or a joke he could understand for light-years. He yawned, rolled over on his stomach, tried to sleep, gave up after a while, and began to wish Arghun's reckless counsel would be accepted. Anything to break this dreariness!

It tapped on the door. He started to his feet, bumped his head on a curved ridgepole, swore, and said: "Come in." The caution of years laid his hand on a blaster.

The short day was near an end, only a red streak above one edge of the world. His lamp picked out Bourtai. She entered, closed the door, and stood unspeaking.

"Why . . . hullo." Flandry paused. "What brings you here?"

"I came to see if you were indeed well." Her eyes did not meet his.

"Oh? Oh, yes. Yes, of course," he said stupidly. "Kind of you. I mean, uh, shall I make some tea?"

"If you were bitten, it should be tended," said the girl. "Gurchaku bites can be infectious."

"No, thanks, I escaped any actual wounds." Automatically, Flandry added with a smile: "I could wish otherwise, though. So fair a nurse—"

Again he saw the blood rise in her face. Suddenly he understood. He would have realized earlier, had these people not been more reticent than his own. A heavy pulse beat in his throat. "Sit down," he invited.

She lowered herself to the floor. He joined her, sliding a practiced arm over her shoulder. She did not flinch. He let his hand glide lower, till the arm was around her waist. She leaned against him.

"Do you think we will see another springtime?" she asked. Her tone grew steady once more; it was a quite practical question.

"I have one right here with me," he said. His lips brushed her dark hair.

"No one speaks thus in the ordu," she breathed. Quickly: "We are both cut off from our kindred, you by distance and I by death. Let us not remain lonely."

He forced himself to give fair warning: "I shall return to Terra the first chance I get."

"I know," she cried, "but until then—"

His lips found hers.

There was a thump on the door.

"Go away!" Flandry and Bourtai said it together, looked surprised into each other's eyes, and laughed with pleasure. "My lord," called a man's voice, "Toghrul Gur-Khan sends me. A message has been picked up—a Terran spaceship!"

Flandry knocked Bourtai over in his haste to get outside. But even as he ran, he thought with frustration that this job had been hoodooed from the outset.

XIII

Among the thin winds over Ulan Baligh, hidden by sheer height, a warrior sat in the patient arms of a medusa. He breathed oxygen from a tank and rested numbed fingers on a small radio transceiver. After four hours he was relieved; perhaps no other breed of human could have endured so long a watch.

Finally he was rewarded. His earphones crackled with a faint, distorted voice, speaking no language he had ever heard. A return beam gabbled from the spaceport. The man up above gave place to another, who spoke a halting, accented Altaian, doubtless learned from the Betelgeuseans.

The scout of the Tebtengri dared not try any communication of his own. If detected (and the chances were that it would be) such a call would bring a nuclear missile streaking upward from Ulan Baligh. However, his transceiver could amplify and relay what came to it. Medusae elsewhere carried similar sets: a long chain, ending in the ordu of Toghrul Vavilov. Were that re-transmission intercepted by the enemy, no one would be alarmed. They would take it for some freak of reflection off the ionosphere.

The scout's binoculars actually showed him the Terran spaceship as it descended. He whistled in awe at its sleek, armed swiftness. Still, he thought, it was only one vessel, paying a visit to Oleg the Damned, who had carefully disguised all his modern installations. Oleg would be like butter to his guests, they would see what ho wished them to see and no more. Presently they would go home again, to report that Altai was a harmless half-barbaric outpost, safely forgettable.

The scout sighed, beat gloved hands together, and wished his relief would soon arrive.

And up near the Arctic Circle, Dominic Flandry turned from Toghrul's receiver. A frosted window framed his head with the early northern night. "That's it," he said. "We'll maintain our radio monitors, but I don't expect to pick up anything else interesting, except the moment when the ship takes off again."

"When will that be?" asked the Gur-Khan.

"In a couple of days, I imagine," said Flandry. "We've got to be ready! All the tribesmen must be alerted, must move out on the plains according to the scheme Juchi and I drew up for you."

Toghrul nodded. Arghun Tiliksky, who had also crowded into the kibitka, demanded: "What scheme is this? Why have I not been told?"

"You didn't need to know," Flandry answered. Blandly: "The warriors of Tebtengri can be moving at top speed, ready for battle, on five minutes' notice, under any conditions whatsoever. Or so you were assuring me in a ten-minute speech one evening last week. Very well, move them, noyon."

Arghun bristled. "And then—"

"You will lead the Mangu Tuman varyak division straight south for 500 kilometers," said Toghrul. "There you will await radio orders. The other tribal forces will be stationed elsewhere; you will doubtless see a few, but strict radio silence is to be maintained between you. The less mobile vehicles will have to stay in this general region, with the women and children maneuvering them."

"And the herds," reminded Flandry. "Don't forget, we can cover quite a large area with all the Tebtengri herds."

"But this is lunacy!" yelped Arghun. "If Oleg knows we're spread out in such a manner, and drives a wedge through—"

"He won't know," said Flandry. "Or if he does, he won't know why: which is what counts. Now, git!"

For a moment Arghun's eyes clashed with his.

Then the noyon slapped gauntlets against one thigh, whirled, and departed. It was indeed only a few moments before the night grew loud with varyak motors and lowing battle horns.

When that had faded, Toghrul tugged his beard, looked across the radio, and said to Flandry: "Now can you tell me just what fetched that Terran spaceship here?"

"Why, to inquire more closely about the reported death of me, a Terran citizen, on Altai," grinned Flandry. "At least, if he is not a moron, that is what the captain will tell Oleg. And he will let Oleg convince him it was all a deplorable accident, and he'll take off again."

Toghrul stared, then broke into buffalo laughter. Flandry chimed in. For a while the Gur-Khan of the Mangu Tuman and the field agent of the Imperial Terrestrial Naval Intelligence Corps danced around the kibitka singing about the flowers that bloom in the spring.

Presently Flandry left. There wasn't going to be much sleep for anyone in the next few days. Tonight, though—He rapped eagerly on his own yurt. Silence answered him, the wind and a distant sad mewling of the herds. He scowled and opened the door.

A note lay on his bunk. *My beloved, the alarm signals have blown. Toghrul gave me weapons and a new varyak. My father taught me to ride and shoot as well as any man. It is only fitting that the last of Clan Tumurji go with the warriors.*

Flandry stared at the scrawl for a long while. Finally, "Oh, hell and tiddlywinks," he said, and undressed and went to bed.

XIV

When he woke in the morning, his cart was under way. He emerged to find the whole encampment grinding across the steppe. Toghrul stood to one side, taking a navigational sight on the rings. He greeted Flandry with a gruff: "We should be in our own assigned position tomorrow." A messenger dashed up, something needed the chief's attention, one of the endless emergencies of so big a group on the move. Flandry found himself alone.

By now he had learned not to offer his own unskilled assistance. He spent the day composing scurrilous limericks about the superiors who had assigned him to this mission. The trek continued noisily through the dark. Next morning there was drifted snow to clear before camp could be made. Flandry discovered that he was at least able to wield a snow shovel. Soon he wished he weren't.

By noon the ordu was settled; not in the compact standardized laagers which offered maximum safety, but straggling over kilometers in a line which brought mutinous grumbling. Toghrul roared down all protest and went back to his kibitka to crouch over the radio. After some hours he summoned Flandry.

"Ship departing," he said. "We've just picked up a routine broadcast warning aircraft from the spaceport area." He frowned. "Can we carry out all our maneuvers while we're still in daylight?"

"It doesn't matter," said Flandry. "Our initial pattern is already set up. Once he spots that from space—and he's pretty sure to, because it's routine to look as long and hard as possible at any doubtful planet—the skipper will hang around out there."

His gray eyes went to a map on the desk before him. The positions of all Tebtengri units had now been radio confirmed. As marked by Toghrul, the ordus lay in a heavy east-and-west line, 500 kilometers long across the winter-white steppe. The more mobile varyak divisions sprawled their bunches to form lines slanting past either end of the stationary one, meeting in the north. He stroked his mustache and waited.

"Spaceship cleared for take off. Stand by. Rise, spaceship!"

As the relayed voice trickled weakly from the receiver, Flandry snatched up a pencil and drew another figure under Toghrul's gaze. "This is the next formation," he said. "Might as well start it now, I think; the ship will have seen the present one in a few minutes."

The Gur-Khan bent over the microphone and rapped: "Varyak divisions of Clans Munlik, Fyodor, Kubilai, Tuli, attention! Drive straight west for 100 kilometers. Belgutai, Dagdarin, Chagatai, Kassar, due east for 100 kilometers. Gleb, Jahangir—"

Flandry rolled his pencil in tightened fingers. As the reports came in, over an endless hour, he marked where each unit had halted. The whole device began to look pathetically crude.

"I have been thinking," said Toghrul after a period of prolonged silence.

"Nasty habit," said Flandry. "Hard to break. Try cold baths and long walks."

"What if Oleg finds out about this?"

"He's pretty sure to discover something is going on. His air scouts will pick up bits of our messages. But only bits, since these are short-range transmissions. I'm depending on our own air cover to keep the enemy from getting too good a look at what we're up to. All Oleg will know is, we're maneuvering around on a large scale." Flandry shrugged. "It would seem most logical to me, if I were him, that the Tebtengri were practicing formations against the day he attacks."

"Which is not far off." Toghrul drummed the desk top.

Flandry drew a figure on his paper. "This one next," he said.

"Yes." Toghrul gave the orders. Afterward: "We can continue through dark, you know. Light bonfires. Send airboats loaded with fuel to the varyak men, so they can do the same."

"That would be well."

"Of course," frowned the chief, "it will consume an unholy amount of fuel. More than we can spare."

"Don't worry about that," said Flandry. "Before the shortage gets acute, your people will be safe, their needs supplied from outside—or they'll be dead, which is still more economical."

The night wore on. Now and then Flandry dozed. He paid scant heed to the sunrise; he had only half completed his job. Sometime later a warrior was shown in. "From Juchi Shaman," he reported, with a clumsy salute. "Airscouts watching the Ozero Rurik area report massing of troops, outrider columns moving northward."

Toghrul smote the desk with one big fist. "Already?" he said.

"It'll take them a few days to get their big push this far," said Flandry, though his guts felt cold at the news. "Longer, if we harry them from the air. All I need is one more day, I think."

"But when can we expect help?" said Toghrul.

"Not for another three or four weeks at the very least," said Flandry. "Word has to reach Catawrayannis Base, its commandant has to patch together a task force which has to get here. Allow a month, plus or minus. Can we retreat that long, holding the enemy off without undue losses to ourselves?"

"We had better," said Toghrul, "or we are done."

XV

Captain Flandry laid the rifle stock to his shoulder. Its plastic felt smooth and uncold, as nearly as his numbed cheek could feel anything. The chill of the metal parts, which would skin any fingers that touched them, bit through his gloves.

Hard to gauge distances in this red half-light, across this whining scud of snow. Hard to guess windage; even trajectories were baffling, on this miserable three-quarter-gee planet. . . . He decided the opposition wasn't close enough yet, and lowered his gun.

Beside him, crouched in the same lee of a snowbank, the Dweller turned dark eyes upon the man. "I go now?" he asked. His Altaian was even worse than Flandry's, though Juchi himself had been surprised to learn that any of the Ice Folk knew the human tongue.

"I told you no." Flandry's own accent was

thickened by the frostbitten puffiness of his lips.
"You must cross a hundred meters of open
ground to reach those trees. Running, you would
be seen and shot before going half way. Unless we
can arrange a distraction—"

He peered again through the murk. Krasna had
almost vanished from these polar lands for the
winter, but was still not far below the horizon.
There were still hours when a surly gleam in the
south gave men enough light to see a little distance.

The attacking platoon was so close now that
Flandry could make out blurred individuals, out-
lined against the great vague lake. He could see
that they rode a sort of modified varyak, with
runners and low-powered negagrav thrust to
drive them across the permasnow. It was sheer ill
luck that he and his squad had blundered into
them. But the past month, or however long, had
been that sort of time. Juchi had withdrawn all his
people into the depths of the Ice Lands, to live off
a few kine slaughtered and frozen while their
herds wandered the steppes under slight guard
. . . while a front line of Tebtengri and Dwellers
fought a guerrilla war to slow Oleg Khan's advance. . . . Skulk, shoot, run, hide, bolt your
food, snatch a nap in a sleeping bag as dank as
yourself, and go forth to skulk again. . . .

Now the rest of Flandry's party lay dead by
Tengri Nor. And he himself, with this one companion, was trapped by a pursuit moving faster on
machine than he could afoot.

He gauged his range afresh. Perhaps. He got his
sights on a man in the lead and jerked his head at

the Dweller, who slipped from him. Then he fired.

The southerner jerked in the saddle, caught at his belly, and slid slowly to the ground. Even in this glum light, his blood was a red shout on the snow. Through the wind, Flandry heard the others yell. They swept into motion, dispersing. He followed them with his sights, aimed at another, squeezed trigger again. A miss. This wasn't enough. He had to furnish a few seconds' diversion, so the Dweller could reach those crystalline trees at his back.

Flandry thumbed his rifle to automatic fire. He popped up, shooting, and called: "My grandmother can lick your grandmother!"

Diving, he sensed more than heard the lead storm that went where he had been. Energy bolts crashed through the air overhead, came down again and sizzled in the snow. He breathed hot steam. Surely that damned Dweller had gotten to the woods now! He fired blind at the inward-rushing enemy. *Come on, someone, pull me out of this mess!—What use is it, anyhow? The little guy babbled about calling through the roots, letting all the forest know*—Through gun-thunder, Flandry heard the first high ringing noise. He raised his eyes in time to see the medusae attack.

They swarmed from above, hundreds upon hundreds, their tentacles full of minor lightning. Some were hit, burst into hydrogen flame, and sought men to burn even as they died. Others snatched warriors from the saddle, lifted them, and dropped them in the mortally cold waters of Tengri Nor. Most went efficiently about a task of electrocution. Flandry had not quite understood what happened before he saw the retreat begin. By the time he had climbed erect, it was a rout.

"Holy hopping hexaflexagons," he mumbled in awe. "Now why can't I do that stunt?"

The Dweller returned, small, furry, rubbery, an unimpressive goblin who said with shyness: "Not enough medusa for do this often. Your friends come. We wait."

"Huh? Oh . . . you mean a rescue party. Yeh, I suppose some of our units would have seen that flock arrive here and will come to investigate." Flandry stamped his feet, trying to force circulation back. "Nice haul," he said, looking over strewn weapons and vehicles. "I think we got revenge for our squad."

"Dead man just as dead on any side of fight," reproached the Dweller.

Flandry grimaced. "Don't remind me."

He heard the whirr of tow motors. The ski patrol which came around the woods was bigger than he had expected. He recognized Arghun and Bourtai at its head. It came to him, with a shock, that he hadn't spoken to either one, except to say hello-goodbye, since the campaign began. Too busy. That was the trouble with war. Leave out the toil, discipline, discomfort, scant sleep, lousy food, monotony, and combat, and war would be a fine institution.

He strolled to meet the newcomers, as debonairly as possible for a man without cigarets. "Hi," he said.

"Dominic . . . it was you—" Bourtai seized his hands. "You might have been killed!" she gasped.

"Occupational hazard," said Flandry. "I

thought you were in charge of our western division, Arghun."

"No more fighting there," said the noyon. "I am going about gathering our troops."

"What?"

"Have you not heard?" The frank eyes widened. Arghun stood for a moment in the snow, gaping. Then a grin cracked his frozen mustache; he slapped Flandry's back and shouted: "The Terrans have arrived!"

"Huh?" Flandry felt stunned. The blow he had taken—Arghun owned a hefty set of muscles—wait, *what* had he said?

"Yesterday," chattered the Altaian. "I suppose your portable radio didn't pick up the news, nor anyone in that company you were fighting. Reception is poor in this area. Or maybe they were fanatics. There are some, whom we'll have to dispose of. But that should not be difficult."

He brought himself under control and went on more calmly: "A task force appeared and demanded the surrender of all Yesukai forces as being Merseian clients. The commander at Ulan Baligh yielded without a fight—what could he have done? Oleg Khan tried to rally his men at the front . . . oh, you should have been listening, the ether was lively last night! . . . but a couple of Terran spaceships flew up and dropped a demonstration bomb squarely on his headquarters. That was the end of that. The tribesmen of the Khanate are already disengaging and streaming south. Juchi Shaman has a call from the Terran admiral at Ulan Baligh, to come advise him what to do next—oh yes, and bring you along—"

Flandry closed his eyes. He swayed on his feet, so that Bourtai caught him in her arms and cried, "What is it, my dear one?"

"Brandy," he whispered. "Tobacco. India tea. Shrimp mayonnaise, with a bottle of gray Riesling on the side. Air conditioning. . . ." He shook himself. "Sorry. My mind wandered."

He scarcely saw how her lip trembled. Arghun did, gave the Terran a defiant look, and caught the girl's hand in his own. She clung to that like a lost child.

This time Flandry did notice. His mouth twitched upward. "Bless you, my children," he murmured.

"What?" Arghun snapped it in an anger half bewilderment.

"When you get as old and battered as I," said Flandry, "you will realize that no one dies of a broken heart. In fact, it heals with disgusting speed. If you want to name your first-born Dominic, I will be happy to mail a silver spoon, suitably engraved."

"But—" stammered Bourtai. "But—" She gave up and held Arghun's hand more tightly.

The noyon's face burned with blood. He said hastily, seeking impersonal things: "Now will you explain your actions, Terra man?"

"Hm?" Flandry blinked. "Oh. Oh, yes. To be sure."

He started walking. The other two kept pace, along the thin blue Lake of Ghosts, under a lacework of icy leaves. The red halfday smoldered toward night. Flandry spoke, with laughter reborn in his voice:

"Our problem was to send a secret message. The most secret possible would, of course, be one which nobody recognized as a message. For instance, Mayday painted on the Prophet's Tower. It looked like gibberish, pure spiteful mischief . . . but all the city could see it. They'd talk. How they'd talk! Even if no Betelgeuseans happened to be at Ulan Baligh just then, there would soon be some who would certainly hear news so sensational, no matter how closely they were guarded. And the Betelgeuseans in turn would carry the yarn home with them—where the Terrans connected with the Embassy would hear it. And the Terrans would understand!

"You see, Mayday is a very ancient code call on my planet. It means, simply, *Help me.*"

"Oh!" exclaimed Bourtai.

"Oh-ho," said Arghun. He slapped his thigh and his own laughter barked forth, "Yes, I see it now! Thanks, friend, for a joke to tell my grandchildren!"

"A classic," agreed Flandry with his normal modesty. "My corps was bound to send a ship to investigate. Knowing little or nothing, its men would be alert and wary. Oleg's tale of my accidental death, or whatever he told them, would be obvious seafood in view of that first message; but I figured I could trust them to keep their mouths shut, pretend to be taken in by him, until they could learn more. The problem now was, how to inform them exactly what the situation was—without Oleg knowing.

"Of course, you can guess how that was done: by maneuvering the whole Tebtengri Shamanate across the plain, to form Terran letters visible through a telescope. It could only be a short, simple note; but it served."

He filled his lungs with the keen air. Through all his weariness, the magnificence of being alive flowed up into him. He grinned and added, half to himself: "Those were probably the first secret messages ever sent in an alphabet ranging from one to five hundred kilometers tall."

THE PLAGUE
OF MASTERS

THE PLAGUE OF MASTERS

First he was aware of rain. Its noise filled the opened airlock chamber, a great slow roar that reverberated through the spaceship's metal. Light struck outward, glinted off big raindrops crowded together in their falling. Each globule shone quicksilver. But just beyond that curtain was total night. Here and there in blackness a lamp could be seen, and a watery glimmer reflected off the concrete under its pole. The air that gusted into the lock chamber was as warm as wet, and full of strange smells; Flandry thought some were like jasmine and some like rotting ferns, but couldn't be sure.

He tossed his cigaret to the dark and ground it under his heel. The hooded raincape which he slipped on seemed useless in such weather. *Diving suit might help*, he grumbled to himself. All his careful elegance had gone for naught: from the peaked cap with the sunburst of Empire, down past flowing silkite blouse and embroidered blue doublet, red sash with the fringed ends hanging just so, to sleek white trousers tucked in soft but shiny leather halfboots. He pressed a control button and descended from the lock. As he reached ground, the ladder retreated, the valve closed, lights went out in the ports of the flitter. He felt very much alone.

The rain seemed even louder here in the open. It must be striking on foliage crowding every side of the field. Flandry heard water gurgle in gutters and drains. He could make out several buildings now, across the width of concrete, and started toward them. He hadn't gone far when half a dozen men approached from that direction. *It must be the receiving committee,* he thought, and halted so that they might be the ones coming to him. Imperial prestige and so forth, what?

As they neared, he saw they were not an especially tall race. He, who was about three-fourths caucasoid, topped the biggest by half a head. But they were wide-shouldered and well-muscled, walking lithely. A nearby lamp showed them to be tawny brown of skin, with black hair banged across the forehead and falling past the ears, a tendency toward almond eyes and flattish noses. They wore a simple uniform: green pocketed kilt of waterproof synthetic, sandals on their feet, a medallion around each neck. They moved with a confident semi-military stride, and haughtiness marked the beardless faces. Yet they were armed only with truncheon and dagger.

Odd. Flandry noted the comforting weight of the blaster at his own hip.

The squad reached him and deployed. There had been another man with them. One of the squad continued to hold a gracefully shaped umbrella over this one's head. It was a head shaven smooth, with a symbol tattooed on the brow in fluorescing gold. The man was short and slender, but seemed athletic. Hard to judge his age; the

face was unlined, but sharper and with more pro-
file than the others, a sensitive mouth and discon-
certingly steady eyes. He wore a robe which flared
outward from the shoulders (held by a yoke,
Flandry judged, to permit free air circulation
around the body) and fell in simple white folds to
the ankles. On its breast was the image of a star.

He regarded Flandry for several seconds before
speaking, in archaic and thickly accented Anglic:
"Welcome to Unan Besar. It is long since an . . .
outsider . . . has been on this planet."

The newcomer sketched a bow and answered in
Pulaoic, "On behalf of His Majesty and all the
peoples of the Terran Empire, greetings to your
world and yourself. I am Captain Sir Dominic
Flandry of the Imperial Navy." Intelligence
Corps, field division, he did not add.

"Ah. Yes." The other man seemed glad to slip
back into his own language. "The dispatcher did
mention to me that you spoke our tongue. You
honor us by taking the trouble to learn."

Flandry shrugged. "No trouble. Neural
educator, don't y' know. Doesn't take long. I got
the implantation from a Betelgeusean trader on
Orma, before I came here."

The language was musical, descended from
Malayan but influenced by many others in the
past. The ancestors of these people had left Terra
to colonize New Djawa a long time ago. After the
disastrous war with Gorrazan, three centuries
back and a bit, some of those colonists had gone
on to Unan Besar, and had been isolated from the
rest of the human race ever since. Their speech
had evolved along its own track.

Flandry was more interested in the reaction of

the robed man. His beautifully curved lips drew taut, for just an instant, and a hand curved its fingers to claws before withdrawing into the wide sleeve. The others stood impassive, rain running off their shoulders, but their eyes never left Flandry.

The robed man exclaimed, "What were you doing on Orma? It's no planet of the Empire. We're beyond the borders of any empire!"

"More or less." Flandry made his tone careless. "Terra is a couple of hundred light-years away. But you must be aware how indefinite interstellar boundaries are—how entire hegemonies can interpenetrate. As for Orma, well, why shouldn't I be there? It has a Betelgeusean trading base, and Betelgeuse is friendly to Terra."

"The real question," said the other, hardly audible above the rainfall, "is why you should be here."

And then, relaxing, donning a smile: "But no matter. You are most welcome, Captain. Permit self-introduction. I am Nias Warouw, director of the Guard Corps of the Planetary Biocontrol."

Chief of detectives, translated Flandry. *Or . . . chief of military intelligence? Why else should the Emperor's representative—as they must figure I am—be met by a policeman rather than the head of government?*

Unless the police are the government.

Warouw startled him by switching briefly to Anglic: You might call me a physician."

Flandry decided to take things as they came. *As the tourist in the sultan's harem said.* A folk out of touch for three hundred years could be expected to develop some strange customs.

"Do you always get these rains?" He drew his cloak tighter. Not that it could prevent his collar from wilting. He thought of Terra, music, perfumed air, cocktails at the Everest House with some bit of blonde fluff, and wondered dismally why he had ever come to this sinkhole planet. It wasn't as if he had orders.

"Yes—normally about nightfall in these latitudes," said Warouw.

Unan Besar has a mere ten-hour rotation period, thought Flandry. *They could easily have waited another five of those hours, till their one and only spaceport came around into daylight again. I'd have been glad to stay in orbit. They kept stalling me long enough as it was; and then suddenly their damn dispatcher ordered me down on the instant. Five extra hours—why, I could have spent them cooking myself a really decent dinner, and eating it at a decent speed, instead of gobbling a sandwich. What kind of manners is this, anyhow?*

I think they wanted me to land in darkness and rain.

Why?

Warouw reached beneath his robe and took out a vial. It held some large blue pills. "Are you aware of the biochemical situation here?" he asked.

"The Betelgeuseans mentioned something about it, but they weren't too clear or thorough on the subject."

"They wouldn't be. Having a nonhuman immunochemistry, they are not affected, and thus are not very interested. But to us, Captain, the very air of this planet is toxic. You have already absorbed enough to cause death in a few days."

Warouw smiled sleepily. "Of course, we have an antitoxin," he went on. "You will need one of these pills every thirty or so of our days while remaining here, and a final dose before you leave."

Flandry gulped and reached for the vial. Warouw's movement of withdrawal was snake smooth. "Please, Captain," he murmured. "I shall be happy to give you one now. But only one at a time. It is the law, you understand. We have to keep a careful record. Can't be careless, you know."

The Terran stood motionless for what seemed a long while. At last he grinned, without much jollity. "Yes," he said, "I believe I do understand."

II

The spaceport was built on a hill, a hundred jungled kilometers from the planet's chief city, for the benefit of the Betelgeuseans. A few ancient Pulaoic ships were also kept at that place, but never used.

"A hermit kingdom," the bluefaced skipper had growled to Flandry in the tavern on Orma. "We don't visit them very often. Once or twice a standard year a trading craft of ours stops by." The Betelgeuseans were ubiquitous throughout this sector of space. Flandry had engaged passage on one of their tramp ships, as the quickest way to get from his completed assignment on Altai to the big Imperial port at Spica VI. There he would catch the *Empress Maia*, which touched on the home-

ward leg of her regular cruise. He felt he deserved
to ride back to Terra on a luxury liner, and he was
an accomplished padder of expense accounts.

"What do you trade for?" he asked. It was idle
curiosity, filling in time until the merchant ship
departed this planet. They were speaking Alfza-
rian, which scratched his throat, but the other
being had no Anglic.

"Hides, natural fibers, and fruits, mostly.
You've never eaten *modjo* fruit? Humans in this
sector think it's quite a delicacy; me, I wouldn't
know. But I guess nobody ever thought to take
some as far as Terra. Hm-m-m." The Betelgeusean
went into a commercial reverie.

Flandry sipped raw local brandy and said,
"There are still scattered independent colonies
left over from the early days. I've just come from
one, in fact. But I've never heard of this Unan
Besar."

"Why should you? Doubtless the astronautical
archives at sector HQ, even at Terra, contain mention of it. But it keeps to itself. And it's of no real
importance, even to us. We sell a little machinery
and stuff there; we pick up the goods I mentioned;
but it amounts to very little. It could amount to
more, I think, but whoever controls the planet
doesn't want that."

"Are you sure?"

"It's obvious. They have one wretched little
spaceport for the whole globe. Antiquated
facilities, a few warehouses, all stuck way to
chaos out in the woods—as if spaceships were
still spewing radiation! Traders aren't permitted
to go anywhere else. They aren't even furnished a
bunkhouse. So naturally, they only stay long

enough to discharge a consignment and load the exchange cargo. They never meet anyone except a few officials. They're not supposed to speak with the native longshoremen. Once or twice I've tried that, in private, just to see what would happen. Nothing did. The poor devil was so frightened that he ran. He knew the law!"

"Hm." Flandry rubbed his chin. Its scratchiness reminded him he was due for his bimonthly dose of antibeard enzyme, and he shifted to stroking his mustache. "I wonder they even let you learn their language."

"That happened several generations ago, when our traders first made contact. Anglic was inconvenient for both parties—Oh, yes, a few of their aristocrats know Anglic. We sell them books, newstapes, anything to keep their ruling class up to date on what's happening in the rest of the known galaxy. Maybe the common people on Unan Besar are rusticating. But the overlords are not."

"What are they doing, then?"

"I don't know. From space, you can see it's a rich world. Backward agricultural methods, odd-looking towns, but crammed with natural resources."

"What sort of planet is it? What type?"

"Terrestroid. What else?"

Flandry grimaced and puffed a cigaret to life. "You know how much that means!"

"Well, then, it's about one A.U. from its sun. But that's an F2 star, a little more massive than Sol, so the planet's sidereal period is only nine months and its average temperature is higher than Terra or Alfzar. No satellites. Very little axial tilt.

About a ten-hour rotation. A trifle smaller than Terra, surface gravity oh-point-eight gee. As a consequence, fewer uplands: smaller continents, lots of islands, most areas rather low and swampy. Because of the weaker gravity and higher irradiation, it actually has less hydrosphere than Terra. But you'd never know that, what with shallow seas and heavy clouds everywhere you look. . . . Uh, yes, there's something the matter with its ecology also. I forget what, because it doesn't affect my species, but humans need to take precautions. Can't be too serious, though, or the place wouldn't have such a population. I estimate a hundred million inhabitants—and it was only colonized three centuries ago."

"Well," said Flandry, "people have to do something in their spare time."

He smoked slowly, thinking. The self-isolation of Unan Besar might mean nothing, except to its dwellers. On the other hand, he knew of places where hell's own kettle had simmered unnoticed for a long time. It was hard enough—impossible, actually—to keep watch on those four million suns estimated to lie within the Imperial sphere itself. Out here on the marches, where barbarism faded into unknownness, and the agents of a hostile Merseia prowled and probed, any hope of controlling all situations grew cold indeed.

Wherefore the thumb-witted guardians of a fat and funseeking Terra had stopped even trying, thought Flandry. They should make periodic reviews of the archives, sift every Intelligence report, investigate each of a billion mysteries. But that would require a bigger Navy, he thought, which would require higher taxes, which would deprive too many Terran lordlings of a new skycar and too many of their mistresses of a new syntha-gem bracelet. It might even turn up certain facts on which the Navy would have to act, which might even (horrors!) lead to full-scale fighting somewhere. . . .

Ah, the devil with it, he thought. *I've just come from a mission the accounts of which, delicately exaggerated, will make me a celebrity at Home. I have several months' unspent pay waiting. And speaking of mistresses—*

But it is not natural for a human planet to cut itself off from humanity. When I get back, I'd better file a recommendation that this be checked up on.

Though I'm hardly naive enough to think that anyone will act on my bare suspicion.

"Where," said Captain Flandry, "can I rent a space flitter?"

III

The aircar was big, modern, and luxuriously outfitted. A custom job from Betelgeuse, no doubt. Flandry sat among deadpan Guard Corpsmen who said never a word, beside Warouw who was almost as quiet. Rain and wind were noisy as the car got under way, but when it slanted toward Kompong Timur, the weather had cleared. Flandry looked down upon a sprawling constellation of lights. He could see that the city borders faded into a broad lake, and that it was everywhere threaded with canals, which shimmered under mercury and neon glare. An experienced eye recognized certain other signs, such as the clustering of radiance near the central and tallest buildings, the surrounding zones of low roofs and infrequent lamps. That usually meant slums, which in turn suggested a concentration of wealth and power among the few.

"Where are we going?" he asked.

"To an interview. The governing board of Biocontrol is most anxious to meet you, Captain." Warouw lifted one eyebrow. It gave his smooth oval face a flicker of sardonicism. "You are not weary, I trust? What with the short day and night here, our people have gotten into the habit of taking several naps throughout the rotation period, rather than one long rest. Perhaps you feel ready for bed?"

Flandry tapped a cigaret on one thumbnail. "Would it do me much good to say yes?"

Warouw smiled. The aircar glided down to a landing terrace, high on one of the biggest buildings—a structure important enough to have been erected on a piece of solid land, rather than on the piles driven into mud which upheld most of the city.

As Flandry stepped out, the Guards closed in around him. "Call off the Happiness Boys, will you?" he snapped. "I want a quiet smoke." Warouw jerked his head. The silent men withdrew, but not very far. Flandry walked across the terrace to its rail.

Clouds banked high on the eastern horizon. Lightning flickered in their depths. Overhead, the sky was clear, though a dim violet haze wavered among unearthly star-patterns—fluorescence in the upper atmosphere, due to the hidden but brilliant sun. Flandry identified the red spark of Betelgeuse, and yellow Spica, with a certain wistfulness. God knew if he'd ever drink beer again on any planet of either. He had stumbled into something unmerciful.

This building must be a hundred meters square. It rose in many tiers, pagoda fashion, the curved roofs ending in elephant heads whose tusks were lamps. The rail beneath Flandry's hand was sculptured scaly. The dome which topped the whole enormous edifice was created with an arrogant image: the upraised foot of some bird of prey, talons grasping at heaven. The walls were gilt, dazzling even at night. From this terrace it was a fifty-meter drop to the oily waters of a major canal. On the other side rose a line of palaces. They were airy, colonnaded structures, their roofs leaping gaily upward, their walls painted with multi-armed figures at play. Lights glowed from several; Flandry heard twanging minor-key music.

Even here, in the city's heart, he thought he could smell the surrounding jungle.

"If you please." Warouw bowed at him.

Flandry took a final drag on his cigaret and followed the other man. They went through an archway shaped like the gaping mouth of a monster and down a long red hall beyond. Several doors stood open to offices, where kilted men sat tailorwise on cushions and worked at low desks. Flandry read a few legends: Interisland Water Traffic Bureau, Syncretic Arbitration Board, Seismic Energy Commission—yes, this was the seat of government. Then he was in an elevator, purring downward. The corridor into which he was finally guided stretched black between whitely fluorescing pillars.

At its end, a doorway opened on a great blue room. It was almost hemispherical, with an outsize window overlooking the night of Kompong Timur. To right and left stood banks of machinery: microfiles, recorders, computers, communicators. In the center was a table, black wood inlaid with native ivory. Behind it sat the overlords of Unan Besar.

Flandry stepped closer, studying them from the camouflage of a nonchalant grin. Cross-legged on a padded bench, all twenty had shaven heads and white robes like Warouw, the same tattooed mark on their brows. It was a gold circle with a cross beneath and an arrow slanting upward. The breast insignia varied—a cogwheel, a triode circuit diagram, an integral dx, conventionalized waves and grain sheafs and thunderbolts—the heraldry of a government which at least nominally emphasized technology.

Mostly, these men were older than Nias Warouw, and not in such good physical shape. The one who sat in the middle must be the grand panjandrum, Flandry thought: a petulant fat face, and the vulture-claw sign of mastery on his robo.

Warouw had been purringly urbane, but there was no mistaking the hostility of these others. Here and there a cheek gleamed with sweat, eyes narrowed, fingers drummed the tabletop. Flandry made the muscles around his shoulderblades relax. It was no easy job, since the knife-wielding Strength Through Joy squad stood immediately behind him.

The silence stretched.

Someone had to break it. "Boo," said Flandry. The man at the center stirred. "What?"

"A formula of greeting, your prominence," bowed Flandry.

"Address me as Tuan Solu Bandang." The fat man switched eyes toward Warouw. "Is this the, ah, the Terran agent?"

"No," snorted Flandry, "I'm a cigar salesman." But he didn't snort it very loudly, or in Pulaoic.

"Yes, Tuan." Warouw inclined his head briefly above folded hands.

They continued to stare. Flandry beamed and pirouetted for them. He was worth looking at, he assured himself smugly, being of athletic build (thanks to calisthenics, which he loathed but forced himself to keep up) and high-boned, straight-nosed, aristocratic features (thanks to one of Terra's most fashionable biosculptors). His eyes were gray, his brown hair cut close about the ears in Imperial style but sleek on top.

Bandang pointed uneasily. "Take that, ah, gun from him," he ordered.

"Please, Tuan," said Flandry. "It was bequeathed me by my dear old grandmother. It still smells of lavender. If anyone demanded it from me, my heart would be so broken I'd blow his guts out."

Someone else turned purple and said shrilly. "You foreigner, do you realize where you are?"

"Let him keep it if he insists, Tuan," said Warouw indifferently. He met Flandry's gaze with the faintest of smiles and added: "We should not disfigure this reunion moment with quarrels."

A sigh went down the long table. Bandang pointed to a cushion on the floor. "Sit."

"No, thank you." Flandry studied them.

Warouw seemed the most intelligent and formidable of the lot, but after their initial surprise, they had all settled back into a disquieting habitual scornfulness. Surely the only firearm in the whole room didn't count for that little!

"As you wish." Bandang leaned forward, assuming unctuousness. "See here, ah, Captain— you'll understand, I trust, how . . . how . . . delicate? Yes, how delicate a matter this is. I'm, ah, sure your discretion—" His voice trailed off in a smirk.

"If I'm causing any trouble, Tuan, I apologize," said Flandry. "I'll be glad to depart at once." *And how!*

"Ah . . . no. No, I fear that isn't er, practicable. Not for the present. My implication is quite simple actually, and I, ah, have no doubt that a man of your obvious sophistication can, er, grasp?—yes, can grasp the situation." Bandang drew a long breath. His colleagues looked resigned. "Consider this planet, Captain: its people, its culture, isolated and autonomous for more than four hundred years." (That would be local years, Flandry reminded himself, but still, a long time.) "The, ah, distinctive civilization which has inevitably developed—the special values, beliefs, customs, ah, and . . . achievements—the socioeconomic balance—cannot lightly be upset. Not without, er, great suffering. And loss. Irreparable loss."

Having an inside view of the Empire, and unprejudiced eyes, Flandry could understand the reluctance of some worlds to have anything to do with same. But there was more here than a simple desire to preserve independence and dignity. If these characters had any knowledge at all of what was going on elsewhere in the universe—and certainly they did—then they would know that Terra wasn't a menace to them. The Empire was old and sated; except when driven by military necessity, it didn't want any more real estate. Something big and ugly was being kept hidden on Unan Besar.

"What we, ah, wish to know," continued Bandang, "is, er, do you come here with official standing? And if so, what message do you convey from your, um, respected superiors?"

Flandry weighed his answer, thinking of knives at his back and night beyond the windows. "I have no message, Tuan, other than friendly greetings," he said. "What else can the Imperium offer until we are able to get to know your people better?"

"But you *have* come here under orders, Captain? Not by chance?"

"My credentials are in my spaceship, Tuan." Flandry hoped his commission, his field agent's open warrant, and similar flashy documents might impress them. For an unofficial visitor could end up in a canal with his throat cut, and no one in all the galactic vastness would care.

"Credentials for what?" It was a nervous croak from the end of the table.

Warouw scowled. Flandry could sympathize with the Guard chief's annoyance. This was no way to conduct an interrogation. Biocontrol was falling all over its own flat feet: crude bluster and cruder insinuation. To be sure, they were amateurs at this job—Warouw was their tame professional—but the lowest-echelon politician in the Empire would have had more understanding of men, and made a better attempt at questioning such a quasi-prisoner.

"If the Tuan pleases," Warouw interposed, "we seem to be giving Captain Flandry an unfortunate impression of ourselves. May my unworthy self be permitted to discuss the situation with him privately?"

"No!" Bandang stuck his head forward, like a flabby bull. "Let's have none of your shilly-shally. I'm a man of few words, yes, few words and—Captain, I, ah, trust you'll realize . . . will not take offense . . . we bear responsibility for an entire planet and—ah—well, as a man of sophistication, you will not object to narcosynthesis?"

Flandry stiffened. "What?"

"After all—" Bandang wet his lips. "You come unheralded . . . ah . . . without the expected, er, preliminary fanfare or—Conceivably you are a mere imposter. Please! Please do not resent my, um, necessary entertaining of the possibility. If you actually are an official, ah, delegate—or agent—naturally, we will wish to ascertain—"

"Sorry, Tuan," said Flandry. "I've been immunized to truth drugs."

"Oh? Oh. Oh, yes. Well, then . . . we do have a hypnoprobe—yes, Colleague Warouw's department is not altogether behind the times. He obtains goods on order from the Betelgeuseans. . . . Ah, I realize that a hypnoprobing is, er, an uncomfortable experience—"

To put it mildly, thought the Terran. His spine crawled. *I see. They really are amateurs. Nobody who understood politics and war would be so reckless. Mind-probing an Imperial officer! As if the Empire could let anyone live who heard me spill half of what I know! Yes, amateurs.*

He stared into the eyes of Warouw, the only man who might realize what this meant. And he met no pity, only a hunter's wariness. He could guess Warouw's calculations:

If Flandry has chanced by unofficially, on his own, it's simple. We kill him. If he's here as an advance scout, it becomes more complicated. His "accidental" death must be very carefully faked. But at least we'll know that Terra is interested in us, and can start taking measures to protect our great secret.

The worst of it was, they would learn that this visit had indeed been Flandry's own idea, and that if he died on Unan Besar a preoccupied Service wouldn't make any serious investigation.

Flandry thought of wines and women and adventures yet to be undertaken. Death was the ultimate dullness.

He dropped a hand to his blaster. "I wouldn't try that, sonny boy," he said.

From the corner of an eye, he saw one of the Guards glide forward with a raised truncheon. He sidestepped, hooked a foot before the man's ankles, shoved, and clipped behind the ear with his free hand as the body fell. The Guard hit the floor and stayed there.

His comrades growled. Knives flashed clear. "Stop!" yelled an appalled Bandang. "Stop this instant!" But it was Warouw's sharp whistle, like a man calling a dog to heel, which brought the Guards crouching in their tracks.

"Enough," said Warouw. "Put that toy away, Flandry."

"But it's a useful toy." The Terran skinned teeth in a grin. "I can kill things with it."

"What good would that do you? You would never get off this planet. And in thirty days—two Terrestrial weeks, more or less—Watch."

Ignoring stunned governors and angry Guards, Warouw crossed the floor to a telecom screen. He twirled the dials. Breath wheezed from the Biocontrol table; otherwise the room grew very quiet.

"It so happens that a condemned criminal is on public exhibition in the Square of the Four Gods." Warouw flicked a switch. "Understand, we are not inhuman. Ordinary crime is punished less drastically. But this man is guilty of assault on a Biocontrol technicial. He reached the state of readiness for display a few hours ago."

The screen lit up. Flandry saw an image of a plaza surrounded by canal water. A statue loomed in each corner, male figures dancing with many arms radiating from their shoulders. In the middle stood a cage. A placard on it described the offense. A naked man lay within.

His back arched, he clawed the air and screamed. It was as if his ribs must break with the violence of breath and heartbeat. Blood trickled out of his nose. His jaw had dislocated itself. His eyes were blind balls starting from the sockets.

"It will progress," said Warouw dispassionately. "Death in a few more hours."

From the middle of nightmare, Flandry said, "You took his pills away."

Warouw turned down the dreadful shrieking and corrected: "No, we merely condemned him not to receive any more. Of course, an occasional criminal under the ban prefers to commit suicide. This man gave himself up, hoping to be sentenced to enslavement. But his offense was too great. Human life on Unan Besar depends on Biocontrol, which must therefore be inviolable."

Flandry took his eyes from the screen. He had thought he was tough, but this was impossible to watch. "What's the cause of death?" he asked without tone.

"Well, fundamentally the life which evolved on Unan Besar is terrestroid, and nourishing to man. But there is one phylum of airborne bacteria that occurs everywhere on the planet. The germs enter the human bloodstream, where they react with certain enzymes normal and necessary to us and start excreting acetylcholine. You know what an overly high concentration of acetylcholine does to the nervous system."

"Yes."

"Unan Besar could not be colonized until scientists from the mother planet, New Djawa, had developed an antitoxin. The manufacture and distribution of this antitoxin is the responsiblity of Biocontrol."

Flandry looked at the faces behind the table. "What happens to me in thirty days," he said, "would not give you gentlemen much satisfaction."

Warouw switched off the telecom. "You might kill a few of us before the Guards overcame you," he said. "But no member of Biocontrol fears death."

Bandang's sweating countenance belied him. But others looked grim, and a fanatic's voice whispered from age-withered lips: "No, not as long as the holy mission exists."

Warouw extended his hand. "So give me that gun," he finished, almost lightly.

Flandry fired.

Bandang squealed and dove under the table. But the blaster bolt had gone by him anyway. It smote the window. Thunder crackled behind it.

"You *fool!*" shouted Warouw.

Flandry plunged across the floor. A Guard ran to intercept him. Flandry stiff-armed the man and sprang to the tabletop. An overlord grabbed at him. Teeth crunched under Flandry's boot. He leapfrogged a bald head and hit the floor beyond.

A thrown dagger went past his cheek. The broken window gaped before him. He sprang through the hole and hit the roof underneath. It slanted steeply downward. He rolled all the way, tumbled from the edge, and straightened out as he fell toward the canal.

IV

The water was dirty. As he broke its surface, he wondered for one idiotic moment what the chances were of salvaging his clothes. They had cost him a pretty sum. Then alien smells filled his nostrils, and he struck out in search of darkness.

Dreamlike in this hunted moment, a boat glided past. Its stem and stern curved upward, extravagantly shaped, and the sides were gay with tiny electric lamps. A boy and girl snuggled in the waist under a transparent canopy. Their kilts and

Dutch boy bob seemed the universal style here for both sexes, but they had added bangles and had painted intricate designs on their skins. Music caterwauled from a radio. Rich kids, no doubt. Flandry sank back under water as the boat came near. He felt its propeller vibrations in ears and flesh.

When his head came up again, he heard a new sound. It was like a monstrous gong, crashing from some loudspeaker on the golden pagoda. An alarm! Warouw's corps would be after him in minutes. Solu Bandang might be content to wait, expecting the Terran to die in two weeks—but Nias Warouw wanted to quiz him. Flandry kicked off his boots and began swimming faster.

Lights blazed overhead at the intersection of the next canal. Every one seemed focused on him. There was a thick traffic of boats, not only pleasure craft but water buses and freight carriers. Pedestrians crowded the narrow walks that ran along the housefronts, and the high bridges crossing the waterways. The air was full of city babble. Flandry eased up against the weed-grown brick of an embankment.

Four young men stood on the walk opposite. They were muscular, the look of illiterate commoners in their mannerisms and the coarse material of their kilts. But they talked with animation, gesturing, possibly a little drunk. Another man approached. He was a small fellow, distinguished only by robe and shaven pate. But the four big ones grew still the moment they saw him. They backed against the wall to let him go by and bent their heads over folded hands. He paid no atten-

tion. When he was gone, it took them a few minutes to regain their good humor.

So, thought Flandry.

The chance he had been waiting for came, a
freight boat putt-putting close to the canal bank in
the direction he wanted. Flandry pushed away
from the bricks, seized a rope bumper hung from
the rail, and snuggled close to the hull. Water
streamed silkily around his body and trailing
legs. He caught smells of tar and spice. Somewhere above, the steersman tapped a gamelan and
crooned to himself.

Within two kilometers, the boat reached an invisible boundary common to most cities. On one
side of a cross-canal, an upper-class apartment
house lifted tiers of delicate red columns toward a
gilt roof. On the other side there was no solid land,
only endless pilings to hold structures above the
water. There the lamps were few, with darknesses
between, and the buildings crouched low. Flandry could just see that those warehouses and
tenements and small factories were not plas-
tifaced like the rich part of town. This was all
sheet metal and rough timber, thatch roofs, dim
light glowing through little dirty-paned windows. He saw two men pad by with knives in their
hands.

The truckboat continued, deeper into slum.
Now that the great gong was stilled and the heavy
traffic left behind, it was very quiet around Flandry. He heard only a muted background growl of
distant machines. But if the canals had been dirty
before, they were now disgusting. Once something brushed him in the night; with skin and

nose he recognized it as a corpse. Once, far off, a
woman screamed. And once he glimpsed a little
girl, skipping rope all alone under a canalside
lamp. Its harsh blue glow was as solitary as a star.
Darkness enclosed the child. She didn't stop
jumping as the boat passed, but her eyes followed
it with a hag's calculation. Then Flandry was
beyond her and had lost her.

About time to get off, he thought.

Suddenly the stillness and desertion were broken. It began as a faint irregular hooting, which
drew closer. Flandry didn't know what warned
him—perhaps the way the truck pilot stopped
musicking and revved up the motor. But his
nerves tingled and he knew: *School's out.*

He let go the bumper. The boat chugged on in
haste, rounded a corner and was gone. Flandry
swam through warm slimy water till he grasped a
ladder. It led up to a boardwalk, which fronted a
line of sleazy houses with tin sides and peaked
grass roofs and lightless windows. The night was
thick and hot and stinking around him, full of
shadows. No other human stirred. But the animal
hooting came nearer.

After a moment, their hides agleam in the light
of one lamp twenty meters away, the pack swam
into sight. There were a dozen, about the size and
build of Terrestrial sea lions. They had glabrous
reptile skins, long necks and snaky heads. Ton-
gues vibrated between rows of teeth. Tasting the
water? Flandry didn't know how they had traced
him. He crouched on the ladder, the canal lapping
about his ankles, and drew his gun.

The swimmers saw him, or smelled him, and
veered. Their high blasts of sound became a shrill

ululation. *Give tongue, the fox is gone to earth!*

As the nearest of them surged close, Flandry's blaster fired. Blue lightning spat in the dark, and a headless body rolled over. He scrambled up onto the walk.

The beasts kept pace as he ran, reaching up to snap at his feet. The planks resounded. He fired again, and missed. Once he stumbled, hit a corrugated metal wall, and heard it boom.

Far down the canal, engines whined and the fierce sun of a searchlight waxed in his eyes. He didn't need to be told it was a police boat, tracking him with the help of the swimmers. He stopped before a doorway. The animals churned the water below the pier. He felt its piles tremble from the impact of heavy bodies. Their splashing and whistling filled his skull. Where to go, what to do?—Yes. He turned the primitive doorknob. Locked of course. He thumbed his blaster to narrow beam and used it as a cutting torch, with his body between the flame and the approaching speedboat.

There! The door opened under his pressure. He slipped through, closed it, and stood in the dark. An after-image of the gunbeam still flickered across his blindness, and his pulse was loud.

Got to get out of here, he thought. *The cops won't know offhand precisely where I went, but they'll check every door in this row and find the cut lock.*

He could just make out a gray square of window across the room, and groped toward it. Canal water dripped off his clothes.

Feet pattered on bare boards. "Who goes?" An instant later, Flandry swore at himself for having spoken. But there was no answer. Whoever else was in this room—probably asleep till he came—was reacting to his intrusion with feline presence of mind. There was no more noise.

He barked his shins on a low bedstead. He heard a creak and saw an oblong of dull shimmering light appear. A trapdoor in the floor had been opened. "Stop!" he called. The trapdoor was darkened with a shadow. Then that was gone too. Flandry heard a splash below. He thought he heard the unknown start swimming quickly away. The trapdoor fell down again.

It had all taken a bare few seconds. He grew aware of the animals, hooting and plunging outside. The unknown had nerve, to dive into the same water as that hell-pack! And now engine-roar slowed to a whine, a sputter, the boat had arrived. A voice called something, harsh and authoritative.

Flandry's eyes were adapting. He could see that this house—cabin, rather—comprised a single big room. It was sparsely furnished: a few stools and cushions, the bed, a brazier and some cooking utensils, a small chest of drawers. But he sensed good taste. There were a couple of exquisitely arabesqued wooden screens; and he thought he could identify fine drawing on a scroll which decorated one wall.

Not that it mattered! He stepped to the window on the side through which he had come. Several Guards crouched in the boat, flashing its search-light around. A needle gun was mounted on its prow, but otherwise the men were armed only with their knives and nightsticks. There might be another boatload along soon, but for the moment—

Flandry set his blaster to full power, narrow beam, and opened the door a crack. *I couldn't get more than one or two men at this range*, he calculated, *and the others would radio HQ that they'd found me. But could be I can forestall that with some accurate shooting. Very accurate. Fortunately, I count marksmanship among my many superiorities.*

The weapon blazed.

He chopped the beam down, first across cockpit and dashboard to knock out the radio, then into the hull itself. The Guards bellowed. Their searchlight swung blindingly toward him and he heard needles thunk into the door panels. Then the boat was pierced. It filled and sank like a diving whale.

The Guards had already sprung overboard. They could come up the ladder, dash at their quarry, and be shot down. Wherefore they would not come very fast. They'd most likely swim around waiting for reinforcements. Flandry closed the door with a polite "*Auf Wiedersehen*" and hurried across the room. There was no door on that side, but he opened a window, vaulted to the boardwalk beneath, and loped off fast and quietly. With any luck, he'd leave men and sealhounds milling about under the place he'd just quitted until he was safely elsewhere.

At the end of the pier, a bridge arched across to another row of shacks. It wasn't one of the beautiful metallic affairs in the center part of town. This bridge was of planks suspended from vine cables.

But it had a grace of its own. It swayed under
Flandry's tread. He passed the big pillars anchor-
ing the suspension at the far end—

One brawny arm closed around his neck. The
other hand clamped numbingly on his gun wrist.
A bass voice told him, very low, "Don't move,
outlander. Not till Kemul says you can."

Flandry, who didn't wish a fractured larynx,
stood deathstill. The blaster was plucked from his
hand. "Always wanted one of these," the mugger
chuckled. "Now, who in the name of fifty million
devils are you, and what d' you mean breaking
into Luang's crib that way?"

The pressure tightened around his throat.
Flandry thought in bitterness, *Sure, I get it. Luang
escaped down the trap and fetched help. They
figured I'd have to come in this direction, if I
escaped at all. I seemed worth catching. This ape
simply lurked behind the pillar waiting for me.*

"Come now." The arm cut off all breath. "Be
good and tell Kemul." Pressure eased a trifle.

"Guards—Biocontrol agents—back there," rattled Flandry.

"Kemul knows. Kemul isn't blind or deaf. A
good citizen should hail them and turn you over
to them. Perhaps Kemul will. But he is curious.
No one like you has ever been seen on all Unan
Besar. Kemul would like to hear your side of the
tale before he decides what to do."

Flandry relaxed against a bare chest solid as a
wall. "This is hardly the place for long stories," he
whispered. "If we could go somewhere and
talk—"

"Aye. If you will behave." Having tucked the
blaster in his kilt, Kemul patted Flandry in search

of other goods. He removed watch and wallet, released the Terran, and stepped back, tigerishly fast, ready for counterattack.

Vague greasy light fell across him. Flandry saw a giant by the standards of any planet, an ogre among these folk: 220 centimeters high, with shoulders to match. Kemul's face had from time to time been slashed with knives and beaten with blunt instruments; his hair was grizzled; but still he moved as if made of rubber. He wore body paint that wove a dozen clashing colors together. A kris was thrust in the garish batik of his kilt.

He grinned. It made his ruined countenance almost human. "Kemul knows a private spot," he offered. "We can go there if you really want to talk. But so private is it, even the house god wears a blindfold. Kemul must blindfold you too."

Flandry massaged his aching neck. "As you will." He studied the other man a moment before adding, "I had hoped to find someone like you."

Which was true enough. But he hadn't expected to meet Kompong Timur's underworld at such a severe disadvantage. If he couldn't think of something to bribe them with—his blaster had been the best possibility, and it was gone now—they'd quite likely slit his weasand. Or turn him over to Warouw. Or just leave him to die screaming, a couple of weeks hence.

V

Boats clustered around a long two-story building which stood by itself in the Canal of the Fiery Snake. Everywhere else lay darkness, the tenements of the poor, a few sweatshop factories, old

warehouses abandoned to rats and robbers. But
there was life enough on the first floor of the
Tavern Called Swampman's Ease. Its air was thick
with smoke, through which grinned jack-o'-
lantern lights, and with the smells of cheap arrack
and cheaper narcotics. Freightboat crewmen,
fishers, dock wallopers, machine tenders, hunters
and loggers from the jungle, bandits, cutpurses,
gamblers, and less identifiable persons lounged
about on the floor mats: drinking, smoking, quar-
reling, plotting, rattling dice, watching a dancer
swing her hips to plang of gamelan and squeal of
flute and thump-thump of a small drum. Occasionally, behind a beaded curtain, one of the joy
girls giggled. High on her throne, Madame Ud-
jung watched with jet eyes nearly buried in fat.
Sometimes she spoke to the noseless daggerman
who crouched at her feet in case of trouble, but
mostly she drank gin and talked to the ketjil bird
on her wrist. It was not large, but its tail swept
down like a rain of golden fire and it could sing in
a woman's voice.

Flandry could hear enough of the racket to
know he was in some such place. But there were
probably a hundred like it, and his eyes had only
been unbandaged when he reached this second-
floor room. Which was not the sort of layout he
would have expected. It was clean, and much like
the one he'd blundered onto earlier: simple fur-
nishings, a decorative scroll, a couple of screens, a
shallow bowl holding one stone and two white
flowers. A glowlamp in the hand of a small,
blindfolded wooden idol on a shelf showed that
every article was of exquisite simplicity. One
window stood open to warm breezes, but incense
drowned the garbage smell of the canal.

Kemul tossed Flandry a kilt, which the Terran was glad enough to belt around his middle. "Well," said the giant, "what are his things worth after they've been cleaned, Luang?"

The girl studied the clothes Flandry had been forced to take off. "All synthetic fiber . . . but never have color and fineness like this been seen on Unan Besar." Her voice was husky. "I should say they are worth death in the cage, Kemul."

"What?"

Luang threw the garments to the floor and laughed. She sat on top of the dresser, swinging bare feet against its drawers. Her kilt was dazzling white, her only ornament the ivory inlay on her dagger hilt. Not that she needed more. She wasn't tall, and her face had never been sculpted into the monotonous beauty of all rich Terran women. But it was a vivid face, high cheekbones, full mouth, delicately shaped nose, eyes long and dark under arched brows. Her bobbed hair was crow's-wing color, her complexion dull gold, and her figure reminded Flandry acutely that he had been celibate for months.

"Reason it out, mugger," she said with a note of affectionate teasing. She took a cigaret case from her pocket and offered it to the Terran. Flandry accepted a yellow cylinder and inhaled. Nothing happened. Luang laughed again and snapped a lighter for him and herself. She trickled smoke from her nostrils, as if veiling her expression. Flandry tried it and choked. If this was tobacco, then tobacco on Unan Besar had mutated and crossed itself with deadly nightshade.

"Well, Captain, as you style yourself," said Luang, "what do you suggest we do with you?"

Flandry regarded her closely, wishing the local

costume weren't quite so brief. Dammit, his life depended on cool thinking. "You might try listening to me," he said.

"I am. Though anyone who breaks in on my rest as you did—"

"I couldn't help that!"

"Oh, the trouble you caused isn't held against you." Luang raised her feet to the dresser top, hugged her legs and watched him across rounded knees. "On the contrary, I haven't had so much fun since One-Eyed Rawi went amok down on Joy Canal. How those fat frumps squealed—and dove into the water in all their finery!" Malice faded and she sighed. "It ended unhappily, though, when poor old Rawi must needs be killed. I hope this adventure doesn't end likewise."

"I hope so too," Flandry agreed. "Let's work together very hard to prevent any such outcome."

Kemul, who was hunkered on the floor, snapped his fingers. "Ah! Kemul understands!"

She smiled. "What do you mean?"

"About his clothes and other valuables. They would be noticed, Luang, and Biocontrol would ask questions, and might even trace them back to us. And if it turned out we had failed to give Biocontrol this man they were hunting, it would be the cage for both of us."

"Congratulations," said Flandry.

"Best we surrender him at once." Kemul shifted uneasily on his haunches. "There might even be a reward."

"We shall see." Luang inhaled thoughtfully—and, to the Terran, most distractingly. "Of course," she mused, "I had best go back to my other place soon. The Guard Corps must be swarming all over it. They'll establish my identity from fingerprints." She looked at Flandry through drooping lashes. "I *could* tell them that when you broke in, I was frightened and escaped through the trap and don't know anything about the affair."

He leaned against the wall near the window. It was very dark outside. "But I have to make it worth your while to take the risk they won't believe you, eh?" he said.

She made a face. "Poo! That's no risk. Whoever heard of a Guard able to think past the end of his own snout? The real danger would come later, in keeping you hidden, outworld man. Swamp Town is full of eyes. It would be expensive, too."

"Let's discuss the matter." Flandry took another puff of his cigaret. It wasn't so bad the second time; probably his taste buds were stunned. "Let's get acquainted, at least. I've told you I'm an Imperial officer, and explained a little of what and where the Empire is nowadays. So let me learn something about your own planet. Check my deductions against the facts for me, will you?

"Biocontrol manufactures the antitoxin pills and distributes them through local centers, right?" She nodded. "Every citizen gets one, every thirty days, and has to swallow it there on the spot." Again she nodded. "Obviously, even infants must have a ration in their milk. So every person on this world can be fingerprinted at birth. The prints are kept in a central file, and automatically checked every time anyone comes in for his pill. Thus no one gets more than his ration. And anyone in trouble with the law had better surrender very meekly to the Guards . . . or he won't get the next dose." This time her nod included a faint, derisive smile.

"No system ever worked so well that there wasn't some equivalent of an underworld," Flandry continued. "When the authorities began to get nasty, I struck out for the slums, where I figured your criminal class must center. Evidently I was right about that. What I don't yet know, though, is why as much freedom as this is allowed. Kemul, for example, seems to be a full-time bandit; and you, m'lady, appear to be a, ahem, private entrepreneur. The government could control your people more tightly than it does."

Kemul laughed, a gusty noise overriding that mumble and tinkle which seeped through the floorboards. "What does Biocontrol care?" he said. "You pay for your medicine. You pay plenty, each time. Oh, they make some allowance for hardship cases, where such can be proven, but that puts you right under the Guards' nosy eye—" *Wow!* thought Flandry. "Or a slave owner gets a reduction on the pills he buys for his folk. Bah! Kemul would rather slash his own belly like a free man. So he pays full price. Most people do. So Biocontrol gets its money. How that money is earned in the first place, Biocontrol doesn't care."

"Ah." Flandry stroked his mustache. "A single tax system."

The socio-economics of it became obvious enough now. If every person, with insignificant exceptions, had to pay the same price for life every two weeks, certain classes were placed at a severe disadvantage. Men with large families, for example: they'd tend to put the kids to work as young as possible, to help meet the bills. This would mean an ill-educated younger generation, still less able to maintain its place on the economic ladder. Poor people generally would suffer; any run of hard luck would land them in the grip of the loan sharks for life. The incentive toward crime was enormous, especially when there was no real policing.

Over lifetimes, the rich got richer and the poor got poorer. At last a small class of billionaires—merchants, big manufacturers and landholders—lorded it over a beaten-down peasantry and a turbulent city proletariat. These distinctions became hereditary, simply because no one ever got far enough ahead to rise above his father's status. . . . If there had been contact with other planets, the necessities of interstellar competition would have forced Unan Besar into a more efficient pattern. But except for the occasional unimportant visit of a strictly segregated Betelgeusean trader, Unan Besar had been isolated these past three centuries.

Flandry realized he was oversimplifying. A planet is a world, as big and diverse as ever Terra was. There had to be more than one social structure, and within any sub-culture there must be individuals who didn't fit the pattern. Luang, for instance; he didn't know quite what to make of her. But no matter for now. He was in Kompong Timur, where life was approximately as he had deduced.

"I take it, then, that failure to respect Biocontrol personnel is the only serious crime here," he said.

"Not quite." Kemul's fist clenched. "Biocontrol is chummy with the rich. Burgle a rich man's

house and see what happens. Ten years in the
quarries, if you're lucky. Enslavement, more
likely."

"Only if you are caught," purred Luang. "I remember once—But that was then."

"I see why Guards don't bother carrying
firearms," said Flandry.

"They do in this section of town." Kemul
looked still grimmer. "And they go in teams. And
still they're apt to end up floating in the canal,
with none to say who did it to them. So many
people might, you see. Not so much for the money
they have. But might be a husband, after some rich
boy come slumming saw his wife and ordered her
aboard his boat. Or a palace servant, whipped
once too often. Or a sometime engineer, what lost
his post and sank down to our level, because he'd
not wink at a defective load of cement. Cases like
that."

"He speaks of people he knows," said Luang.
"He hasn't imagination enough to invent examples." Her tone remained bantering.

"But most times," Kemul finished doggedly,
"the Guards don't come into Swamp Town. No
reason for it. We buy our pills and stay out of the
palace section. What we do to each other, nobody
cares."

"Have you never thought of—" Flandry groped
in his Pulaoic vocabulary, but couldn't find any
word for revolution. "You commoners and pau-
pers outnumber the ruling class. You have
weapons, here and there. You could take over,
you know."

Kemul blinked. Finally he spat. "Ah, what use

has Kemul for fancy eats and a fancy harem?
Kemul does well enough."

Luang caught Flandry's real meaning. He saw
that she was a little shocked; not that she found
any sacredness in the existing order of things, but
the idea of complete social change was too radical. She lit another cigaret from the butt of the first
and fumed a while with eyes closed, forehead
bent on her knees. When she glanced up again,
she said:

"I remember now, outworld man. Things I have
read in books. Even a few very old ones, that
Biocontrol must think were all burned long ago.
Unlike most, I know how the masters first came to
power. And we can't overthrow them. At least,
not without dying." She stretched like a cat. "And
life amuses me." ·

"I realize Biocontrol has the sole knowledge of
how to manufacture the antitoxin," Flandry said.
"But once you stood over their technicians with a
gun—"

"Listen to me," said Luang. "When Unan Besar
was first colonized, Biocontrol was merely one
arm of the government. Troubles came that I don't
quite know about: foolishness and corruption.
Biocontrol was staffed by men who were very
clever and . . . what word? . . . saintly? They
wanted the best for this planet, so they issued a
proclamation calling for a certain program of re-
form. The rest of the government didn't like this.
But Biocontrol was standing by the great vats
where the antitoxin is made. The process must be
watched all the time, you understand, or it goes
bad. One man, pulling the wrong switch, can ruin

an entire batch. Biocontrol could not be attacked without danger of wrecking those vats. The people were afraid they would get no more medicine. They forced the government men to lift the seige of Biocontrol, and yield.

"Then Biocontrol was the whole government. They said they would not rule forever, only long enough to establish the best social order for Unan Besar. One that was carefully planned and would endure."

"I see." Flandry spoke with a coyote grin. "They were scientists, and wanted a rationalized civilization. Probably they subscribed to some version of Psychotechnocracy. It was a popular theory in those days. When will the intellectuals learn that scientific government is a contradiction in terms? Since people didn't fit into this perfect scheme—and the scheme being perfect by definition, this must be the fault of the people— Biocontrol never did find an occasion to give up its power. After a few generations, it evolved into an old-fashioned oligarchy. Such governments always do."

"Not quite." He wasn't sure how closely the girl had followed him. Perforce he used many Anglic words; hoping Pulaoic had cognates. But her gaze was steady on him and she spoke with almost a scholar's detachment. "Biocontrol was forever Biocontrol. I mean, they have always recruited promising boys and trained them to tend the vats. Only after a long period of service, rising from grade to grade, can a member hope to get on the governing board."

"So . . . it *is* still a rule by technicians," he said. "Odd. The scientific mentality isn't well suited to governing. I'd expect Biocontrol would hire administrators, who would eventually make all the real decisions."

"That did happen once, about two hundred years ago," she said. "But a dispute arose. The corps of hireling experts started giving orders independently. Several Biocontrol people realized that Biocontrol had become a mere figurehead. One of them, Weda Tawar—there are statues to him all over the planet—waited until his turn to go on watch. Then he threatened to destroy the vats, unless the hireling corps surrendered itself to him. His fellow conspirators had already seized the few spaceships and were prepared to blow them up. Every human on Unan Besar would have died. The hirelings capitulated.

"Since then, Biocontrol has done its own governing. And during his novitiate, every member is trained and sworn to destroy the vats—and, thus, all the people—if the power of his fellowship is threatened."

That explains the general sloppiness, Flandry thought. *There's no bureaucracy to control things like slums and crime rates. By the same token, Biocontrol itself no longer exists for any reason except to man the brewery and perpetuate its own meaningless power.*

"Do you think they actually would carry out their threat, if it came to that?" he asked.

"Many of them, at least," said Luang. "They are very harshly trained as boys." She shivered. "It's not a risk to take, outworld man."

Kemul stirred on the floor. "Enough of this buttertonguing!" he grumbled. "We've still not learned what you really came here for."

"Or why the Guards want you," said Luang.

It grew most quiet. Flandry could hear the lapping of oily water against the piles below him. He thought he could hear thunder, far out over the jungle. Then someone cursed down in the tavern, there was a scuffle, a joy girl screamed and a body splashed in the canal. Only a minor argument: the loser could be heard swimming away, and the music resumed.

"They want me," said Flandry, "because I can destroy them."

Kemul, who had ignored the fight under his broad bottom, half rose. "Don't joke Kemul!" he gasped. Even Luang's cool eyes widened, and she lowered her feet to the floor.

"How would you like to be free men?" Flandry asked. His gaze returned to Luang. "And women," he added. "Obviously."

"Free of what?" snorted Kemul.

"*Most* obviously . . . Oh. Yes. How would you like to be done with Biocontrol? To get your antitoxin free, or for a very low price that anyone can afford? It's possible, you know. You're being outrageously overcharged for the stuff, as a form of taxation which, I'm sure, has been screwed higher each decade."

"It has," said Luang. "But Biocontrol possesses the vats, and the only knowledge of their use."

"When Unan Besar was colonized," Flandry said, "this whole sector was backward and anarchic. The pioneers seem to have developed some elaborate process, probably biosynthetic, for preparing the antitoxin. A process which even in that day would have been clumsy, old-fashioned. Any decent laboratory—on Spica VI, for instance—can now duplicate any organic molecule. The apparatus is simple and foolproof, the quantity that can be manufactured is unlimited."

Luang's lips parted to show small white teeth. "You want to go there," she whispered.

"Yes. At least, that's what Brothers Bandang and Warouw are afraid I want to. Not a bad idea, either, Mitsuko Laboratories on Spica VI would pay me a handsome commission for calling as juicy a market as Unan Besar to their attention. Hm, yes-s-s," said Flandry dreamily.

Kemul shook his head till the gray hair swirled. "No! Kemul doesn't have it badly, the way things are. Not badly enough to risk the cage for helping you. Kemul says turn him in, Luang."

The girl studied Flandry for a long minute. Her face was not readable. "How would you get off this planet?" she asked.

"Details." Flandry waved a hand in an airy gesture.

"I thought so. If you don't know, how can we? Why should we hazard anything, least of all our lives?"

"Well—" Flandry flexed his arms, trying to work out some of the tension that stiffened them and made his voice come out not quite natural. "Well, we can discuss that later."

She blew smoke. "For you," she said, "will there be a later?"

He donned the smile which had bowled over female hearts from Scotha to Antares. "If you wish it, my lady."

She shrugged. "I might. If you make it worth the risk and trouble. But Kemul already took everything you were carrying. What can you buy your next thirty days with?"

That was a good question.

VI

The part of Swamp Town between Lotus Flower Canal, the great spice warehouse of Barati & Sons, the Canal of the Drowned Drunkard, and those miserable tenement rafts where Kompong Timur faded into unreclaimed watery wastes was ruled by Sumu the Fat. Which is to say, every resident with a noticeable income—artisan, rentier, joy girl, bazaar keeper, freight hauler, priest, wizard, coiner, et multifarious cetera—paid regular tribute to him. It was shrewdly calculated according to ability to pay, so no one resented it dangerously. Sumu even made some return. His bully boys kept rival gangs out of the district; sometimes they caught lone-wolf robbers and made examples of them. He was an excellent fence for goods stolen from other parts of town. With his connections, he could even help a legitimate merchant make an extra profit, or find a buyer for the daughter of some impoverished man who didn't know where his next pill was coming from. In such cases, Sumu didn't charge an exorbitant commission. He offered rough-and-ready justice to those who wanted to lay their quarrels before him. Every year at the Feast of Lanterns, he bore the whole expense of decorating the quarter and went about giving candy to small children.

In short, he was hated no more than any other overlord would have been.

Wherefore Sumu's man Pradjung, making his regular rounds to collect the tribute, was distressed to hear that a new storyteller had been operating on Indramadju Square for two whole days without so much as a by-your-leave.

Pradjung, who was of ordinary size but notoriously good with a knife, went thither. It was a clear day. The sun stood high and white in a pale sky. Sheet metal walls, canal water, even thatch and wood cast back its radiance until all things swam in that fierce light, wavered with heat haze but threw hard blue shadows. Far off above the roofs, Biocontrol Pagoda reared as if molten, too dazzling to look at. Sound of squalling voices and rumbling motors seemed baked out of the air; women squatted in doorways nursing their babies and gasping. As he hurried past the booths of listless potters, Pradjung heard his own sandals go *slap-slap* on planks where tar bubbled.

He crossed a suspension bridge to the hummock where Indramadju Square had been constructed, so long ago that the stone dragons on the central fountain were weathered into pug dogs. The fountain was dry, its plumbing had been stolen generations back, but fruit and vegetable vendors from the outlying paddy-farms still brought their produce here to sell. Their booths surrounded the square with thatch and tiny red flags. Because it was cooler here than many other places, and the chance of stealing an occasional *modjo* not too bad, children and idlers could always be found by the score. Which made it a good location for storytellers.

The new one sat under the basin. He had the usual fan in one hand and the usual bowl set out for contributions. But nothing else about him was normal. Pradjung must push through a crowd six deep before he could even see the man.

Then he gaped. He had never known anyone like this. The fellow was tall, reasonably young, and very well-muscled. But his skin was pale, his face long, his nose a jutting beak, his eyes deepset and of altogether wrong shape. He had hair on his upper lip, which was uncommon but not unknown; however, this mustache was brown, like the close-cropped hair peeping from beneath his turban. He spoke with a strong, unidentifiable accent, and had none of the traditional storyteller mannerisms. Yet he was outrageously at ease.

Which well he might be, for he spoke not of the Silver Bird or Polesotechnarch Van Rijn or any ancient themes known everywhere by heart. He told new stories, most of them indecent and all impudently funny. The crowd shrieked laughter.

"—Now after this long and mighty career, warring in the air for his country, Pierre the Fortunate was granted leave to come home and rest. No honor, no reward was considered too great for this prince among pilots." The storyteller glanced modestly downward. "But I am a poor man, O gentle and generous people. Weariness overwhelms me."

Money tinkled into his bowl. After pouring it into a bulging purse, the storyteller leaned back, lit a cigaret, swigged from a wineskin, and resumed: "The home of Pierre the Fortunate was called Paris and was the richest, most beautiful of cities. There, and there alone, had men altogether mastered the arts of pleasure: not mere wallowing in quantity, but the most subtle refinements, the most elegant and delicious accompaniments. For example, the tale is told of a stranger from an uncouth land called Texas, who was visiting in Paris—"

"Hold!"

Pradjung muscled past the inner circle and confronted the newcomer. He heard a growl behind him, and touched his knife. The noise subsided to angry mutters. A few people on the fringes began to drift away, elaborately inconspicuous.

"What is your name, stranger, and where are you from?" snapped Pradjung.

The storyteller looked up. His eyes were an eerie gray color.

"That's no way to begin a friendship," he reproved.

Pradjung flushed. "Do you know where you are? This is Sumu's territory, may his progeny people the universe. Who told an outland wretch like you to set up shop?"

"None told me not to."

The answer was soft enough for Pradjung to concede—after all, the storyteller was earning at a rate which promised a good rakeoff—"New arrivals of good will are never unwelcome. But my master Sumu must decide. He will surely fine you for not coming to him at once. But if you are courteous to him and—ahem!—his faithful men, I do not think he will have you beaten."

"Dear me, I hope not." The storyteller rose to his feet. "Come, then, take me to your leader."

"You could show his men the politeness they deserve, and gain friends," Pradjung said, glancing at the full purse.

"Of course." The storyteller raised his wineskin. "Your very good health, sir." He took a long drink and hung the skin on his back.

"What of our story?" cried some rustic, too indignant to remember Pradjung's knife.

"I fear I am interrupted," said the stranger.

The crowd made a sullen way. Pradjung was

feeling surly enough himself, now, but held his peace. Wait till they came to Sumu.

The great man dwelt in a wooden house unpretentious on the outside, except for its dimensions and the scarfaced guards at every door. But the interior was so full of furniture, drapes, rugs, incense burners, caged songbirds, aquaria, and assorted crockery that you could easily get lost. The harem wing was said to possess a hundred inmates, though not always the same hundred. What most impressed a visitor was the air conditioning system, bought at fabulous expense in the palace section of town.

Sumu lolled in a silkite campaign chair, riffling through some papers with one hand and scratching his belly with the other. A pot of sweet black herb tea and a bowl of cookies stood in easy reach. Two daggermen squatted behind him, and he personally packed a gun. It was an archaic snubnosed chemical weapon throwing lead slugs, but it would kill you as dead as any blaster.

"Well?" Sumu raised his bulldog face and blinked nearsightedly.

Pradjung shoved the storyteller forward with a rough hand. "This outland *sarwin* has been narrating on Indramadju for two days, tuan. See how plump his purse has grown! But when I asked him to come pay his respects to my noblest of masters, he refused with vile oaths until I compelled him at dagger point."

Sumu peered at the stranger and inquired mildly, "What is your name, and where are you from?"

"Dominic is my name." The tall man shifted in Pradjung's grip, as if uneasy.

"A harsh sound. But I asked where you were from."

"Pegunungan Gradjugang—ouch!—It lies beyond the Tindjil Ocean."

"Ah. So." Sumu nodded wisely. One knew little about the dwellers on other continents. Their overlords sometimes came here, but only by air and only to visit the overlords of Kompong Timur. Poor folk rarely traveled far. One heard that strange ways of life had grown up under alien conditions. Doubtless generations of poor diet and insufficient sunlight had bleached this man's people. "Why did you not seek me out as soon as you arrived? Anyone could have told you where I live."

"I did not know the rule," said Dominic pettishly. "I thought I was free to earn a few honest coins."

"More than a few, I see," Sumu corrected. "And is it honest to deny me my right? Well, ignorance may pass for an excuse this time. Let us count what you have gotten thus far today. Then we can decide on a proper weekly sum for you to contribute, as well as the fine for not reporting immediately."

Pradjung grinned and snatched after Dominic's purse. The tall man stepped back and cast it himself into Sumu's lap. "Here, tuan," he exclaimed. "Don't trust this ugly man. He has reptile eyes. Count the coins yourself. But this is not one day's take. It's two days, yes, and a good part of one night. Ask in the square. They'll tell you how long I worked."

"Will they tell how much else you have hidden about you, begetter of worms?" sneered Pradjung.

"Off with your garments! A fortune could lie in that turban."

Dominic backed further. Pradjung signaled to the daggermen, who closed in on the storyteller and seized his arms. As he went to his knees, lest bones break, Pradjung kicked him in the stomach. "Strip," said Pradjung. Sumu continued sorting coins into his sarong.

Dominic groaned. There proved to be nothing in his kilt except himself, but wound into the turban was a package. Pradjung unfolded it before Sumu's eyes. An awed silence fell on the room.

The wrapping was a blouse: some fabric hitherto unheard of, colored like the palest dawn, fine enough to fold into cubic centimeters but utterly wrinkleproof. Inside the package lay a multiple-dialed watch of incredibly beautiful workmanship, and a wallet not made from leather or any recognized plastic. The wallet held cards and money, whose papery substance was equally strange, whose engraving was lovely but whose legends were in a peculiar form of the alphabet and an altogether foreign language.

VII

Sumu made a sign against evil. "Nine sticks of incense to the gods at Ratu Temple!" He swung on Dominic, who had been released and knelt shuddering. "Well?"

"Tuan!" Dominic flopped on his face. "Tuan, take all my cash!" he wailed. "I am a poor man and the humblest of your slaves. Give me back those valueless trinkets bequeathed me by my poor old mother!"

"Valueless, I think not." Sumu mopped the

sweat of excitement from his forehead. "We shall have a little truth out of you, storyteller."

"Before the Three Headed One himself, you have the truth!"

"Come now," said Sumu in his kindliest tone. "I am not cruel. I should not like to have you questioned. Especially since I would have to entrust the questioning to Pradjung, who seems to have taken a dislike to you."

Pradjung licked his lips. "I know these stubborn cases, mighty master," he said. "It may take me a while. But he will still be able to talk when he decides to. Come along, you!"

"Wait, wait, wait," said Sumu. "Not that quickly. Give him a few swats of the cane across his feet and see if his tongue loosens. Every man deserves a chance to be heard, Pradjung."

Dominic beat his brow against the floor. "It is a family secret, nothing but a family secret," he begged. "Your nobleness could not profit by hearing it."

"If that is so, rest assured I shall keep your secret inviolate," promised Sumu magnanimously. "Anyone here who cannot keep a secret goes straight into the canal."

Pradjung, who saw an opportunity slipping past, seized the bastinado and applied it. Dominic cried out. Sumu told Pradjung to stop, and offered Dominic wine.

Eventually the story came out.

"My brother George found the ship," Dominic said between gulps for air and gulps of drink. His hands trembled. "He was a timber cruiser, and often went far into the mountains. In one deep, misty ravine, he found a spaceship."

"A ship from the stars?" Sumu made violent

signs and promised another dozen joss sticks. He had heard of the Betelgeuseans, of course, in a vague way, and even seen a few of their goods. But nonetheless he bore a childhood of myth about the Ancestors, the Stars, and the Monsters, which a sketchy education had not removed.

"Just so, tuan. I do not know if the vessel came from the Red Star, whence they say Biocontrol receives visitors on certain nights, or from some other. It might even have been from Mother Terra, for this shirt fits me. It must have crashed out of control long ago, long ago. Jungle had covered it, but could not destroy the metal. Wild animals laired within. Doubtless they had eaten the bones of the crew, but they could not open the hatches to the holds. Those were not locked, however, only dogged shut. So my brother George went down and saw wonders beyond reckoning—"

It took half an hour to elaborate on the wonders.

"Of course, he could not carry such things on his back," said Dominic. "He took only these articles, for proof, and returned home. It was his thought that he and I should raise enough money somehow for vehicles to get the cargo out. How, I knew not, for we were poor. But surely we would never tell our overlord, who would take all the treasure for himself! Long we discussed the matter in secret. George never told me where the ship lay." Dominic sighed. "He knew me well. I am not a resolute man. The secret was safest with him."

"Well?" Sumu dithered in his chair. "Well? What happened?"

"Ah, what happens all too often to poor folk. I was a tenant farmer of Proprietor Kepuluk. George, as I told you, was a timber cruiser for the master's lumbering operations. Because of our scheming to get money, we neglected our work. Frequently our overseers reproved us with a touch of the electrostick. But the dream we had would not let us rest in peace. George was at last dismissed. He brought his family to live with me. But my plot of ground was so small it would barely support my own wife and children. We went swiftly into debt to Proprietor Kepuluk. George had a young and beautiful wife, whom Kepuluk seized for the debt. Then George went amok and fell upon Kepuluk. It took six men to drag him away."

"So Djordju is dead?" cried an appalled Sumu.

"No. He was sentenced to enslavement. Now he toils as a field hand on one of Kepuluk's plantations. Of course, my farm was taken from me, and I must make my way as best I could. I found places for the women and children, then set out alone."

"Why?" demanded Sumu.

"What was there for me in Pegunungan Gradjugang, except a lifetime's toil for barely enough wages to buy my pills? I had always had a talent for storytelling, so I yarned my way to the ocean. There I got a scullery job on a watership bound for this continent. From Tandjung Port I came afoot to Kompong Timur. Here, I thought, I could make a living—even save a little money—and inquire with great discretion, until at last—"

"Yes? Yes? Speak up!"

Pradjung reached for the cane again, but Sumu waved him back. Dominic sighed heartbreakingly. "My tale is ended, tuan."

"But your plan! What is it?"

"Ah, the gods hate me. It seemed easy enough,

once. I would find a patron, a kind man who would not begrudge me a good payment and a position in his household, in exchange for what I could tell him. He must be rich, of course. Rich enough to buy George from Kepuluk and outfit an expedition under George's guidance. Oh, my lord—" Dominic lifted streaming eyes—"do you perchance know of some wealthy man who would listen to my tale? If you could arrange it for me, I would reward you with half of what I was paid myself."

"Be still," commanded Sumu.

He lay back in his chair, thinking furiously. In the end: "Perhaps your luck has turned, Dominic. I have some small savings of my own, and am always ready to venture what I can afford in the hope of an honest profit."

"Oh, my lord!"

"You need not kiss my feet yet. I have made no promises. But let us take our ease and share a midday meal. Afterward we can talk further."

The talk stretched on. Sumu had learned caution. But Dominic had answers for all questions; "I have had two years now, largest of masters, to think this out."

An expedition into the mountains would be costly. It should not be outfitted here in Kompong Timur. That would not only add the expense of transporting equipment across the ocean, but would attract far too much notice. (Sumu agreed. Some palace-dwelling *sarwin* like Nias Warouw would hear about it, investigate, and claim a major share of the loot.) Nor was it a good idea to use the primitive banking facilities of Unan Besar: too traceable. No, the cash itself must be smug-

gled out of town, across the lake and down the
Ukong River to Tandjung, where Sumu's trusty
men would take it across the ocean in their baggage. Once arrived in Pegunungan Gradjugang,
they would pose as entrepreneurs hoping to establish a hardwood trade with the Selatan Islands,
a market which the local bigwigs had neglected.
They would buy a few experienced slaves as assis-
tants, who would just happen to include Djordju.
Then in secret, Djordju would guide Sumu's rep-
resentatives to the ship.

The new hardwood company would buy some
thousands of hectares from the immense Kepuluk
holdings, and also acquire the flyers, junglecats,
and similar machinery needed to exploit a forest.
That would be expensive, but it couldn't be
helped; any other way, Kepuluk would smell a
rat. But thereafter, under cover of their logging
operations, the expedition could plunder the ship
at leisure. Doubtless its cargo should be sold very
gradually, over a period of years, so as to avoid
undue attention and to keep up the price of such
exotic stuffs.

"I see." Sumu wiped curry from his chins,
belched, and called for a girl to pick his teeth.
"Yes. Good."

"George is a very resolute man," said Dominic.
"His hope was always to lift our family out of
tenantdom. He would die before telling anyone
where the ship lies, unless I persuade him first."
Slyly: "If Proprietor Kepuluk does not remember
his face, I alone could identify my dear brother
among all the plantation slaves."

"Yes, yes, yes," snapped Sumu. "I am a fair
man. Ask anyone if I am not fair. You and Djordju

shall have proper shares in the loot. Enough to go into business, under my protection. But now, about the cost—''

That night Dominic stayed in the house of Sumu. He was, in fact, a guest for several days. His chamber was pleasant, though it lacked windows, and he had enough company, for it opened directly on a barrackroom where the bachelor daggermen lived. No one got past that room without a key to the automatic lock, which Dominic didn't ask for. He messed with the daggermen, traded jokes, told them stories, and gambled. Cards on Unan Besar had changed faces, but were still essentially the same old pack of fifty-two. Dominic taught the boys a game called poker. They seized on it avidly, even though he won large amounts from them. Not that he cheated— that would have been fatal, under so many experienced eyes. He simply understood the game better. The daggermen accepted the fact, and were willing to pay for instruction. It would take many years to get back from neophytes elsewhere all that Dominic eventually won, but the Pulaoic mentality was patient.

Sumu shared that patience. He did not rush into Dominic's project, but made inquiries. A thornfruit dealer was located who had bought occasional shipments originating on Proprietor Kepuluk's holdings in Pegunungan Gradjugang. Hm, yes, they were mountaineers and forest dwellers there mostly, weren't they? The climate made them pale-skinned, if that hadn't simply been genetic drift. Sumu had no idea what genetic drift might be: the term impressed him enough that he didn't stop to ask exactly how light a complexion was meant. He was shrewd, but no intellecutal heavyweight. He was convinced.

The investment was considerable, a hundred thousand silvers to start with. Two men were needed to lift the chest holding it. Those were Pradjung and a butcher boy named Mandau, both tough and strong and utterly reliable—especially since Pradjung still spat at Dominic's name. They would accompany the chest and the storyteller to Tandjung, where several others traveling by more open routes would meet them on the ship *Sekaju*.

About this time, when Dominic was again interviewed, he voiced a mild complaint at his detention and said he was due for his pill. Also, was it fitting that a loyal (however humble) servant of the famous Sumu went about in these dirty old clothes? Sumu shrugged and allowed Dominic to go, accompanied by a daggerman just in case. Dominic was in a happy mood. He spent a long time shopping for garments, while the daggerman yawned and sweated. Dominic made up for it by buying them both large quantities of wine. Afterward the luckless daggerman admitted he'd been too tired and drunk when Dominic went off to get his pill. He stayed in the tavern and never actually saw the storyteller go to the district dispensary. But Dominic soon came back to him and the fun resumed.

The next night had been set for departure. Dominic whiled the hours away with a new game. As the bravos came into the bunkroom for their naps, one by one during the course of the day, Dominic bet them he could make five pat five-card poker hands out of any twenty-five cards. He let his incredulous friends provide the pack, shuffle, and deal. Once or twice he lost, but the net sum he tucked away in several already fat purses was rather fantastic. Next day a bully who had once studied some arithmetic figured out that the odds in Dominic's favor had been about fifty to one. By then Dominic was gone.

He left the house after sunset. Rain sluiced from a hidden sky, roaring on the canal surface and drowning distant lamps. A speedboat waited with Pradjung, Mandau, and the chest of silvers. Dominic kissed Sumu's unclipped toenails and embarked. The boat slipped into darkness.

Several days previously, Dominic had proposed a route of his own as the least dangerous way out of town. Sumu had grinned and told him to stick to his storytelling. Dominic became so insistent that Sumu was forced to explain in detail precisely why a route down Burning Torch Canal and so out into the lake would attract less notice.

Now, when the boat planed close to the Bridge Where Amahai Wept, Dominic said a polite, "Excuse me." He reached across the cockpit and switched off motor and headlights.

"What in all hells—!" Pradjung leaped to his feet. Dominic slid back the canopy. Rain cataracted hot and heavy upon them. The boat glided toward a halt.

Pradjung snatched for the revolver Sumu had lent him. Dominic, timid spinner of yarns, failed to cower as expected. The chopping motion of his hand was instantaneous. A hard edge smacked on Pradjung's wrist. The gun clattered free.

The boat went slowly under the Bridge Where Amahai Wept. Someone leaped from the span. The deck thundered beneath that gorilla impact.

Mandau snarled and tried to grapple. Kemul the mugger brushed his arms aside, put Mandau across one knee, broke his back, and threw him overboard.

Pradjung had drawn a knife. He stabbed underhanded at Dominic's belly. But Dominic wasn't there any more. He was a few centimeters to one side. His left wrist struck out, deflecting the blade. His right hand took Pradjung's free arm and spun the daggerman around. They fell together, but Dominic had the choking hold. After a few seconds, Pradjung turned blue and lay quietly.

Dominic got off. Kemul picked up the bravo. "No, wait," protested Dominic, "he's still alive—" Kemul threw Pradjung into the canal. "Oh, well," said Dominic and gunned the engine.

Headlights strengthened from behind, through the rain. "Kemul thinks Sumu had you followed," said the mugger. "It would make sense. Now they want to catch up with us and find why your lights went out. Shall we fight?"

"Can you lift a chest with a hundred thousand silvers?" asked Captain Sir Dominic Flandry.

Kemul whistled. Then: "Yes, Kemul can carry it a ways."

"Good. We needn't fight."

Flandry steered close to the left pier. As they went by a ladder, Kemul stepped off with the chest under one arm. Flandry revved the motor and went over the side. Treading water in the dark, he watched the second boat pursue his own out of sight.

Half an hour later, he stood in Luang's quarters above the Tavern Called Swampman's Ease and gestured at the open chest. "A hundred thousand," he said grandly. "Plus a good bit extra I made gambling. And a firearm, which I understand is hard for commoners to come by." It was thrust firmly into his own belt.

The girl lit a cigaret. "Well," she said, "the usual black market price for a pill is two thousand." She put a vial on the table. "Here are ten capsules. You have credit with me for forty more."

The lamp in the hooded god's hands threw soft coppery light across her. She wore a little paint on the amber skin, which was not her custom, luminous blue outlining eyes and breasts. There was a red blossom in her hair. For all its coolness, he thought her voice was not entirely level.

"When the boy brought us your note," said Kemul, "it seemed foolishness to wait in ambush where you desired. Even though we were surprised to hear from you at all. When you first left us to win your fortune, Kemul thought you a dead man already."

"You have more than common luck, I think." Luang frowned at her cigaret, avoiding Flandry's look. "In the past two or three days, there have been public announcements in the name of Nias Warouw. A reward is offered for you dead and a bigger one for you alive. The loudspeaker boats have not yet gotten as far as Sumu's district. It's plain to see, nobody who heard the criers had chanced to spy you, or knew you were with him. But he must soon have realized."

"I made the swindle move as fast as possible," Flandry said. The air was so hot and damp that he hoped they wouldn't notice the sweat on him was suddenly rather cold. "I'm an experienced con man. It's half my profession, one way or another. To be sure, I was a bit nervous about pulling a Spanish Prisoner here. You must have some home-grown version. But with refinements—" He broke off. They didn't follow his words, full of Anglic phrases as was necessary. "What do I owe you for my shirt and watch and wallet? It was good of you to give them back to me for a stake."

"Nothing," said Kemul. "They were useless to us, as Luang explained."

The girl bit her lip. "I hated for you to go out like that—all alone—" She put the cigaret to her mouth and inhaled so hard that her cheeks filled with shadow. Abruptly and roughly: "You are very clever, Terra man. I never had allies, except Kemul. They always betray you. But I think you could be a profitable associate."

"Thanks," said Flandry.

"One question yet. I forgot to ask you before. You knew Biocontrol makes all the antitoxin. What gave you the idea you could get any from us?"

Flandry yawned. He felt tired after all the strain and watchfulness. It was good to lounge back on the bed and look up at Luang, where she paced back and forth. "I felt confident someone would have some extras for sale," he answered. "Human cussedness is bound to find ways, when anything as valuable as this drug is to be had. For instance, armed raids on dispensaries, by masked men. Or the hijacking of shipments. Not often, I suppose, but it must happen occasionally. Or . . . well, there must be hunters, sailors, prospectors, and so on . . . men who have legitimate reasons for not coming near a dispensary every thirty days, and are allowed an advance supply of antitoxin. Once in a while they will be murdered, or robbed, or will die naturally and be stripped. Or simple corruption: a local dispenser juggles his records and peddles a few extra pills. Or he is bribed or blackmailed into doing it."

Luang nodded. "Yes," she said, "you are wise in such matters." With a sudden, odd defiance: "I get some capsules myself, now and then, from a certain dispenser. He is a young man."

Flandry chuckled. "I'm sure he gets more than value in return."

She stubbed out her cigaret with a savage gesture. Kemul rose, stretching. "Time for Kemul's nap," he said. "Around sunrise we can talk of what's to be done. The Captain is wily, Luang, but Kemul thinks best he be gotten out of Kompong Timur and used elsewhere for a time. Till Warouw and Sumu forget him."

Her nod was curt. "Yes. We will talk about it tomorrow."

"Good rest, Luang," said Kemul. "Are you coming, Captain? Kemul has an extra bed."

"Good rest, Kemul," said Luang.

The giant stared at her.

"Good rest," she repeated.

Kemul turned to the door. Flandry couldn't see his face; not that Flandry particularly cared to, just then. "Good rest," said Kemul, barely audible, and went out.

Someone laughed like a raucous bird, down in the joyhouse. But the rain was louder, filling all the night with a dark rushing. Luang did not smile at Flandry. Her mouth held a bitterness he did not

quite understand, and she switched off the light
as if it were an enemy.

VIII

Two thousand kilometers north of Kompong
Timur, a mountain range heaved itself skyward. It
was dominated by Gunung Utara, which was also
a city.

The morning after he arrived, Flandry stepped
out on the ledge fronting his hostel. Behind him, a
tunnel ran into black basalt, looping and twisting
and branching, for it was an ancient fumarole.
Rooms had been excavated along that corridor;
airblowers and fluorescent tubes had been installed; plastisurfacing and tapestries softened
bare rock. Most of the city was built into such
natural burrows, supplemented with artificial
caves—up and down the slopes of Gunung Utara.

Flandry could just see the cliff behind him, and
about ten meters downward where the ledge tumbled below his feet. Otherwise his world was
thick white mist. It distorted sounds; he heard
machines and voices as if from far away and from
impossible directions. The air was thin and cool,
his breath smoked. He shivered and drew tighter
about him the hooded cloak which local people
added to kilt, stockings, and shirt. After all, they
lived a good 2,500 meters above sea level.

There was a rumbling underfoot, deeper than
any engine, and the ground quivered a little.
Gunung Utara dreamed.

Flandry lit an atrocious native cigaret. Luang
had promptly sold all his Terran supply. Presently he would go look for some breakfast. Food

in the lowlands had been heavy on rice and fish, but Luang said meat was cheaper in the mountains. Bacon and eggs? No, that would be too much to hope for. Flandry sighed.

It had been a pleasant trip here, though. Extremely pleasant, on admirably frequent occasions. The girl had not merely sent him off to hide, but come along herself, with Kemul at heel. They had been ferried across the lake at night by someone who would keep his mouth shut. At the depot on the far side, she engaged a private cabin on one of the motorized rafts which plied the Ukong River. He stayed inside that, and she spent most of her time with him, while the raft chugged them slowly northeast to Muarabeliti. (Kemul slept outside the door, and said little in waking hours, spending most of his time with a marijuana pipe.) There they could have gotten an airliner, but since that was only for the wealthy, it seemed safer to go by monorail. Not that they jammed themselves into a thirdclass car like ordinary peasants; they got a compartment, suitable conveyance for petty bourgeoisie. Across a continent of jungle, plantation, and drowned lowland, Flandry had once more paid less attention to the scenery than a dutiful tourist should. And now they were holed up in Gunung Utara until the heat went off, with Biocontrol certain that Flandry must be dead.

And then?

He heard the lightest clack of shoes on stone and turned around. Luang emerged from the tunnel. She had yielded to this climate with a flame-red tunic and purple tights, but the effect was still remarkable, even before breakfast. "You should have called me, Dominic," she said. "I rapped on

Kemul's door, but he is still snoring.'' She yawned, curving her back and raising small fists into the fog. "This is no town for long naps. Here men work hard and wealth flows quickly. It has grown much since I visited it last, and that was only a few years ago. Let me get well established, and I can hope to earn—''

"Oh, no, you don't!" Somewhat to his own astonishment, Flandry discovered that he retained a few absurd prejudices. "Not while we're partners.''

She laughed, deep in her throat, and took his arm. It was not a very gentle gesture, though. She was curt and fierce with him, and would never say much about herself. "As you wish. But what then shall we do?''

"Live quietly. We've more than enough funds.''

She let him go and snatched a cigaret out of a pocket. "Bah! Gunung Utara is rich, I tell you! Lead, silver, gems, I know not what else. Even a common miner may go prospecting and gain a fortune. It's soon taken from him. I want to do some of the taking.''

"It is quite safe for me to show myself?" he asked cautiously.

She looked at him. With his beard still inhibited, he needed only to shave his upper lip each day. Dye had blackened his hair, whose shortness he explained to the curious as due to a bout of jungle fungus, and contact lenses made his eyes brown. The harsh sunlight had already done the same for his skin. There remained his height and the unPulaoic cast of his face, but enough caucasoid genes floated around in the population that such features, though rare, were not freakish.

"Yes," she said, "if you remember that you are from across the ocean."

"Well, the chance must be taken, I suppose, if you insist on improving the shining hour with racketeering." Flandry sneezed. "But why did we have to come here, of all drizzly places?"

"I told you a dozen times, fool. This is a mining town. New men arrive each day from all over the planet. No one notices a stranger." Luang drew smoke into her lungs, as if to force out the mist. "I like not the god-hated climate myself, but it can't be helped."

"Oh, right-o." Flandry glanced up. A light spot showed in the east, where sun and wind were breaking the mists. A warm planet like Unan Besar could expect strong moist updrafts, which would condense into heavy clouds at some fairly constant altitude. Hereabouts, that was the altitude at which the mines happened to lie. The area was as foggy as a politician's brain.

It seemed reckless to build a town right into a volcano. But Luang said Gunung Utara was nearly extinct. Smoldering moltenness deep underneath it provided a good energy source, and thus another reason for this settlement; but the crater rarely did more than growl and fume. It was unusually active at the present time. There was even a lava flow. But the same engineers whose geophysical studies proved there would never again be a serious eruption, had built channels for such outpourings.

As the fog lightened, Flandry could see the ledge below this one, and the head of a crazily steep trail which wound down past tunnel mouths. He caught a sulfurous whiff.

"We should find it interesting for a while," he said. "But what do we do afterward?"

"Go back to Kompong Timur, I suppose. Or anywhere else in the world that you think there may be a profit. Between us we will always do well."

"That's just it." He dropped his cigaret butt and ground it under his sandal. "Here I am, the man who can free your whole people from Biocontrol—I don't believe in false modesty, or even in true modesty—"

"Biocontrol never troubled me very much." Her tone grew sharp. "Under a new arrangement . . . oh, yes, I can easily foresee what an upheaval your cheap antitoxin would bring . . . would I survive?"

"You could prosper in any situation, my dear." Flandry's grin died away. "Until you get old."

"I don't expect to reach old age," she snapped, "but if I do, I'll have money hoarded to live on."

The clouds rifted, and one sunbeam dashed itself blindingly along the mountainside. Far down the slope, among ledges and crags and boulders, a rolling road was being installed to carry ore from a minehead to a refinery. Antlike at this distance, men crawled about moving rock by hand. Flandry had no binoculars, but he knew very well how gaunt those men were, how often they lost footing and went over a cliff, how their overseers walked among them with electric prods. But still the sunbeam raced downward, splitting the fog like a burning lance, until it touched the valley under the mountain. Impossibly green that valley was, green fire streaked with mist and streams, against the bare red and black rock which surrounded it. Down there, Flandry knew, lay rice paddies, where the wives and children of the construction gang stooped in the mud as wives and children had since the Stone Age. *Yet once upon a time, for a few generations, it wasn't done this way.*

He said, "The hand labor of illiterates is so cheap, thanks to your precious social system, that you're sliding back from the machine era. In another several centuries, left to yourselves, you'll propel your rafts with sweeps and pull wagons with animals."

"You and I will be soundly asleep in our graves then, Dominic," said Luang. "Come, let's find a tea house and get some food."

"Given literacy," he persisted, "machines can work still cheaper. Faster, too. If Unan Besar was exposed to the outside universe, labor such as those poor devils are doing would be driven off the market in one lifetime."

She stamped her foot and flared: "I tell you, I don't care about them!"

"Please don't accuse me of altruism. I just want to get home. These aren't my people or my way of life . . . good God, I'd never find out who won this year's meteor ball pennant!" Flandry gave her a shrewd glance. "You know, you'd find a visit to some of the more advanced planets interesting. And profitable. D' you realize what a novelty you'd be to a hundred jaded Terran nobles, any of whom could buy all Unan Besar for a yo-yo?"

Her eyes lit up momentarily. Then she laughed and shook her head. "Oh, no, Dominic! I see your bait and I won't take your hook. Remember, there is no way off this planet."

"Come, now. My own spaceship is probably still at the port, plus several left over from pioneering days, plus the occasional Betelgeusean visitor. A raid on the place—or, more elegantly, the theft of a ship—"

"And how long until you returned with a cargo of capsules?"

Flandry didn't answer. They had been through this argument before. She continued, jetting smoke between phrases like a slender dragon: "You told me it would take several days to reach Spica. Then you must get the ear of someone important, who must come investigate and satisfy himself you are right, and go back, and report to his superiors, who will wrangle a long time before authorizing the project. And you admitted it will take time, perhaps many days, to discover exactly what the antitoxin is and how to duplicate it. Then it must be produced in quantity, and loaded aboard ships, and brought here, and—Oh, by every howling hell, you idiot, what do you think Biocontrol will do meanwhile? They will destroy the vats the moment they know you have escaped. There is no reserve supply worth mentioning. No one here could hope to live more than a hundred of our days, unless he barricaded himself in a dispensary. Your precious Spicans would find a planetful of bones!"

"You could escape with me," he said, chiefly to test her reaction.

It was as he had hoped: "I don't care what happens to all these stupid people, but I won't be a party to murdering them!"

"I understand all that," he said hastily. "We've been over this ground often enough. But can't you see, Luang, I was only talking in general terms. I didn't mean anything as crude as an open breakaway. I'm sure I can find a way to slip off without Biocontrol suspecting a thing. Smuggle myself aboard a Betelgeusean ship, for instance."

"I've known Guards, some of whom have been on spaceport duty. They told me how carefully the Red Star folk are watched."

"Are you sure Biocontrol will pull the switch?"

"Sure enough. They can take a final dose of medicine and flee in the other ships."

"If those were sabotaged, though—?"

"Oh, not every man of them would ruin the world for sheer spite. Perhaps not even most. Especially if it meant their own deaths. But they all stand watches at the vats . . . and Dominic, all it needs is one fanatic, and there is more than one. No!" Luang discarded her cigaret and took his arm again, digging sharp nails into his flesh. "If ever I find you scheming any such lunacy, I will tell Kemul to break your neck. Now I am starving, and this is also the day when I should get my pill."

Flandry sighed.

He let her go first down the ladder to the trail. They walked precariously, unused to such steepness, and entered the crowds at lower levels. An engineer, in gaily embroidered tunic and the arrogance of a well-paid position, had a way cleared for him by two brawny miners. A yellow-robed priest walked slowly, counting his beads and droning a charm; from a cave mouth several meters above the path, a wrinkled wizard in astrological cloak made faces at him. A vendor cried his wares of fruit and rice, carried up from the valley at the ends of a yoke. A mother screamed and snatched her child from the unfenced edge of a precipice. Another woman squatted in a tunnel entrance and cooked over a tiny brazier. A third stood outside a jabbering joy cave and propositioned a gaping yokel from some jungle village. A smith sang invocations as he thrust a knife blade into the tempering solenoid. A rug seller sat in a booth and called his bargains to every passerby. High overhead, a bird of prey soared among the last ragged mists. Sunlight struck its wings and made them gold.

From a vantage point Flandry could see how the city came to an end and the raw mountain slope stretched northward: cinders, pinnacles, and congealed lava flows. Across a few kilometers of wasteland he spied a concrete dyke, banking the magma channel. Smoke hazed it, as the liquid rock oozed downward and froze. Above all tiers of city and all naked scaurs lifted the volcanic cone. The wind was blowing its vapors away, which was one thing to thank the lean cold wind for.

"Oh. This is the dispensary. I may as well get my medicine now."

Flandry stopped under the Biocontrol insigne. Actually, he knew, Luang had a couple of days' grace yet, but the law permitted that much overlap. He also knew she had illicit pills and didn't really need to buy her ration—but only a dead man could fail to do so without drawing the instant notice of the authorities. He accompanied her through the rock-hewn entrance.

The office beyond was small, luxuriously furnished in the low-legged cushions-and-matting style of Unan Besar. A door led to the living quarters which went along with this job; another door

was built like a treasury vault's. Behind a desk sat
a middle-aged man. He wore a white robe with an
open hand pictured on the breast, and his pate
was shaven; but the golden brand was not on his
brow, for employees like him were not ordained
members of Biocontrol.

"Ah." He smiled at Luang. Most men did.
"*Good* day. I have not seen you before, gracious
lady."

"My friend and I are newly arrived." With her
to look at, Flandry didn't think the dispenser
would notice him much. She counted ten silvers,
the standard price, down on the table. The dispenser didn't check them for genuineness, as
anyone else would have. If you passed bad money
to Biocontrol, you'd be in trouble enough the next
time! He activated a small electronic machine.
Luang put her hands flat on a plate. The machine
blinked and hummed, scanning them.

Flandry could imagine the system for himself.
Her print pattern was flashed by radio to a central
electronic file in Kompong Timur. In seconds the
file identified her, confirmed that she was indeed
ready for her ration, established that she was not
wanted by the Guards, made the appropriate addi-
tion to her tape, and sent back its okay. As the
machine buzzed, Luang removed her hands from
it. The dispenser took her money and went to the
vault, which scanned his own fingers and opened
for him. He came back without the coins, the door
closed again, he gave Luang a blue capsule.

"One moment, my dear, one moment. Allow
me." He bustled over to fill a beaker with water.
"There, now it will go down easier. Eh-h-h?"
Flandry doubted if he was as attentive to the aver-

age citizen. At least, not judging from the way he used the opportunity to do a little pinching.

"Where are you staying in our city, gracious lady?" he beamed.

"For now, noble sir, at the Inn of the Nine Serpents." Luang was plainly unhappy at having to linger—but, equally plainly, you were never impolite to a dispenser. In law he had no rights over you. In practice, it was not unknown for a dispenser to block the signaler, so that GHQ never recorded a given visit, and then hand his personal enemy a capsule without contents.

"Ah, so. Not the best. Not the best. Not suitable at all for a damsel like yourself. I must think about recommending a better place for you. Perhaps we could talk it over sometime?"

Luang fluttered her lashes. "You honor me, sir. Alas, business compels me to hurry off. But . . . perhaps, indeed, later—?" She left while he was still catching his breath.

Once outdoors, she spat. "Ugh! I'll want some arrack in my tea, to get the taste out!"

"I should think you would be used to that sort of thing," said Flandry.

He meant it in all thoughtless innocence, but she hissed like an angry snake and jerked free of him. "What the blue deuce?" he exclaimed. She slipped into the crowd. In half a minute, he had lost sight of her.

IX

He checked his stride. Chattering brown people thronged by, forcing him off the trailstreet and onto a detritus slope. After some while, he realized he was staring past the stone wall which kept these rocks off terraces below, downward to an ore processing plant. Its stack drooled yellow smoke, as if ambitious to be a volcano too. Nothing about it merited Flandry's unbroken attention.

Well, he thought in a dull and remote fashion, *I still haven't had my breakfast.*

He began trudging over the scree, paralleling the trail but in no mood to go back and jostle his way along it. The downslope on the other side of the low wall became steeper as he went, until it was a cliff dropping fifty meters to the next level of dwellings. Stones scrunched underfoot. The mountain filled half his world with black massiveness, the other half was sky.

His first dismay—and, yes, he might as well admit it, his shock of pity for Luang and loneliness for himself—had receded enough for him to start calculating. Trouble was, he lacked data. If the girl had simply blown a gasket when he touched some unsuspected nerve, that was one thing. He might even use the reconciliation to advance his argument again, about escaping from Unan Besar. But if she had dropped him for good and all, he was in a bad situation. He couldn't guess if she had or not. A man thought he understood women, more or less, and then somebody like Luang showed up.

Of course, if the worst comes to the worst—but that's just what it's likely to do—

Hoy! What's this?

Flandry stopped. Another man had left the trail and was walking across the slope. A boy, rather: couldn't be more than sixteen, with so round a face and slender a body. He looked as if he hadn't eaten lately and had hocked everything but his kilt. Yet that was of shimmery velvety cloth, not cheap at all. Odd.

Something about his blind purposefulness jabbed understanding into Flandry. The Terran began to run. The boy sprang up on the wall. He stood there a moment, gazing into the wan sky of Unan Besar. Sunlight flooded across him. Then he jumped.

Flandry did a bellywhopper across the wall and caught an ankle. He almost went over too. "Oof!" he said, and lay draped with the boy squirming and swinging at the end of his arm. When his breath returned, he hauled his burden back over and dumped it on the ground. The boy gave one enormous shudder and passed out.

A crowd was gathering, quite agog. "All right," panted Flandry, "all right, the show's over. I thank you for your kind attention. Anyone who wishes to pass the hat is free to do so." A Guard shoved through. No mistaking that green kilt and medallion, the knife and club, or the built-in swagger.

"What's this?" he said, in the manner of policemen the universe over.

"Nothing," said Flandry. "The boy got a little reckless and nearly had an accident."

"So? Looked to me as if he jumped."

"Only a game. Boys," said Flandry with sparkling wit, "will be boys."

"If he's contracted or enslaved, suicide would be an evasion of obligations and attempted suicide would rate a flogging."

"No, he's free. I know him, Guardsman."

"Even a free man has no right to jump within city limits. He might have hit somebody underneath him. He'd have made a mess for someone to clean up, that's certain. Both of you come with me now, and we'll look into this."

Flandry's spine tingled. If he got himself arrested on so much as a malicious mopery charge, that was the end of the party. He smiled and reached inside his kilt pocket. "I swear it was only a near accident, Guardsman," he said. "And I'm a busy man." He extracted one of his purses. "I haven't time to argue this officially. Why don't you . . . ah . . . take ten silvers and go settle any claims there may be? It would be so much easier all around."

"What? Do you mean—"

"Quite right. The aggrieved parties ought to have at least two goldens between them. You know this city, Guardsman, and I'm a newcomer. You can find who deserves the payment. I beg you, do not burden my soul with debts I cannot settle." Flandry thrust the coins into his hand.

"Ah. Ah, yes." The Guard nodded. "Yes, it would be best that way, wouldn't it? Seeing that no actual damage was done."

"I am always pleased to meet a man of discretion." Flandry bowed. The Guard bowed. They parted with murmurs of mutual esteem. The crowd lost interest and continued on its various ways. Flandry knelt beside the boy, who was coming to, and cradled the dark head in his arms.

"Take it easy, son," he advised.

"Oa-he, tuan, why did you stop me?" A shaken whisper. "Now I must nerve myself all over again."

"Ridiculous project," snorted Flandry. "Here, can you get up? Lean on me."

The boy staggered to his feet. Flandry supported him. "When was your last meal?" he inquired.

"I don't remember." The boy knuckled his eyes, like a small child.

"Well, I was on my way to breakfast, which by now is more like luncheon. Come join me."

The thin body stiffened. "A man of Ranau takes no beggar's wage."

"I'm not offering charity, you gruntbrain. I want to feed you so you can talk rationally, which is the only way I can learn whether you're the person I want to hire for a certain job."

Flandry looked away from the sudden, bitterly resisted tears. "Come!" he snapped. His guess had been right, the youngster was out of work and starving. A stranger to this area: obviously so, from the intricate foreign pattern of his batik and from his dialect. Well, an outlander might prove of some use to a stranded Imperialist.

A tea house wasn't far off. At this sunny time of day, most of its customers sat on a ledge outside beneath giant red parasols, and looked down on a ravine full of clouds. Flandry and the boy took cushions at one table. "Tea with a jug of arrack to lace it," Flandry told the waiter. "And two of your best rijstaffels."

"*Two*, sir?"

"To begin with, anyhow." Flandry offered the boy a cigaret. It was refused. "What's your name, younker?"

"Djuanda, son of Tembesi, who is chief ecologist on the Tree Where the Ketjils Nest, which is in Ranau." The head bowed above folded hands. "You are kind to a stranger, tuan."

"I'm one myself." Flandry lit his own tobacco and reached for his tea cup as it arrived. "From, ah, Pegunungan Gradjugang, across the Tindjil Ocean. Name's Dominic. I came here in hopes of my fortune."

"Half the world does, I think." Djuanda slurped his tea in the approved Pulaoic manner. His voice had strengthened already, which underlined the anger in it. "So half the world are fools."

"Commoners have become rich men here, I am told."

"One in a million, perhaps . . . for a while . . . until he loses it to a cheat. But the rest? They rot their lungs in the mines, and their wives and children cough like amphibians in the rice pad-dies, and at the end they are so far in debt they must become slaves. Oh, tuan, the sun hates Gunung Utara!"

"What brought you, then?"

Djuanda sighed. "I thought the Trees of Ranau were not high enough."

"Eh?"

"I mean . . . it is a saying of my folk. A tree which grows too high will topple at last. Surulan-gun Ridge is the earth-buried bole of such a tree. It fell a thousand years ago, three hundred meters tall, and the forest still bears the scars of its falling, and the Ridge is still hot from its slow decay. The old people made a parable of it, and told us not to strive beyond reason. But I always thought—how splendid the great tree must have been while it lived!"

"So you ran away from home?"

Djuanda looked at the fists clenched in his lap.
"Yes. I had a little money, from my share of our
trade with outland merchants. It got me passage
here. Tuan, believe I never scorned my folk. I only
thought they were too stiff in their ways. Surely
modern engineering skills could be of value to us.
We might build better houses, for example. And
we ought to start industries which would bring
more cash money to Ranau, so we could buy more
of what the merchants offered—not merely toys
and baubles, but better tools. This I told my father,
but he would not hear of it, and at last I departed
without his blessing."

Djuanda glanced up again, anxious to justify
himself. "Oh, I was not altogether foolish, tuan. I
had written to the mine chiefs here, offering myself as an engineer apprentice. One of them had
written back, agreeing to give me a position. I
knew it would be humble, but I could learn in it.
So I thought."

"Have a drink," said Flandry, sloshing arrack
into his guest's cup. "What happened?"

Djuanda demurred. It took several minutes and
numerous sips of the now high-octane tea before
he broke down and admitted he'd been played for
a sucker. The job was as advertised—but he had to
buy equipment like respirators out of the company slop chest, at a staggering markup. Before
long he was in debt. Someone took him out on a
bender to forget his troubles, and steered him into
a clip joint. What with one thing and another,
Djuanda lost what he had, borrowed from a loan
shark to recoup, lost that too, and finally faced the
prospect of crawling back to the loan shark to
borrow ten silvers for his next pill.

"Couldn't you write home for help?" Flandry asked.

The immature face grew stiff with pride. "I had defied my father's will, tuan. In the hearing of all our Tree, I said I was now a man able to look after myself. Did I not at least make my own way home again, his dignity would suffer as much as mine. No. I found another eager young man, the gods be pitiful toward him, who wanted my position and could pay me somewhat for it. I sold all I owned. It was still not enough. I went to the dispenser and told him he could keep my last pill, recording it as issued to me, for fifty goldens. He would only give me five." (*Black market resale value, one hundred goldens,* Flandry remembered. *The poor rube from Ranau had had no concept of haggling.*) "So I could not buy passage home. But at least I now had enough to clear my name from debt. I flung the coins in the moneylender's face. Then for days I tried to find other work, any work, but it was only offered to me if I would become a slave. No man of Ranau has ever been a slave. I went forth at last to die honorably. But you came by, tuan. So I suppose the gods do not want me yet," finished Djuanda naively.

"I see." To cover his own need for a thinking space, as well as the boy's, Flandry raised his cup. "Confusion to moneylenders!"

"Damnation to Biocontrol," said Djuanda, with a slight hiccough.

"What?" Flandry set down his own cup and stared.

"Nothing!" Fear rose in the dark liquid eyes. "Nothing, tuan! I said not a word!"

This might bear further investigation, Flandry thought with excitement. *I was wondering what*

*the hell to do about this lad—couldn't have him
tagging along with his big wet ears a-flap in the
breeze—not when my scalp is still wanted—But
this makes him, perhaps, a lucky find. The first
I've heard who's said anything against Biocontrol
itself. He's too young to have thought of it on his
own. So . . . somewhere in his home town, at
least one older person—probably more—has
daydreamed about a revolution—*

The soup arrived. Djuanda forgot his terrors in
attacking it. Flandry poured more liquor and ate
at a calmer pace. While they waited for the main
course, he said conversationally, "I've never
heard of Ranau. Tell me about it. . . ."

A rijstaffel, properly made, is a noble dish re-
quiring a couple of hours to eat. Then there was
sherbet, with more tea and arrack. And a pair of
strolling dancers came up to earn a few coppers by
entertaining the wealthy man. And another jug of
arrack seemed indicated. And there was a never
ending string of toasts to drink.

The white sun climbed to the zenith and toppled. Shadows rose under the mountain. When
the sun went behind the crater, the sky was still
blue, but it duskened rapidly and the evening star
was kindled over eastern ridges. A low cold wind
piped along ashen slopes, whipping the first
streamers of cloud before it.

Flandry stood up, relieving cramped muscles
in a giant yawn. "We'll go back to my room," he
suggested. Djuanda, unhardened to drinking,
gave him a blurry look. Flandry laughed and
tossed the boy his cloak. "Here, better put this on.
You look as if you can stand an overnight nap.
We'll talk further after sunrise."

It seemed as good a way as any of putting

Djuanda on the shelf while he assessed his own situation with respect to Luang. (And to Kemul. Never forget those enormous strangler's hands.) Alcohol glowed along Flandry's veins, but his new confidence could also be justified logically. If Luang had indeed decided to hate him—or even if she remained too stubborn about an escape attempt—Djuanda offered a ready-made entree to Ranau. What hints he had gotten suggested to Flandry that Ranau could prove useful. Very useful, perhaps.

Below the retaining wall, where shadows had already engulfed the slopes, lamps were twinkling to life. But fog rose up, to blur and finally smother those tiny strewn stars. Flandry guided a somewhat wobbly Djuanda, who sang songs, up the sharp trail toward the Inn of the Nine Serpents. Having negotiated the last ladder and crossed the terrace, he went down the fumarole to his door. It had an ancient type of lock, he must grope for his key . . . no, wait, it wasn't locked after all, so his companions must be in there expecting his return. . . . With a split second's hesitation, Flandry opened the door and stepped through.

Two green-kilted men snatched at his arms. Across the chamber, Flandry saw a dozen more. Kemul and Luang sat with ankles lashed together. Flandry got one look at the girl's face turned toward his. "*Get out!*" he heard her scream. A Guard smacked his stick against her temple. She sagged into Kemul's lap. The mugger roared.

Nias Warouw leaned against the farther wall, smoking an outplanet cigaret and smiling.

Flandry had barely glimpsed the men closing in on either side. His reaction was too fast for thought. Spinning on his heel, he drove stiff-held fingers into the throat before him. It was one way to break your hand, unless you struck your enemy with a vector precisely normal to the skin. Flandry opened the throat and tore the windpipe across.

The other man was upon his back. Arms closed around the Terran's neck. Flandry's head was already down, chin protecting larynx. He dropped straight through the hug, hit the floor and rolled over.

The Guard backed into the doorway. His knife gleamed forth. The rest of Warouw's troop stalked closer, their own blades drawn.

Flandry bounced to his feet, reached in his shirt, and yanked out the pistol he had captured.

He didn't waste his breath crowing. Not when knives and clubs could be hurled from every side. He shot.

Four men went down in as many explosions. The others milled back. Flandry's eyes searched through a reeking haze of cordite. Where was their chief now—? Warouw looked out from behind one of the rough pillars upholding the ceiling. Still he smiled. Flandry fired and missed. Warouw's right hand emerged, with a modern Betelgeusean blaster.

Flandry didn't stop for heroics. He didn't even stop to make a conscious decision. His chance of hitting Warouw with his own clumsy weapon was negligible. A single wide-beam low-energy blaster shot couldn't possibly miss. It would roll him screaming on the floor. Later, if he wanted to take the trouble, Warouw could have his seared prisoner treated in some hospital.

The Guard at the door was down with a slug in

his chest. The door stood open. Flandry went
through it.

As he burst out on the terrace again, Warouw
was close behind. The rest of the Guards swarmed
shouting in their wake. The dusk was cool and
blue, almost palpable, surrounding all things and
drowning them. Mist and smoke hung in it. Flandry bounded down the ladder to the trailstreet.

There went a rumbling through air and earth.
Briefly, flame gushed in the sky. From an open
doorway came the sound of crockery falling and
smashing; a woman ran out with a scream. Flandry glimpsed several men halted in their tracks,
looking up toward the crater. Their bodies were
shadows in this vague twilight, but the gleam of a
lamp touched white eyeballs. Further down the
trail, the barely visible mass of the crowds had
stopped seething. Their mutter lifted between
black walls.

Gunung Utara was angry.

Warouw paused only an instant at the foot of
the ladder. Then a flashbeam sprang from his left
hand and speared Flandry. The Terran whirled,
dashed from the light, over the pebbles to the
retaining wall. He heard footfalls rattle behind
him.

At this point, he remembered, the downslope
beyond the wall was steep and rugged. He made
out a boulder, and leaped from the wall to its top.
Another shock went through the ground. The
boulder stirred beneath him and he heard lesser
stones grind valleyward. Warouw's flash darted
from the wall, here, there, hunting him. Where to
go? He could see naught but darkness and thick-
ening fogs. No, wait . . . was that another jut of

rock, two meters away? No time to wonder. He sprang. Almost, he missed, and heard below him the shifting of debris which would cut his feet to rags if he landed in it. He grasped an invisible roughness, pulled himself up on top of the crag, spied another mass below him, and jumped to that.

Warouw's light bobbed in pursuit.

Flandry realized he was cutting across town. He didn't know how long he sprang from coign to coign. It was all mist and darkness. Somehow he crossed another safety wall, landed on a terrace, scrambled to the trail beneath, and sped among emptied caves.

Panther to his mountain goat, Warouw followed. Once in a while, for a fractional second, his light picked out the Terran.

Then Flandry was beyond the city. The trail petered out. He ran across a bare slope, over black cinders and among crags like tall ghosts.

He could just see how sharply the ground rose on his left, almost a cliff, up to the crater rim. Gunung Utara thundered. Flandry felt the noise in his teeth and marrow. Cinders shifted, dust filled his nostrils. Somewhere a bouldor went hurtling and bouncing down toward the valley. Smoke boiled from the crater, a solid column three kilometers high, lit from beneath with dull flickering red.

Flandry looked back. The flashbeam jiggled in a gloom where streamers of mist seemed to glow white. He lurched onward. A few times he stumbled, teetered on the uneasy slope, and heard a roar as the scree slid downward. No use heading that way, unless he wanted to die in chunks. He sobbed for air, his lungs were twin deserts and his gullet afire.

A sheer wall rose before him. He ran into it and stared stupidly for seconds before he comprehended. The magma dyke. Yes. Yes, that was it. Must be some way up . . . here, a ladder, iron rungs set into the concrete. . . .

He stood on a railed platform and looked down into the channel. The molten rock threw gusts of heat and poison gas at him. It growled and glowed, ember colored, but he thought he could see tiny flames sheet back and forth across its current. If he wasn't crazy. If he wasn't dreaming.

There was no way to go from here. No bridge, no catwalk to the other side. Not even a flat top on the levee itself. Only the platform, where the engineers could stand to check the stone river. Why should there be more? Flandry leaned on the rail and fought to breathe.

A voice from below, hardly discernible through racing blood and the snarl of Gunung Utara—but cool, almost amused: "If you wish to immolate yourself in the lava, Captain, you still have time. Or you can stay there, holding us off, till the fumes have overcome you. Or, of course, you can surrender now. In that case, the persons who assisted you will not be put in the cage."

Flandry croaked, "Will you let them go?"

"Come, come," chided Warouw. "Let us be sensible. I promise nothing except to spare them the ultimate punishment."

Somewhere in the pounding weariness of his brain, Flandry thought that he should at least make an epigram. But it was too much like work.

He threw his gun into the lava. "I'll be down in a minute," he sighed.

X

Awakening was slow, almost luxurious until he realized the aches and dullnesses in him. He sat up with a groan which turned into an obscenity.

But the chamber was large and cool. Its view of gardens, pools, and small arched bridges was very little spoiled by a wrought-iron grille set in the window frame. A clean outfit of kilt and sandals lay waiting next to the low bedstead. An alcove behind a screen held a bathroom, complete with shower.

"Well," murmured Flandry to himself, as he let hot needles of water wash some of the stiffness out, "it's the minimum decent thing they can do for me . . . after last night." That memory brought a shiver, and he hurriedly continued his graveyard whistling: "So let's hope they do the most. Breakfast, dancing girls, and a first-class one-way ticket to Terra."

Not that they had tortured him. Warouw wasn't that crude. Flandry hoped. Most of the physical suffering had been due his own exhaustion. They didn't let him sleep, but hustled him straight to a highspeed aircar and questioned him all the way to wherever-this-was. Thereafter they continued the grilling, established that he was indeed immune to any drug in their inquisitorial pharmacopeia, but did their best to break his will with his own sheer grogginess. Flandry was on to that method, having applied it himself from time to time; he'd been able to cushion the worst effects by relaxation techniques.

Still, it had been no fun. He didn't even remember being conducted to this room when the party broke up.

He examined himself in the mirror. His dyed hair was showing its natural hue at the roots, his mustache was noticeable again, and the high cheekbones stood forth under a skin stretched tight. Without their lenses, his eyes revealed their own color, but more washed out than normal. *I was interrogated a long time*, he thought. *And then, of course, I may easily have slept for twenty hours.*

He was scarcely dressed when the door opened. A pair of Guards glowered at him. There were truncheons in their hands. "Come," snapped one. Flandry came. He felt inwardly lepidopteral. And why not? For a captain's lousy pay, did the Imperium expect courage too?

He seemed to be in a residential section—rather luxurious, its hallways graciously decorated, servants scurrying obsequiously about—within a much larger building. Or . . . not exactly residential. The apartments he glimpsed didn't look very lived in. Transient, yes, that must be it. A hostel for Biocontrol personnel whose business brought them here. He began to realize precisely where he must be, and his scalp prickled.

At the end of the walk, he was shown into a suite bigger than most. It was fitted in austere taste: black pillars against silvery walls, black tables, one lotus beneath a scroll which was a calligraphic masterpiece. An archway opened on a balcony overlooking gardens, a metal stockade, jungled hills rolling into blue distances. Sunlight and birdsong came through.

Nias Warouw sat on a cushion before a table set for breakfast. He gestured at the Guards, who bowed very low and departed. Flandry took a place opposite their master. Warouw's short supple body was draped in a loose robe which showed the blaster at his hip. He smiled and poured Flandry's tea with his own hands.

"Good day, Captain," he said, "I trust you are feeling better?"

"Slightly better than a toad with glanders," Flandry admitted.

A servant pattered in, knelt, and put a covered dish on the table. "May I recommend this?" said Warouw. "Filet of badjung fish, lightly fried in spiced oil. It is eaten with slices of chilled coconut—so."

Flandry didn't feel hungry till he began. Then he became suddenly sharkish. Warouw crinkled his face in a still wide smile and heaped the Terran's plate with rice, in which meat and baked fruits were shredded. By the time a platter of tiny omelets arrived, Flandry's animal needs were satisfied enough that he could stop and ask for the recipe.

Warouw gave it to him. "Possibly the aspect of your wideranging career most to be envied by a planet-bound individual such as myself, Captain," he added, "is the gastronomical. To be sure, certain crops of Terran origin must be common to a great many human-colonized planets. But soil, climate, and mutation doubtless vary the flavors enormously. And then there are the native foods. Not to mention the sociological aspect: the local philosophy and practice of cuisine. I am happy that our own developments apparently find favor with you."

"Ummm, grmff, chmp," said Flandry, reaching for seconds.

"I myself could wish for more intercourse between Unan Besar and the rest of the galaxy," said Warouw. "Unfortunately, that is impracticable." He poured himself a cup of tea and sipped it, watching the other man with eyes as alert as a squirrel's. He had not eaten heavily.

The Terran finished in half an hour or so. Not being accustomed from boyhood to sit crosslegged, he sprawled on the floor in his relaxation. Warouw offered him Spican cigarillos, which he accepted like his soul's salvation.

Inwardly, he thought: *This is an old gimmick. Make things tough for your victim, then quickly ease off the pressure and speak kindly to him. It's broken down a lot of men. As for me . . . I'd better enjoy it while it lasts.*

Because it wasn't going to.

He drew blessedly mild smoke into his throat and let it tickle his nose on the way out. "Tell me, Captain, if you will," said Warouw, "what is your opinion of the Terran poet L. de le Roi? I have gotten a few of his tapes from the Betelgeuseans, and while of course a great many nuances must escape me—"

Flandry sighed. "Fun is fun," he said, "but business is business."

"I don't quite understand, Captain."

"Yes, you do. You set an excellent table, and I'm sure your conversation is almost as cultural as you believe. But it's hard for me to expand like a little flowerbud when I don't know what's happening to my friends."

Warouw stiffened, it was barely perceptible, and the first syllable or two of his answer was ever so faintly off key. However, it came smoothly enough, with an amiable chuckle: "You must allow me a few items in reserve, Captain. Accept my word that they are not at the moment suffering at the hands of my department, and let us discuss other things."

Flandry didn't press his point. It would only chill the atmosphere. And he wanted to do as much probing as he could while Warouw was still trying the benevolent uncle act.

Not that anything he learned would help him much. He was thoroughly trapped, and in a while he might be thoroughly destroyed. But action, any action, even this verbal shadowboxing, was one way to avoid thinking about such impolite details.

"Professionally speaking," he said, "I'm interested to know how you trapped me."

"Ah." Warouw gestured with his own cigarillo, not at all loath to expound his cleverness. "Well, when you made your . . . eh . . . departure in Kompong Timur, it might have been the hysterical act of a fool who had simply blundered onto us. If so, you were not to be worried about. But I dared not assume it. Your whole manner indicated otherwise—not to mention the documents, official and personal, which I later studied on your ship. Accordingly, my working hypothesis was that you had some plan for surviving beyond the period in which your first antitoxin dose would be effective. Was there already an underground organization of extraplanetary agents, whom you would seek out? I admit the search for such a group took most of my time for numerous days."

Warouw grimaced. "I pray your sympathy for my plight," he said. "The Guards have faced no serious task for generations. No one resists Biocontrol! The Guards, the entire organization, are escorts and watchdogs at best, idiots at worst. Ignoring the proletariat as they do, they have no experience of the criminal subtleties developed by the proletariat. With such incompetents must I chase a crafty up-to-date professional like yourself."

Flandry nodded. He'd gotten the same impression. Modern police and intelligence methodology—even military science—didn't exist on Unan Besar. Poor, damned Nias Warouw, a born detective forced to re-invent the whole art of detection!

But he had done a disquietingly good job of it.

"My first break came when a district boss named Sumu—ah, you remember?" Warouw grinned. "My congratulations, Captain. He was unwilling to admit how you had taken him, but afraid not to report that he had unwittingly entertained a man of your description. I forced the whole tale from him. Delicious! But then I began to think over the datum it presented. It took me days more; I am not used to such problems. In the end, however, I decided that you would not have carried out so risky an exploit except for money, which you doubtless needed to buy illegal antitoxin. (Oh, yes, I know there is some. I have been trying to tighten up controls on production and distribution. But the inefficiency of centuries must be overcome.) Well, if you had to operate in such fashion, you were not in touch with a secret organization. Probably no such organization existed! However, you must have made some contacts in Swamp Town."

Warouw blew smoke rings, cocked his head at the trill of a songbird, and resumed: "I called for the original reports on the case. It was established that in fleeing us you had broken into the establishment of a certain courtesan. She had told the Guards that she fled in terror and knew nothing else. There had been no reason to doubt her. Nor was there now, a priori, but I had no other lead. I ordered her brought in for questioning. My squad was told she had left several days before, destination unknown. I ordered that a watch be kept on her antitoxin record. When she appeared at Gunung Utara, I was informed. I flew there within the hour.

"The local dispenser remembered her vividly, and had a recollection of a tall man with her. She had told him where she was staying, so we checked the inn. Yes, she had been careless enough to tell the truth. The innkeeper described her companions, one of whom was almost certainly you. We arrested her and the other man in their rooms and settled back to await you."

Flandry sighed. He might have known it. How often had he told cubs in the Service never to underestimate an opponent?

"You almost escaped us again, Captain," said Warouw. "A dazzling exhibition, though not one that I recommend you repeat. Even if, somehow, you broke loose once more, all aircars here are locked. The only other way to depart is on foot, with 400 kilometers of dense rain forest to the nearest village. You would never get there before your antitoxin wore off."

Flandry finished his cigarillo and crushed it with regret. "Your only reason for isolating this place that much," he said, "is that you make the pills here."

Warouw nodded. "This is Biocontrol Central. If you think you can steal a few capsules for your jungle trip, I suppose you can try. Pending distribution, they are kept in an underground vault protected by identification doors, automatic guns, and—as the initial barrier—a hundred trusted Guards."

"I don't plan to try," said Flandry.

Warouw stretched; muscles flowed under his hairless brown skin. "There is no harm in showing you some of the other sections, though," he said. "If you are interested."

I'm interested in anything which will postpone the next round of unfriendliness, acknowledged Flandry. Aloud: "Of course. I might even talk you into dropping your isolationist policy."

Warouw's smile turned bleak. "On the contrary, Captain," he said, "I hope to prove to you that there is no chance of its being dropped, and that anyone who tries to force the issue is choosing a needlessly lingering form of suicide. Come, please."

XI

Two Guards padded silently behind, but they were no more heeded than Warouw's blaster. The chief took Flandry's arm with a delicate, almost feminine gesture and led him down a hall and a curving ramp to the garden. Here it was cool and full of green odors. Immense purple blooms drooped overhead, scarlet and yellow flowerbeds lined the gravel walks like a formal fire, water plashed high out of carved basins and went rilling under playfully shaped bridges, ketjils were little gold songsparks darting in and out of willow groves. Flandry paid more attention to the building. He was being led across from one wing to the center. It reared huge, the changing styles of centuries discernible in its various parts. Warouw's goal was obviously the oldest section: a sheer black mountain of fused stone, Guards at the doors and robot guns on the battlements.

An attendant in an anteroom bowed low and issued four suits. They were coveralls, masked and hooded, of a transparent flexiplast which fitted comfortably enough, though Warouw must leave off his robe. Gloves, boots, and snouted respirators completed the ensemble.

"Germs in there?" asked Flandry.

"Germs on us." For a moment, the nightmare of a dozen generations looked out of Warouw's eyes. He made a sign against evil. "We dare not risk contaminating the vats."

"Of course," suggested Flandry, "you could produce a big enough reserve supply of antitoxin to carry you through any such emergency."

Warouw's worldliness returned. "Now, Captain," he laughed, "would that be practical politics?"

"No," admitted Flandry. "It could easily lead to Biocontrol having to work for a living."

"You never gave the impression of possessing any such peasantish ideal."

"Fate forbid! My chromosomes always intended me for a butterfly, useful primarily as an inspiration to others. However, you must admit a distinction between butterflies and leeches."

Since Flandry had used the name of equivalent native insects, Warouw scowled. "Please, Captain!"

The Terran swept eyes across one horrified attendant and two indignant Guards. "Ah, yes," he said, "Little Eva and the Sunshine Twins. Sorry, I forgot about them. Far be it from me to do away with anyone's intellectual maidenhead."

Warouw put his hands to a scanner. The inner door opened for his party and they entered a sterilizing chamber. Beyond its UV and ultrasonics, another door led them into a sort of lobby. A few earnest young shavepates hurried here and there with technical apparatus. They gave the sense of a task forever plagued by clumsy equipment and clumsier organization. Which was to be expected, of course. Biocontrol was not about to modernize its plant. And, like all hierarchies not pruned by incessant competition, Biocontrol had proliferated its departments, regulations, chains of command, protocols, office rivalries, and every other fungus Flandry knew so well on Terra.

A creaky old slideramp bore Warouw's group

up several floors. Two purely ornamental Guards lounged on blast rifles outside a gilded door of vast proportions. Several men cooled their heels in the room beyond, waiting for admission to the main office. Warouw brushed past them, through a small auxiliary sterilizing chamber and so into the sanctum.

Solu Bandang himself sat among many cushions. He had removed his flexisuit but not donned a robe again. His belly sagged majestically over his kilt. He looked up, heavy-lidded, and whined, "Now what is the meaning of this? What do you mean? I gave no appointment to—Oh. You."

"Greeting, Tuan," said Warouw casually. "I had not expected to find you on duty."

"Yes, it is my turn, my turn again. Even the highest office, ah, in the . . . the world, this world . . . does not excuse a man from a tour of— Necessary to keep one's finger on the pulse, Captain Flandry," said Bandang. "Very essential. Oh, yes, indeed."

The desk didn't look much used. Flandry supposed that the constant presence of some member of the governing board was a survival of earlier days when Biocontrol's stranglehold wasn't quite so firm.

"I trust, ah, you have been made to . . . see the error of your ways, Captain?" Bandang reached for a piece of candied ginger. "Your attitude has, I hope, become—realistic?"

"I am still arguing with our guest, Tuan," said Warouw.

"Oh, come now!" said Bandang. "Come now! Really, Colleague, this is deplorable, ah, dilatoriness on your part. Explain to the Captain,

Warouw, that we have methods to persuade recal-
citrants. Yes, methods. If necessary, apply those
methods. But don't come in here disturbing me!
He's not in my department. Not my department at
all."

"In that case, Tuan," said Warouw, his exasper-
ation hardly curbed, "I beg you to let me proceed
with my work in my own fashion. I should like to
show the Captain one of our vats. I think it might
prove convincing. But of course, we need your
presence to get into that section."

"What? What? See here, Warouw, I am a busy
man. Busy, do you hear? I have, er, obligations. It
is not my duty to—"

"Perhaps," snapped Warouw, "the Tuan feels
he can take care of the situation single-handed,
when the outworlders arrive?"

"What?" Bandang sat up straight, so fast that
his jowls quivered. The color drained from them.
"What's that? Do you mean there *are* outworlders? Other, that is, than the Betelgeuseans—uncontrolled outworlders, is that, ah,
is that—"

"That is what I have to find out, Tuan. I beg you
for your kind assistance."

"Oh. Oh, yes. Yes, at once. Immediately!" Bandang rolled to his feet and fumbled at his hung-up
flexisuit. The two Guards hastened to assist him
in donning it.

Warouw checked an electronic bulletin board.
"I see Genseng is on watch at Vat Four," he said.
"We'll go there. You must meet Colleague Gen-
seng, Flandry."

The Terran made no answer. He was considering what he had seen. Bandang was a fat fool, but
without too many illusions. His horror at the idea

of out-planet visitors proved he knew very well what Flandry had already deduced:

God, what an overripe plum! If only the pills could come from somewhere else, this Biocontrol boobocracy and its comic opera Guards wouldn't last a week.

If any adventurers do learn the truth, they'll swarm here from a score of planets. Unan Besar is rich. I don't know how much of that wealth is locked in Biocontrol vaults, but it must be plenty. Enough to make the fortune of an experienced fighting man (like me) who'd serve as a revolutionary officer for a share in the loot.

Unless the revolution happens too fast to import filibusters. I suspect that would be the actual case. The people of Unan Besar would rip their overlords apart bare-handed. And, of course, the real money to be made here is not from plundering, but from selling cheap antitoxin without restrictions. . . . Which is less my line of work than a spot of piracy would be. But I'd still like to get that juicy commission from Mitsuko Laboratories.

The lightness faded in him, less because he remembered his immediate problems than because of certain other recollections. The man who screamed and died in a cage where the stone gods danced. Swamp Town, and humans turned wolf to survive. Hungry men chipping a mountainside by hand, women and children in rice paddies. Djuanda, with nothing left him but pride, leaping off the wall. Luang's eyes, seen across the room where she sat bound. The Guard who struck her with a club.

Flandry had no patience with crusaders, but there are limits to any man's endurance.

"Come, then," puffed Bandang. "Yes, Captain, you really must see our production facilities. A, ah, an achievement. A most glorious achievement, as I am sure you will agree, of our, ah, pioneering ancestors. May their, their work . . . ever remain sacred and undefiled, their blood remain, er, pure."

Behind the plump back, Warouw winked at Flandry.

Passing through the office sterilizer, and the waiting technicians who bowed to Bandang, the conducted tour took a slideway down corridors where faded murals depicted the heroic founders of Biocontrol in action. At the slideway's end, a glassed-in catwalk ran above a series of chambers.

They were immense. Up here near the ceilings, Flandry saw technicians down on the floor scuttle like bugs. Each room centered on a gleaming alloy vat, ten meters high and thirty in diameter. With the pipes that ran from it like stiff tentacles, with the pumps and stirrers and testers and control units and meters clustered around, it could have been some heathen god squatting amidst attendant demons. And on more than one face, among the men who went up and down the catwalks, Flandry thought he recognized adoration.

Warouw said in a detached tone: "As you may know, the process of antitoxin manufacture is biological. A yeast-like native organism was mutated to produce, during fermentation, that inhibitor which prevents the bacterial formation of acetylcholine. The bacteria themselves are destroyed within a few days by normal human antibodies. So, if you left this planet, you would need one final pill to flush out the infection. Thereafter you would be free of it. But as long as you are on Unan Besar—each breath you take, each bite you eat or drop you drink, maintains an equilibrium concentration of germs in your system.

"Unfortunately, these omnipresent germs kill the yeast itself. So it is critically important to keep this place sterile. Even a slight contamination would spread like fire in dry grass. The room where it occurred would have to be sealed off, everything dismantled and individually sterilized. It would take a year to get back in operation. And we would be lucky to have only one vat idled."

"A molecular synthesizing plant could turn out a year's biological production in a day, and sneer at germs," said Flandry.

"No doubt. No doubt, Captain," said Bandang. "You are very clever in the Empire. But cleverness isn't all, you know. Not by any means. There are other virtues. Ah . . . Warouw, I think you should not have called the circumstance of, um, easy contamination . . . unfortunate. On the contrary, I would call it most fortunate. A, ah, a divine dispensation, bringing about and protecting the, er, social order most suitable for this world."

"A social order which recognizes that worthiness is heritable, and allows every blood line to find its natural status under the benevolent guardianship of a truly scientific organization whose primary mission has always been to preserve the genetic and cultural heritage of Unan Besar from degradation and exploitation by basically inferior outsiders," droned Flandry.

Bandang looked surprised. "Why, Captain, have you come to so good an understanding already?"

"Here is Vat Four," said Warouw.

In each chamber, a stairway, also glassed in, led down from the catwalk. Flandry was taken along this one. It ended at a platform several meters above the floor, where a semi-circular board flashed with lights and quivered with dials. Flandry realized the instruments must report on every aspect of the vat's functioning. Underneath them was a bank of master controls for emergency use. At the far left projected a long double-pole switch, painted dead black. A light at its end glowed like a red eye.

The man who stood motionless before the board would have been impressive in his white robe. Seen kilted through a flexisuit, he was much too thin. Every rib and vertebra could be counted. When he turned around, his face was a skull in sagging skin. But the eyes lived; and, in an eerie way, the glowing golden brand.

"You dare—" he whispered. Recognizing Bandang: "Oh. Your pardon, Tuan." His scorn was hardly veiled. "I thought it must be some fool of a novice who dared interrupt a duty officer."

Bandang stepped back. "Ah . . . really, Genseng," he huffed. "You go too far. Indeed you do. I, ah, I demand respect. Yes."

The eyes smoldered at them. "I am duty officer here until my relief arrives." The murmur of pumps came more loudly through the glass cage than Genseng's voice. "You know the Law."

"Yes. Yes, indeed. Of course. But—"

"The duty officer is supreme at his station, Tuan. My decisions may not be questioned. I could kill you for a whim, and the Law would uphold me. Holy is the Law."

"Indeed. Indeed." Bandang wiped his countenance. "I too . . . after all. I too have my watches to stand—"

"In an office," sneered Genseng.

Warouw trod cockily to the fore. "Do you remember our guest, Colleague?" he asked.

"Yes." Genseng brooded at Flandry. "The one who came from the stars and leaped out the window. When does he go in the cage?"

"Perhaps never," said Warouw. "I think he might be induced to cooperate with us."

"He is unclean," mumbled Genseng. The hairless skull turned back toward the dance of instruments, as if beauty dwelt there alone.

"I thought you might wish to demonstrate the controls to him."

"S-s-s-so." Genseng's eyes filmed over. He stood a long while, moving his lips without sound. At last: "Yes, I see."

Suddenly his gaze flamed at the Terran. "Look out there," the parchment voice ordered. "Watch those men serving the vat. If any of them makes an error—if any of a hundred possible errors are made, or a thousand possible misfunctions of equipment occur—the batch now brewing will spoil and a million people will die. Could you bear such a burden?"

"No," said Flandry, as softly as if he walked on fulminate.

Genseng swept one chalky hand at the panel. "It is for me to see the error or the failure on these dials, and correct it in time with these master controls. I have kept track. Three hundred and twenty-seven times since I first became a duty officer, I have saved a batch from spoiling. Three hundred and twenty-seven million human lives are owed me. Can you claim as much, out-worlder?"

"No."

"They owe more than their lives, though," said Genseng somberly. "What use is life, if all that life is for should be lost? Better return the borrowed force at once, unstained, to the most high gods, than dirty it with wretchedness like your own, outworlder. Unan Besar owes its purity to me and those like me. The lives we have given, we can take again, to save that purity."

Flandry pointed to the black switch and asked very low, "What does that connect to?"

"There is a nuclear bomb buried in the foundations of this castle," Genseng breathed. "Any duty officer can detonate it from his station. All are sworn to do so, if the holy mission should ever fail."

Flandry risked cynicism: "Though of course a reserve stock of medicine, and enough spaceships for Biocontrol to escape in, are kept available."

"There are those who would do such a thing," sighed Genseng. "Even here the soul-infection lingers. But let them desert, then, to their own damnation. I can at least save most of my people."

He turned back to his panel with a harsh movement. "Go!" he yelled.

Bandang actually ran back up the stairs.

Warouw came last, smiling. Bandang mopped his face, which poured sweat. "Really!" puffed the governor. "Really! I do think . . . honorable retirement . . . Colleague Genseng does appear to, ah, feel his years—"

"You know the Law, Tuan," said Warouw unctuously. "No one who wears the Brand may be deposed, except by vote of his peers. You couldn't get enough votes to do it, and you would anger the whole extremist faction." He turned to Flandry. "Genseng is a somewhat violent case, I admit. But there are enough others who feel like him, to guarantee that this building would go sky-high if Biocontrol ever seemed seriously threatened."

Flandry nodded. He'd been a bit skeptical of such claims before. Now he wasn't.

"I don't know what good this has done," said Bandang softly.

"Perhaps the Captain and I might best discuss that," bowed Warouw.

"Perhaps. Good day, then, Captain." Bandang raised one fat hand in a patronizing gesture. "I trust we shall meet again . . . ah . . . elsewhere than the cage? Of course, of course! Good day!" He wobbled quickly down the catwalk.

Warouw conducted Flandry at a slower pace. They didn't speak for minutes, until they had turned back their flexisuits and were again in the garden and the blessed sane sunlight.

"What do you actually want to convince me of, Warouw?" asked the Terran then.

"Of the truth," said the other man. Banter had dropped from him; he looked straight ahead, and his mouth was drawn downward.

"Which is short-sighted self-interest utilizing fanaticism to perpetuate itself . . . and fanaticism running away with self-interest," said Flandry in a sharp tone.

Warouw shrugged. "You take the viewpoint of a different culture."

"And of most of your own people. You know that as well as I. Warouw, what have you to gain

by the status quo? Are your money, your fancy
lodging, your servants, that important to you?
You're an able chap. You could gain all you now
have, and a lot more besides, in the modern galactic society."

Warouw glanced back at the two Guards and
answered softly: "What would I be there, another
little politician making dirty little com-
promises—or Nias Warouw whom all men fear?"

He jumped at once to a discourse on willow
cultivation, pointing out with expert knowledge
the local evolution of the original imported stock,
until they were again at Flandry's room.

The door opened. "Go in and rest a while," said
Warouw. "Then think whether to cooperate freely
or not."

"You've been harping for some time on the
need for my cooperation," said Flandry. "But
you've not made it clear what you want of me."

"First, I want to know for certain why you came
here," Warouw met his eyes unblinkingly. "If you
do not resist it, a light hypnoprobing will get that
out of you quite easily. Then you must help me
prepare false evidence of your own accidental
death, and head off any Terran investigation.
Thereafter you will be appointed my special
assistant—for life. You will advise me on how to
modernize the Guard Corps and perpetuate this
world's isolation." He smiled with something like
shyness. "I think we might both enjoy working
together. We are not so unlike, you and I."

"Suppose I don't cooperate," said Flandry.

Warouw flushed and snapped: "Then I must
undertake a deep hypnoprobing and drag your
information out of you. I confess I have had very

little practice with the instrument since acquiring it. Even in skilled hands, you know, the hypno-probe at full strength is apt to destroy large areas of cerebral cortex. In unskilled hands—But I will at least get *some* information out of you before your mind evaporates!"

He bowed. "I shall expect your decision tomorrow. Good rest."

The door closed behind him.

Flandry paced in silence. He would have traded a year of life for a pack of Terran cigarets, but he hadn't even been supplied with locals. It was like a final nail driven into his coffin.

What to do?

Cooperate? Yield to the probe? But that meant allowing his mind to ramble in free association, under the stimulus of the machine. Warouw would hear everything Flandry knew about the Empire in general and Naval Intelligence in particular. Which was one devil of a lot.

In itself, that would be harmless—if the knowledge stayed on this planet. But it was worth too much. A bold man like Warouw was certain to exploit it. The Merseians, for instance, would gladly establish a non-interfering protectorate over Unan Besar—it would only tie down a cruiser or two—in exchange for the information about Terran defenses which Warouw could feed them in shrewd driblets. Or better, perhaps, Warouw could take a ship himself and search out those barbarians with spacecraft Flandry knew of: who would stuff the vessel of Warouw with loot from Terran planets which he could tell them how to raid.

Either way, the Long Night was brought that much closer.

Of course, Dominic Flandry would still be alive, as a sort of domesticated animal. He couldn't decide if it was worth it or not.

Thunder rolled in the hills. The sun sank behind clouds which boiled up to cover the sky. A few fat raindrops smote a darkening garden.

I wonder if I get anything more to eat today, thought Flandry in his weariness.

He hadn't turned on the lights. His room was nearly black. When the door opened, he was briefly dazzled. The figure that stepped through was etched against corridor illumination like a troll.

Flandry retreated, fists clenched. After a moment he realized it was only a Biocontrol uniform, long robe with flaring shoulders. But did they want him already? His heart thuttered in anticipation.

"Easy, there," said a vaguely familiar voice.

Lightning split heaven. In an instant's white glare, Flandry made out shaven head, glowing brand, and the broken face of Kemul the mugger.

XII

He sat down. His legs wouldn't hold him.

"Where in the nine foul hells is your light switch?" grumbled the basso above him. "We've little enough time. They may spare you if we are caught, but the cage for Kemul. Quick!"

The Terran got shakily back on his feet. "Stay away from the window," he said. A dim amazement was in him, that he could speak without stuttering. "I'd hate for some passerby to see us alone together. He might misunderstand the purity of our motives. Ah." Light burst from the ceiling.

Kemul took a rich man's garments from under his robe and tossed them on the bed: sarong, curly-toed slippers, blouse, vest, turban with an enormous plume. "Best we can do," he said. "Biocontrol disguise and a painted brand would not go for you. Your scalp would be paler than your face, and your face itself sticking out for all to see. But some great merchant or landowner, come here to talk of some policy matter—Also, speaking earnestly with you as we go, Kemul will not have to observe so many fine points of politeness and rule which he never learned."

Flandry tumbled into the clothes. "How'd you get in here at all?" he demanded.

Kemul's thick lips writhed upward. "That is another reason we must hurry, you. Two dead Guards outside." He opened the door, stooped, and yanked the corpses in. Their necks were broken with one karate chop apiece. A firearm would have made too much noise, Flandry thought in a daze. Even a cyanide needler with a compressed air cartridge would have to be drawn and fired, which might give time for a warning to be yelled. But a seeming Biocontrol man could walk right past the sentries, deep in meditation, and kill them in one second as they saluted him. That ability of Kemul's must have counted for enough that his cohorts (who?) sent him in rather than somebody of less noticeable appearance.

"But how'd you get this far, I mean?" Flandry persisted a trifle wildly.

"Landed outside the hangar, as they all do. Said to the attendant, Kemul was here from Pegunungan Gradjugang on urgent business and might have to depart again in minutes. Walked into the building, cornered a Guard alone in a hall, wrung from him where you were being kept, threw the body out a window into some bushes. Once or twice a white-robe hailed Kemul, but he said he was in great haste and went on."

Flandry whistled. It would have been a totally impossible exploit on any other world he had ever seen. The decadence of Biocontrol and its Guard Corps was shown naked by this fact of an enemy walking into their ultimate stronghold without so much as being questioned. To be sure, no one in all the history of Unan Besar had ever dreamed of such a raid; but still—

But still it was a fantastic gamble, with the odds against it mounting for each second of delay.

"I sometimes think we overwork Pegunungan Gradjugang." Flandry completed his ensemble. "Have a weapon for me?"

"Here." Kemul drew out of his robe a revolver as antiquated as the one liberated from Pradjung (how many eons ago?). The same gesture showed his Terran blaster in an arm sheath. "Hide it. No needless fighting."

"Absolutely! You wouldn't believe how meek my intentions are. Let's go."

The hall was empty. Flandry and Kemul went down it, not too fast, mumbling at each other as if deep in discourse. At a cross-corridor they met a technician, who bowed his head to Kemul's insigne but couldn't entirely hide astonishment.

The technician continued the way they had come. If he passed Flandry's closed door and happened to know that two Guards were supposed to be outside—

The hall debouched in a spacious common room. Between its pillars and gilded screens, a dozen or so off-duty Biocontrol people sat smoking, reading, playing games, watching a taped dance program. Flandry and Kemul started across toward the main entrance. A middle-aged man with a Purity Control symbol on his robe intercepted them.

"I beg your pardon, Colleague," he bowed. "I have not had the pleasure of meeting you before, though I thought I knew all full initiates." His eyes were lively with interest. A tour of duty here must be a drab chore for most personnel, any novelty welcomed. "And I had no idea we were entertaining a civilian of such obvious importance."

Flandry bent his own head above respectfully folded hands, hoping the plume would shadow his face enough. A couple of men, cross-legged above a chessboard, looked up in curiosity and kept on looking.

"Ameti Namang from beyond the Tindjil Ocean," growled Kemul. "I just came with Proprietor Tasik here. Been on special duty for years."

"Er . . . your accent . . . and I am sure I would remember your face from anywhere—"

Having sidled around to Kemul's other side, so that the giant cut off view of him, Flandry exclaimed in a shocked stage whisper: "I beg you, desist! Can't you tell when a man's been in an accidental explosion?" He took his companion's elbow. "Come, we mustn't keep Tuan Bandang waiting."

The stares which followed him were like darts in his back.

Rain beat heavily on the roof of the verandah beyond. Lamplight glowed along garden paths, but even on this round-the-clock planet they weren't frequented in such weather. Flandry glanced behind, at the slowly closing main doors. "In about thirty seconds," he muttered, "our friend will either shrug off his puzzlement with a remark about the inscrutable ways of his superiors . . . or will start seriously adding two and two. Come on."

They went down the staircase. "Damn!" said Flandry. "You forgot to bring rain capes. Think a pair of drowned rats can reclaim your aircar?"

"With a blaster, if need be," snapped Kemul. "Stop complaining. You've at least been given a chance to die cleanly. It was bought for you at the hazard of two other lives."

"Two?"

"It wasn't Kemul's idea, this, or his wish."

Flandry fell silent. Rain struck his face and turned his clothes sodden. The path was like a treadmill, down which he walked endlessly between wet hedges, under goblin lamps. He heard thunder again, somewhere over the jungle.

Sudden as a blow, the garden ended. Concrete glimmered in front of a long hemicylindrical building. "Here's where everybody lands," grunted Kemul. He led the way to the office door. A kilted civilian emerged and bobbed the head to him. "Where's my car?" said Kemul.

"So soon, tuan? You were only gone a short while—"

"I told you I would be. And you garaged my car anyhow? You officious dolt!" Kemul shoved with a brutal hand. The attendant picked himself up and hurried to the hangar doors.

Whistles skirled through the rain-rushing. Flandry looked back. Mountainous over all bowers and pools, the Central blinked windows to life like opening eyes. The attendant paused to gape. "Get moving!" roared Kemul.

"Yes, tuan. Yes, tuan." A switch was pulled, the doors slid open. "But what is happening?"

I don't know, Flandry thought. *Maybe my absence was discovered. Or else somebody found a dead Guard. Or our friend in the common room got suspicious and called for a checkup. Or any of a dozen other possibilities. The end result is still the same.*

He slipped a hand inside his blouse and rested it on the butt of his gun.

Lights went on in the hangar. It was crowded with aircars belonging to men serving their turns here. The attendant stared idiotically around, distracted by whistles and yells and sound of running feet. "Now, let's see, tuan, which one is yours? I don't rightly recall, I don't—"

Four or five Guards emerged from the garden path into the lamplight of the field. "Get the car, Kemul," rapped Flandry. He drew his revolver and slipped behind the shelter of a door. The attendant's jaw dropped. He let out a squeak and tried to run. Kemul's fist smote at the base of his skull. The attendant flew in an arc, hit, skidded across concrete, and lay without breathing.

"That was unnecessary," said Flandry. It wrenched within him: *Always the innocent get hurt worst.*

The mugger was already among the cars. The squad of Guards broke into a run. Flandry stepped from behind his door long enough to fire several times. One man spun around on his heel, went over backward, and raised himself on all fours with blood smeared over his chest. The others scattered. And they bawled for help.

Flandry took another peek. The opposite side of the landing field was coming alive with Guards. Through their shouts and the breaking of branches under their feet, through the rain, boomed Warouw's voice: "Surround the hangar. Squads Four, Five, Six, prepare to storm the entrance. Seven, Eight, Nine, prepare to fire on emerging vehicles." He must be using a portable amplifier, but it was still like hearing an angered god.

Kemul grunted behind Flandry, shoving parked craft aside to clear a straight path for his own. As the three assault squads started to run across the concrete, Flandry heard him call: "Get in, quick!"

The Terran sent a dozen shots into the nearing troop, whirled, and jumped. Kemul was at the controls of one vehicle, gunning the motor. He had left the door to the pilot section open. Flandry got a foot in it as the car spurted forward. Then they struck the Guards entering the hangar.

Somebody shrieked. Somebody else crunched beneath the wheels, horribly. One man seized Flandry's ankle. Almost, the Terran was pulled loose. He shot, missed, and felt his antique weapon jam. He threw it at the man's contorted brown face. The car jetted antigrav force and sprang upward. Flandry clung to the doorframe with two hands and one foot. He kicked with the captured leg. His enemy hung on, screaming. Somehow Flandry found strength to raise the leg until it pointed almost straight out, then bring it down again to bash his dangling burden against the side.

The Guard let go and fell a hundred meters. Flandry toppled back into the control section.

"They'll have an armed flyer after us in sixty seconds," he gasped. "Gimme your place!"

Kemul glared at him. "What do you know about steering?"

"More than any planet hugger. Get out! Or d' you want us to be overhauled and shot down?"

Kemul locked eyes with Flandry. The wrath in his gaze was shocking. A panel cut off the rear section; this was a rich man's limousine, though awkward and underpowered compared to the Guard ships Flandry had ridden. The panel slid back. Luang leaned into the pilot compartment and said, "Let him have the wheel, Kemul. Now!"

The mugger spat an oath, but gave up his seat. Flandry vaulted into it. "I don't imagine this horse cart has acceleration compensators," he said. "So get astern and buckle down tight!"

He concentrated for a moment on the controls. It was an old-fashioned, unfamiliar make of car, doubtless unloaded by some wily Betelgeusean trader. But having handled many less recognizable craft before, and being in peril of his life, Flandry identified all instruments in a few seconds.

Outside was darkness. Rain whipped the windshield. He saw lightning far off to the left. Making a spiral, he searched with his radar for pursuit. Biocontrol Central glittered beneath him. His detector beeped and registered another vessel on a collision path. The autopilot tried to take over. Flandry cut it out of the circuit and began to climb.

His track was a long slant bearing toward the storm center. The radar on this medieval galley wouldn't show what was behind him, but doubtless the Guard car had him spotted and was catching up fast. A whistling scream reminded Flandry he hadn't slid the door shut. He did so, catching a few raindrops on his face. They tasted of wind.

Up and up. Now the lightning flashes were picking out detail for him, cumulus masses that rolled and reared against heaven and dissolved into a cataract at their base. Gusts thrummed the metal of the car. Its controls bucked. Thunder filled the cabin.

With maximum speed attained. Flandry cut the drive beams, flipped 180 degrees around with a lateral thrust, and went back on full power. An instant he hung, killing velocity. Then he got going downward.

At a kilometer's distance, the other vehicle came into view: a lean shark shape with twice his speed. It swelled monstrously to his eye. There were about ten seconds for its pilot to react. As Flandry had expected, the fellow crammed all he had into a sidewise leap, getting out of the way. Even so, Flandry shot past with about one meter to spare.

Gauging the last possible instant of deceleration was a matter of trained reflex. When he applied the brake force, Flandry heard abused frames groan, and he was almost thrown into his own windshield. He came to a halt just above the tossing jungle crowns. At once he shifted to a horizontal course. Faster than any man not trained in space would have dared—or been able—he flew, his landing gear centimeters from the uppermost leaves. Now and then he must veer, barely missing a higher than average tree. He plunged into the wild waterfall of the storm center, and saw lightning rive one such tree not ten meters away.

But up in the sky, his pursuer, having lost speed and course and object, must be casting about in an ever more desperate search for him.

Flandry continued skimming till he was on the other side of the rain. Only then, a good fifty kilometers from Biocontrol Central, did he venture to rise a little and use his own radar again. It registered nothing. Tropical stars bloomed in the violet night haze. The air alone had voice, as he slipped through it.

"We're the one that got away," he said.

He regained altitude and looked back into the main section. Kemul sagged in his chair. "You could have crashed us, you drunken amokker!" choked the big man. Luang unstrapped herself and took out a cigaret with fingers not quite steady. "I think Dominic knew what he did," she answered.

Flandry locked the controls and went back to join them, flexing sore muscles. "I think so too," he said. He flopped down beside Luang. "Hi, there."

She gave him an unwavering look. The cabin light was lustrous on her dark hair and in the long eyes. He saw developing bruises where the violence of his maneuvers had thrown her against the safety belt. But still she regarded him, until at last he must shift uneasily and bum a cigaret, merely to break that silence.

"Best you pilot us now, Kemul," she said.

The mugger snorted, but moved forward as she desired. "Where are we going?" Flandry asked.

"Ranau," said Luang. She took her eyes from him and drew hard on her cigaret. "Where your friend Djuanda is."

"Oh. I believe I see what happened. But tell me."

"When you escaped from the inn, all those imbecilic Guards went whooping after you," she said, unemotional as a history lesson. "Djuanda had been behind you when you entered, and had stayed in the corridor during the fight. No one noticed him. He was intelligent enough to come in as soon as they were all gone, and release us."

"No wonder Warouw despises his own men," said Flandry. "Must have been disconcerting, returning to find the cupboard bare like that. Though he coolly led me to believe you were still his prisoners. Go on, what did you do next?"

"We fled, of course. Kemul hot-wired a parked aircar. Djuanda begged us to save you. Kemul scoffed at the idea. It looked impossible to me too, at first. It was bad enough being fugitives, who would live only as long as we could contrive to get illicit pills. But three people, against the masters of a planet—?"

"You took them on, though." Flandry brought his lips so close to her ear that they brushed her cheek. "I've no way to thank you for that, ever."

Still she gazed straight before her, and the full red mouth shaped words like a robot: "Chiefly you should thank Djuanda. His life was a good investment of yours. He insisted we would not be three alone. He swore many of his own people would help, if there was any hope at all of getting rid of Biocontrol. So . . . we went to Ranau. We spoke to the boy's father, and others. In the end, they provided this car, with plans and information and disguises such as we would need. Now we are bound back to them, to see what can be done next."

Flandry looked hard at her in his turn. "You made the final decision, to rescue me, Luang." he said. "Didn't you?"

She stirred on the seat. "What of it?" Her voice was no longer under absolute control.

"I'd like to know why. It can't be simple self-preservation. On the contrary. You got black market antitoxin before; you could have kept on doing so. When my knowledge was wrung out of me, Warouw would understand you were no danger to him. He wouldn't have pressed the hunt for you. You could probably even snare some influential man and tease him into getting you pardoned. So—if we're going to work together, Luang—I want to know why you chose it."

She stubbed out her cigaret. "Not for any of your damned causes!" she snarled. "I don't care about a hundred million clods, any more than I ever did. It was only . . . to rescue you, we must have help in Ranau, and those oafs would only help as part of a plot to overthrow Biocontrol. That's all!"

Kemul hunched his great shoulders, turned around and rumbled, "If you don't stop baiting her, Terran, Kemul will feed you your own guts."

"Close your panel," said Luang.

The giant averted his face again, sucked in a long breath, and slid shut the barrier between him and the others.

Wind lulled around the flyer. Flandry turned off the lights and saw stars on either side. It was almost as if he could reach out and pluck them.

"I'll answer no more impertinent questions," said Luang. "Is it not enough that you have gotten your own way?"

He caught her to him and her own question went unanswered.

XIII

Ranau lay on a northeasterly jut of the continent, with Kompong Timur a good thousand kilometers to the southwest. Intervening swamp and mountain, lack of navigable rivers, before all the standoffishness of its people, made it little frequented. A few traders flew in during the year, otherwise the airstrip was hardly used. It was still dark when Flandry's car set down. Several impassive men with phosphorescent globes to light their way met him, and he was horrified to learn it was ten kilometers' walk to the nearest dwelling.

"We make no roads under the Trees," said Tembesi, Djuanda's father. And that was that.

Dawn came while they were still afoot. As the

spectacle grew before him, Flandry's life added one more occasion of awe.

The ground was low, wet, thickly covered with a soft and intensely green moss-like turf. It sparkled with a million water drops. Fog rolled and streamed, slowly breaking up as the sun climbed. The air was cool, and filled the nostrils with dampness. His tread muffled and upborne by the springy growth, his companions unspeaking and half blurred in the mist, Flandry moved through silence like a dream.

Ahead of him, rising out of a fog bank into clear sky, were the Trees of Ranau.

There were over a thousand, but only a few could be seen at one time. They grew too far apart, a kilometer or more between boles. And they were too big.

Hearing Djuanda tell of them, mentioning an average height of two hundred meters and an estimated average age of ten thousand Terrestrial years, Flandry had imagined the redwoods he knew from home. But this was not Terra. The great Trees were several times as thick in proportion—incredibly massive, organic mountains with roots like foothills. They shot straight up for fifty meters or so, then began to branch, broadest at the bottom, tapering to a spire. The slim higher boughs would each have made a Terran oak; the lowest were forests in themselves, forking again and yet again, the five-pointed leaves (small, delicately serrated, green on top but with a golden underside of nearly mirror brightness) outnumbering the visible stars. Even given the lower gravity of Unan Besar, it was hard to imagine how branches so huge could support their own weight. But they had cores with a strength approximating steel, surrounded by a principal thickness of wood as light as balsa, the whole armored in tough gray bark. Tossing in the gentle winds which prevailed here, the upper leaves reflected sunlight downward off their shiny sides, so that the lower foliage was not shadowed to death.

No matter explanations. When Flandry saw the grove itself, filling the sky, sunlight winking and shivering and running like flame in the crowns, he merely stood and looked. The others respected his need. For long, the whole party remained silent where it was.

When they resumed—passing through a stand of tall frond trees without even noticing—the Terran found tongue once more: "I understand your people are freeholders. That's rare, isn't it?"

Tembesi, who was a big stern-faced man, replied slowly: "We are not quite what you think. Early in the history of this planet, it became clear that the free yeoman was doomed. The large plantations were underselling him, so he was driven to subsistence farming, with the price of antitoxin too high for him to afford improvements. Let him have one bad year, and he must sell land to the plantation owner, just to pay for survival. Presently his farm became too small to support him, he fell into the grip of the moneylenders, in the end he was fortunate if he became a tenant rather than a slave.

"Our own ancestors were peasants whose leaders foresaw the loss of land. They sold what they had and moved here. There were certain necessities of survival as free men. First, some means of getting cash for antitoxin and tools. Yet, second, not enough wealth to excite the greed of the great lords, who could always find a pretext to dispossess their inferiors. Third, remoteness from the corruption and violence of the cities, the countryside's ignorance and poverty. Fourth, mutual helpfulness, so that individual misfortunes would not nibble away the new community as the old had been destroyed.

"These things were found among the Trees."

And now they left the minor forest and approached the holy grove. It was not as dark under one of the giants as Flandry had expected. The overshadowing roof of leaves twinkled, flashed, glittered, so that sunspecks went dancing among the shades. Small animals scurried out of the way, around the nearest root which heaved its gray wall up from the pseudomoss. Redbreasted fluter birds and golden ketjils darted in and out of the foilage overhead; their song drifted down through a distant, eternal rustle, that was like some huge waterfall heard across many leagues of stillness. Close to a Tree, you had no real sense of its height. It was too enormous: simply there, blocking off half the world. Looking ahead, down the clear shadowy sward, you got a total effect, arched and whispering vaults full of sun, upheld by columns that soared. The forest floor was strewn with tiny white blossoms.

Djuanda turned worshipful eyes from Flandry and said, reddening: "My father, I am ashamed that ever I wished to change this."

"It was not an ill-meant desire," said Tembesi. "You were too young to appreciate that three hundred years of tradition must hold more wis-

dom than any single man." His gray head inclined
to the Terran. "I have yet to offer my thanks for the
rescuing of my son, Captain."

"Oh, forget it," muttered Flandry. "You helped
rescue me, didn't you?"

"For a selfish purpose. Djuanda, your elders are
not quite such doddering old women as you believed. We also want to change the life of the
Trees—more than you ever dreamed."

"By bringing the Terrans!" The boy's voice
cracked loud and exultant across the quiet.

"Well . . . not exactly," demurred Flandry. He
glanced about at the rest. Eager Djuanda, firm
Tembesi, sullen Kemul, unreadable Luang holding his arm . . . he supposed they could be relied
on. The others, though, soft-spoken men with
lithe gait and bold gaze, he didn't know about.
"Uh, we can't proceed too openly, or word will
get back to Biocontrol."

"That has been thought of," said Tembesi. "All
whom you see here are of my own Tree—or clan, if
you prefer, since each Tree is the home of a single
blood-line. I have talked freedom with them for a
long time. Most of our folk can be trusted equally
well. Timidity, treachery, or indiscretion might
make a few dangerous, but they are very few."

"It only takes one," humphed Kemul.

"How could a traitor get word to the outside?"
replied Tembesi. "The next regular trade caravan
is not due for many weeks. I have taken good care
that no one will depart this area meanwhile. Our
few aircraft are all under guard. To go on foot
would require more than thirty days to the next
communication center . . . hence, would be impossible."

"Unless the local dispenser advanced a few pills, given a reasonable-sounding pretext," said Flandry. "Or—wait—the dispenser is in radio touch with Biocontrol all the time!"

Tembesi's chuckle was grim. "Hereabouts," he said, "unpopular dispensers have long tended to meet with accidents. They fall off high branches, or an adderkop bites them, or they go for a walk and are never seen again. The present appointee is my own nephew, and one of our inner-circle conspirators."

Flandry nodded, unsurprised. Even the most villainous governments are bound to have a certain percentage of decent people in them—who, given a chance, often become the most effective enemies of the regime.

"We're safe for a while, I suppose," he decided. "Doubtless Warouw will check the entire planet, hoping to pick up my trail. But he's not likely to think of trying here until a lot of other possibilities have failed."

Djuanda's enthusiasm broke loose again: "And you will free our people!"

Flandry would have preferred a less melodramatic phrasing, but hadn't the heart to say so. He addressed Tembesi: "I gather you aren't too badly off here. And that you're conservative. If Unan Besar is opened to free trade, a lot of things are going to change overnight, including your own ways of life. Is it worth that much to you to be rid of Biocontrol?"

"I asked him the same question," said Luang. "In vain. He had already answered it for himself."

"It is worth it," Tembesi said. "We have kept a degree of independence, but at a cruel cost of narrowing our lives. For we seldom, if ever, have money to undertake new things, or even to travel outside our own land. A Tree will not support many hundred persons, so we must limit the children a family may have. A man is free to choose his life work—but the choice is very small. He is free to speak his mind—but there is little to speak about. And always we must pay our hard-won silvers for pills which cost about half a copper to produce; and always we must dread that some overlord will covet our country and find ways to take it from us; and always our sons must look at the stars, and wonder what is there, and grow old and die without having known."

Flandry nodded again. It was another common phenomenon: revolutions don't originate with slaves or starveling proletarians, but with men who have enough liberty and material well-being to realize how much more they ought to have.

"The trouble is," he said, "a mere uprising won't help. If the whole planet rose against Biocontrol, it would only die. What we need is finesse."

The brown faces around him hardened, as Tembesi spoke for all: "We do not wish to die uselessly. But we have discussed this for years, it was a dream of our fathers before us, and we know our own will. The People of the Trees will hazard death if they must. If we fail, we shall not wait for the sickness to destroy us, but take our children in our arms and leap from the uppermost boughs. Then the Trees can take us back into their own substance, and we will be leaves in the sunlight."

It wasn't really very cold here, but Flandry shivered.

They had now reached a certain bole. Tembesi

stopped. "This we call the Tree Where the Ketjils Nest," he said. "the home of my clan. Welcome, liberator."

Flandry looked up. And up. Plastic rungs had been set into the ancient rough bark. At intervals a platform, ornamented with flowering creepers, offered a breathing spell. But the climb would be long. He sighed and followed his guide.

When he reached the lowest branch, he saw it stretch like a road, outward and curving gradually up. There were no rails. Looking down, he spied earth dizzily far beneath him, and gulped. This close to the leaves, he heard their rustling loud and clear, everywhere around; they made a green gloom, unrestful with a thousand flickering candle-flames of reflection. He saw buildings along the branch, nestled into its forks or perched on swaying ancillary limbs. They were living houses, woven together of parasitic grasses like enormous reeds rooted in the bark—graceful domes and hemicylinders, with wind flapping dyed straw curtains in their doorways. Against the trunk itself stood a long peak-roofed structure of blossoming ood.

"What's that?" asked Flandry.

Djuanda said in an awed whisper, almost lost under the leaf-voices: "The shrine. The gods are there, and a tunnel cut deep into the wood. When a boy is grown, he enters that tunnel for a night. I may not say more."

"The rest are public buildings, storehouses and processing plants and so on," said Tembesi with an obvious desire to turn the conversation elsewhere. "Let us climb further, to where people dwell."

The higher they ascended, the more light and

airy it became. There the buildings were smaller, often gaily patterned. They stood in clusters where boughs forked; a few were attached to the main trunk. The dwellers were about, running barefoot along even the thin and quivering outermost parts as if this were solid ground. Only very young children were restricted, by leash or wattle fence. Physically, this tribe was no different from any other on Unan Besar; their costume varied in mere details of batik; even most of the homely household tasks their women carried out, or the simple furniture glimpsed through uncurtained doorways, was familiar. Their uniqueness was at once more subtle and more striking. It lay in dignified courtesy, which glanced at the newcomers with frank interest but did not nudge or stare, which softened speech and made way for a neighbor coming down a narrow limb. It lay in the attitude toward leaders like Tembesi, respectful but not subservient; in laughter more frequent and less shrill than elsewhere; in the plunk of a samisen, as a boy sat vine-crowned, swinging his feet over windy nothingness and serenading his girl.

"I see flats of vegetables here and there," Flandry remarked. "Where are the big crops you spoke of, Djuanda?"

"You can see one of our harvesting crews a few more boughs up, Captain."

Flandry groaned.

The sight was picturesque, though. From the outer twigs hung lichenoid beards, not unlike Spanish moss. Groups of men went precariously near, using hooks and nets to gather it in. Flandry felt queasy just watching them, but they seemed merry enough at their appalling work. The stuff was carried down by other men to a processing shed, where it would yield the antipyretic drug (Unan Besar had more than one disease!) which was the chief local cash crop.

There were other sources of food, fiber, and income. Entire species of lesser trees and bushes grew on the big ones; mutation and selection had made them useful to man. Semi-domesticated fowl nestled where a share of eggs could be taken. Eventually, branches turned sick; pruning them, cutting them up, treating the residues, amounted to an entire lumber and plastics industry. Bark worms and burrowing insects were a good source of protein, Flandry was assured—though admittedly hunting and fishing down in the ground was more popular.

It was obvious why the planet had only this one stand of titans. The species was moribund, succumbing to a hundred parasitic forms which evolved faster than its own defenses. Now man had established a kind of symbiosis, preserving these last few: one of the rare cases where he had actually helped out nature. *And so,* thought Flandry, *even if I'm not much for bucolic surroundings myself, I've that reason also to like the people of Ranau.*

Near the very top, where branches were more sparse and even the bole swayed a little, Tembesi halted. A plank platform supported a reed hut overgrown with purple-blooming creepers. "This is for the use of newly wed couples, who need some days' privacy," he said. "But I trust you and your wife will consider it your own, Captain, for as long as you honor our clan with your presence."

"Wife?" Flandry blinked. Luang suppressed a

grin. Well . . . solid citizens like these doubtless had equally well-timbered family lives. No reason to disillusion them. "I thank you," he bowed. "Will you not enter with me?"

Tembesi smiled and shook his head. "You are tired and wish to rest, Captain. There are food and drink within for your use. Later we will pester you with formal invitations. Shall we say tonight, an hour after sunset—you will dine at my house? Anyone can guide you there."

"And we'll hear your plans!" cried Djuanda.

Tembesi remained calm; but it flamed in his eyes. "If the Captain so desires."

He bowed. "Good rest, then. Ah—friend Kemul—you are invited to stay with me."

The mugger looked around. "Why not here?" he said belligerently.

"This cabin only has one room."

Kemul stood hunched, legs planted wide apart, arms dangling. He swung his hideous face back and forth, as if watching for an attack. "Luang," he said, "why did we ever snag the Terran?"

The girl struck a light to her cigaret. "I thought it would be interesting," she shrugged. "Now do run along."

A moment more Kemul stood, then shuffled to the platform's edge and down the ladder.

Flandry entered the cabin with Luang. It was cheerfully furnished. The floorboards rocked and vibrated; leaves filled it with an ocean noise. "Cosmos, how I can sleep!" he said.

"Aren't you hungry?" asked Luang. She approached an electric brazier next to a pantry. "I could make you some dinner." With a curiously shy smile: "We wives have to learn cooking."

"I suspect I'm a better cook than you are," he laughed, and went to wash up. Running water was available, though at this height it must be pumped from a cistern thirty meters below. There was even a hot tap. Djuanda had mentioned an extensive use of solar cells in this community as its prime energy source. The Terran stripped off his bedraggled finery, scrubbed, flopped on the bed, and tumbled into sleep.

Luang shook him awake hours later. "Get up, we'll be late for supper." He yawned and slipped on a kilt laid out for him. To hell with anything else. She was equally informal, except for a blossom in her hair. They walked out on the platform.

A moment they paused, then, to look. There weren't many more branches above them; they could see through the now faintly shining leaves to a deep blue-black sky and the earliest stars. The Tree foamed with foliage on either hand and below. It was like standing above a lake and hearing the waters move. Once in a while Flandry glimpsed phosphor globes, hung on twigs far underfoot. But such lighting was more visible on the next Tree, whose vast shadowy mass twinkled with a hundred firefly lanterns. Beyond was the night.

Luang slipped close to him. He felt her shoulder as a silken touch along his arm. "Give me a smoke, will you?" she asked. "I am out."

" 'Fraid I am too."

"Damn!" Her curse was fervent.

"Want one that bad?"

"Yes. I do not like this place."

"Why, I think it's pleasant."

"Too much sky. Not enough people. None of

them my kind of people. Gods! Why *did* I ever tell Kemul to intercept you?"

"Sorry now?"

"Oh . . . no . . . I suppose not. In a way. Dominic—" She caught his hand. Her own fingers were cold. He wished he could make out her expression in the dusk. "Dominic, have you any plans at all? Any hopes?"

"As a matter of fact," he said, "yes."

"You must be crazy. We can't fight a planet. Not even with this ape-folk to help. I know a city, in the opposite hemisphere—or even old Swamp Town, I can hide you there forever, I swear I can—"

"No," he said. "It's good of you, kid, but I'm going ahead with my project. We won't need you, though, so feel free to take off."

Fear edged her tone, for the first time since he had met her: "I do not want to die of the sickness."

"You won't. I'll get clean away, with no suspicion of the fact—"

"Impossible! Every spaceship on this planet is watched!"

"—or else I'll be recaptured. Or, more likely, killed. I'd prefer being killed, I think. But either way, Luang, you've done your share and there's no reason for you to take further risks. I'll speak to Tembesi. You can get a car out of here tomorrow morning."

"And leave you?"

"Uh—"

"No," she said.

They stood unspeaking a while. The Tree soughed and thrummed.

Finally she asked, "Must you act tomorrow already, Dominic?"

"Soon," he replied. "I'd better not give Warouw much time. He's almost as intelligent as I am."

"But tomorrow?" she insisted.

"Well—no. No, I suppose it could wait another day or two. Why?"

"Then wait. Tell Tembesi you have to work out the details of your scheme. But not with him. Let's be alone up here. This wretched planet can spare an extra few hours till it is free—without any idea how to use freedom—can it not?"

"I reckon so."

Flandry dared not be too eager about it, or he might never get up courage for the final hazard. But he couldn't help agreeing with the girl. One more short day and night? Why not? Wasn't a man entitled to a few hours entirely his own, out of the niggardly total granted him?

XIV

Among other measures, Nias Warouw had had a confidential alarm sent all disponsers, to watch for a fugitive of such and such a description and listen (with judicious pumping of the clientele) for any rumors about him. Despite a considerable reward offered, the chief was in no hopes of netting his bird with anything so elementary.

When the personal call arrived for him, he had trouble believing it. "Are you certain?"

"Yes, tuan, quite," answered the young man in the telecom screen. He had identified himself by radio-scanned fingerprints and secret number as well as by name; in the past, hijacker gangs seeking pills for the black market had sometimes used false dispensers. This was absolutely Siak, stationed in Ranau. "He is right in this community. Being as isolated as we are, the average person here knows him only as a visitor from across the sea. So he walks about freely."

"How did he happen to come, do you know?" asked Warouw, elaborately casual.

"Yes, tuan, I have been told. He befriended a youth of our clan in Gunung Utara. The boy released some prisoners of yours; then, with the help of certain local people, they contrived Flandry's escape from Biocontrol Central."

Warouw suppressed a wince at being thus reminded of two successive contretemps. He went on the offensive with a snap: "How do you know all this, dispenser?"

Siak wet his lips before answering nervously, "It seems Flandry hypnotized the boy with gaudy daydreams of seeing Mother Terra. Through the boy, then, Flandry's criminal friends met several other youths of Ranau—restless and reckless—and organized them into a sort of band for the purpose of liberating Flandry and getting him off this planet. Of course, it would be immensely helpful to have me as part of their conspiracy. The first boy, who is a kinsman of mine, sounded me out. I realized something was amiss and responded as he hoped to his hints, in order to draw him out. As soon as I appeared to be of one mind with them, they produced Flandry from the woods and established him in a house here. They claim he is an overseas trader scouting for new markets. . . . Tuan, we must hurry. They have something afoot already. I do not know what. Neither do most of the conspirators. Flandry says that no man can reveal, by accident or treachery, what he has not been told. I only know they do have some means, some device, which they expect to prepare within a very short time. Hurry!"

Warouw controlled a shudder. He had never heard of any interstellar equivalent of radio. But Terra might have her military secrets. Was that Flandry's trump card? He forced himself to speak softly: "I shall."

"But tuan, you must arrive unobserved. Flandry is alert to the chance of being betrayed. With the help of his rebel friends, he must have established a dozen boltholes. If something goes wrong, they will blast down the vault, take a large stock of antitoxin, and escape through the wilderness to complete their apparatus elsewhere. In that case, I am supposed to cooperate with them and pretend to you that I was overpowered. But it would make no difference if I resisted, would it, tuan?"

"I suppose not." Warouw stared out a window, unheeding of the bright gardens. "Judging from your account, a few well-armed men could take him. Can you invite him to your house at a given time, where we will be in ambush?"

"I can do better than that, tuan. I can lead your men to his own house, to await his return. He has been working constantly at the Tree of the Gnarly Boughs, which has a little electronic shop. But in his guise as a trader, he has been asked to dine at noon with my uncle Tembesi. So he will come back to his guest house shortly before, to bathe and change clothes."

"Hm. The problem is to get my people in secretly." Warouw considered the planetary map which filled one wall of his office. "Suppose I land a car in the woods this very day, far enough out from your settlement not to be seen. My men and I will march in afoot, reaching your dispensary at night. Can you then smuggle us by byways to his house?"

"I . . . I think so, tuan, if there are only a few of you. Certain paths, directly from limb to limb rather than along the trunk, are poorly lighted and little frequented after dark. The cabin he uses is high up on the Tree Where the Ketjils Nest, isolated from any others. . . . But tuan, if there can merely be three or four men with you . . . it seems dangerous."

"Bah! Not when each man has a blaster. I do not want a pitched battle with your local rebels, though; the more quietly this affair is handled, the better. So I will leave most of my crew with the aircar. When we have Flandry secured, I will call the pilot to come get us. The rest of the conspiracy can await my leisure. I doubt if anyone but the Terran himself represents any real danger."

"Oh, no, tuan!" exclaimed Siak. "I was hoping you would understand that, and spare the boys. They are only hot-headed, there is no real harm in them—"

"We shall see about that, when all the facts become known," said Warouw bleakly. "You may expect reward and promotion, dispenser . . . unless you bungle something so he escapes again, in which case there will be no sparing of you."

Siak gulped. Sweat glistened on his forehead. "I wish to all the gods there were time to think out a decent plan," said Warouw. He smiled in wryness. "But as it is, I have not even time to complain about the shortness of time." Leaning forward, like a cat at a mousehole: "Now, there are certain details I must know, the layout of your community and—"

XV

As they neared the heights, the sun—low above gleaming crowns—struck through an opening in those leaves which surrounded her and turned Luang's body to molten gold. Flandry stopped.

"What is it?" she asked.

"Just admiring, my sweet." He drew a lungful of dawn air and savored the sad trilling of a ketjil. *There may not be another chance.*

"Enough," grumbled Kemul. "On your way, Terran."

"Be still!" The girl stamped her foot.

Kemul dropped a hand to his blaster and glared out of red eyes. "You have had plenty of time with her, Terran," he said. "Any more stalling now, and Kemul will know for a fact you are afraid."

"Oh, I am," said Flandry, lightly but quite honestly. His pulse hammered; he saw the great branch, the leaves that flickered around it, the score of men who stood close by, with an unnatural sharpness. "Scared spitless."

Luang snarled at the mugger: "You do not have to go up there and face blaster fire!"

Seeing the ugly face, as if she had struck it and broken something within, Flandry knew a moment's pain for Kemul. He said in haste: "That's my own orders, darling. I thought you knew.

Since you insisted on waiting this close to the scene of action, I told him to stand by and protect you in case things got nasty. I won't hear otherwise, either."

She bridled. "Look here, I have always taken care of myself and—"

He stopped her words with a kiss. After a moment's rigidity, she melted against him.

Letting her go, he swung on his heel, grabbed a rung, and went up the bole as fast as he could. Her eyes pursued him until the leaves curtained her off. Then he climbed alone, among murmurous mysterious grottos.

Not quite alone, he told his fears. Tembesi, Siak, young Djuanda, and their comrades came behind. They were lifetime hunters, today on a tiger hunt. But their number and their archaic chemical rifles were of small account against blaster flames.

Well, a man could only die once.

Unfortunately.

The taste of Luang lingered on his mouth. Flandry mounted a final ladder to the platform, which swayed in morning wind. Before him was the cabin. It looked like one arbor of purple flowers. He stepped to the doorway, twitched the drape aside, and entered.

Because the truncheons whacking from either side were not unexpected, he dodged them. His movement threw him to the floor. He rolled over, sat up, and looked into the nozzles of energy guns.

"Be still," hissed Warouw, "or I will boil your eyes with a low beam."

A disgruntled club wielder peered out a vine-screened window. "Nobody else," he said.

"You!" Another Guard kicked Flandry in the ribs. "Was there not a woman with you?"

"No—no—" The Terran picked himself up, very carefully, keeping hands folded atop his head. His gray eyes darted around the hut. Siak had given him a report on the situation, after leaving Warouw here to wait, but Flandry required precise detail.

Two surly Guards posted at the door, sticks still in hand and blasters holstered. Two more, one in each corner, out of jump range, their own guns drawn and converging on him. Warouw close to the center of the room, and to Flandry: a small, deft, compact man with a smile flickering on his lips, wearing only the green kilt and medallion, a blaster in his clutch. The brand of Biocontrol smoldered on his brow like yellow fire.

It was now necessary to hold all their attention for a few seconds. Tembesi's men could climb over the supporting branches rather than up the ladder, and so attain this platform unobserved from the front of the cabin. But it had a rear window too.

"No," said Flandry, "there isn't anyone with me. Not just now. I left her at—Never mind. How in the name of all devils and tax collectors did you locate me so fast? Who tipped you?"

"I think I shall ask the questions," said Warouw. His free hand reached into a pocket and drew forth the flat case of a short-range radiocom. "The girl does not matter, though. If she arrives in the next several minutes, before the car does, we can pick her up too. Otherwise she can wait. Which will not be for long, Captain. A carful of well-armed men is out in the jungle. When they arrive, I will leave them in charge of the local airstrip—and dispensary, in case your noble young morons retain any ideas about raiding it. Then she can give herself up, or wait for a search party to flush her out of hiding, or run into the jungle and die. That last would be a cruel waste of so much beauty, but I do not care immensely."

He was about to thumb the radiocom switch and put the instrument to his lips. Flandry said with great clearness and expression—rather proud of rendering it so well in Pulaoic—"Pillicock sat on Pillicock-hill: Halloo, halloo, loo loo!"

"What?" Warouw exclaimed.

"Take heed o' the foul fiend," cried Flandry: "obey thy parents; keep thy word justly; swear not; commit not with man's sworn spouse; set not thy sweet heart on proud array. Tom's acold."

He twirled once around, laughing, and saw that he had all their eyes. A Guard made signs against evil. Another whispered, "He is going amok, tuan!"

The Terran flapped his arms. "This is the foul fiend Flibbertigibbet," he crowed: "he begins at curfew, and walks till the first cock; he gives the web and the pin, squints the eye, and makes the hare-lip; mildews the white wheat, and hurts the poor creature of earth." He burst into song:

"Swithold footed thrice the old;

He met the nightmare and her nine-fold—"

"Be still!" Warouw stuck the radiocom back in his pocket, advanced, and thrust expert fingers at Flandry's solar plexus.

Flandry didn't remain in the path of that blow.

He tumbled on his back; just in front of the chief. His feet came up, hard, into the groin. As Warouw lurched forward on top of him, driven by the kick as much as the pain, Flandry got the man's gun wrist between two arms and broke the blaster loose. No chance to use it—the effort sent it across the floor, out of reach.

He clutched Warouw against him, shouted, and wondered icily if the Guards would incinerate their own boss to get him.

The four sprang toward the grappling pair.

A rifle cracked at the rear window. A Guard fell backward, brains splashed from his skull. Tembesi fired again. One of the other Guards managed to shoot. Flame engulfed Tembesi. The whole rear wall went up in smoke and thunder. But even as the ecologist died, the room was exposed to outside view. Guns barked from a dozen surrounding boughs.

Flandry saw the last Guard crash to the boards. Fire sheeted up in the flimsy roof. He relaxed his hold on Warouw, preparatory to hustling the man out of the burning hut.

Warouw yanked his left arm free. His fist struck the angle of Flandry's jaw.

For a moment, the Terran sagged among whirling ringing darknesses. Warouw scrambled clear of him, snatched up his blaster, and bounded to the doorway.

As he emerged, a voice from the leaves cried, "Halt where you are!" Warouw showed his teeth and fired full power into that foliage. The Tree man screamed and fell dead off his branch.

Warouw yanked the radiocom from his pocket. A gun spoke. The instrument shattered in his hand. He looked at his bleeding palm, wiped it, fired a thunderbolt in return, and sped for the ladder. Bullets smote the planks near his feet. The hunters hoped for a disabling shot. But they dared not risk killing him. The whole object had been to lure him here and take him alive.

As he reeled from the cabin, Flandry saw Warouw go over the platform edge. The Terran hefted the blaster he himself had picked up, drew a long breath, and forced clarity back into his head. *Someone has to get him,* he thought in an odd unemotional fashion, *and as I'm the only one on my side who knows much about the care and feeding of spitguns, I seem elected.*

He swarmed down the ladder. "Back!" he called, as supple bodies slipped along the branches on either side of him. "Follow me at a distance. Kill him if he kills me, but hold your fire otherwise."

He set his weapon to full-power needle beam, gaining extreme range at the cost of narrowing his radius of destruction to a centimeter or so. If Warouw wasn't quite as handy with pencil shots, there might be a chance to cripple him without suffering much harm from his own diffuse fire. Or there might not.

Down the holy Tree!

Flandry burst into view of the bough where Luang waited. Warouw confronted her and Kemul. Their hands were in the air; he had taken them by surprise. Warouw backed toward the next set of rungs. "Just keep your places and do not follow me," he panted.

Flandry broke through the leaf cover overhead. Warouw saw him, whipped around and raised gun.

"Get him, Kemul!" shouted Luang.

The giant shoved her behind him and pounced. Warouw glimpsed the motion, turned back, saw the mugger's gun not quite out of its holster, and fired. Red flame enveloped Kemul. He roared, once, and fell burning from the limb.

Having thus been given an extra few seconds, Flandry leaped off the bole rungs onto the bough. Warouw's muzzle whirled back to meet him. Flandry's blazed first. Warouw shrieked, lost his gun, and gaped at the hole drilled through his hand.

Flandry whistled. The riflemen of Ranau came and seized Nias Warouw.

XVI

Dusk once more. Flandry emerged from the house of Tembesi. Weariness lay heavy upon him.

Phosphor globes were kindling up and down the Tree Where the Ketjils Nest, and its sister Trees. Through the cool blue air, he could hear mothers call their children home. Men hailed each other, from branch to branch, until the voices of men and leaves and wind became one. The first stars quivered mistily in the east.

Flandry wanted silence for a while. He walked the length of the bough, and of lesser ones forking from it, until he stood on a narrow bifurcation. Leaves still closed his view on either hand, but he could look straight down to the ground, where night rose like a tide, and straight up to the stars.

He stood a time, not thinking of much. When a light footfall shivered the limb beneath him, it was something long expected.

"Hullo, Luang," he said tonelessly.

She came to stand beside him, another slim shadow. "Well," she said, "Kemul is buried now."

"I wish I could have helped you," said Flandry, "but—"

She sighed. "It was better this way. He always swore he would be content to end in a Swamp Town canal. If he must lie under a blossoming bush, I do not think he would want anyone but me there to wish him good rest."

"I wonder why he came to my help."

"I told him to."

"And why did you do that?"

"I don't know. We all do things without thinking, now and then. The thinking comes afterward. I will not let it hurt me." She took his arm. Her hands were tense and unsteady. "Never mind Kemul. Since you have stopped working on him, I take it you have succeeded with Warouw?"

"Yes," said Flandry.

"How did you do it? Torture?" she asked casually.

"Oh, no," he said. "I didn't even withhold medical care for his injuries: which are minor, anyhow. I simply explained that we had a cage for him if he didn't cooperate. It took a few hours' argument to convince him we meant it. Then he yielded. After all, he's an able man. He can leave this planet—he'd better!—and start again elsewhere, and do rather well, I should think."

"Do you mean to let him go?" she protested.

Flandry shrugged. "I had to make the choice as clear-cut as possible—between dying of the sickness, and starting afresh with a substantial cash stake. Though I wonder if the adventurous aspect of it didn't appeal to him most, once I'd dangled a few exotic worlds before his imagination."

"What of that carful of men out in the forest?"

"Warouw's just called them on the dispenser's radiocom, to come and get me. They're to land on the airstrip—change of plan, he said. Djuanda, Siak, and some others are waiting there, with blasters in their hands and revenge in their hearts. It won't be any problem."

"And then what is to happen?"

"Tomorrow Warouw will call Biocontrol. He'll explain that he has me secure, and that some of my co-conspirators spilled enough of what I'd told them for him to understand the situation pretty well. He and some Guards will take me in my own flitter to Spica, accompanied by another ship. En route he'll hypnoprobe me and get the full details. Tentatively, his idea will be to sabotage the flitter, transfer to the other craft, and let mine crash with me aboard. Somewhat later, he and the Guards will land. They'll tell the Imperial officials a carefully doctored story of my visit, say they're returning what they believe was a courtesy call, and be duly shocked to learn of my 'accidental' death. In the course of all this, they'll drop enough false information to convince everyone that Unan Besar is a dreary place with no trade possibilities worth mentioning."

"I see," nodded the girl. "You only sketched the idea to me before. Of course, the 'Guards' will be Ranau men, in uniforms lifted from the car crew; and they will actually be watching Warouw every second, rather than you. But do you really think it can be done without rousing suspicion?"

"I know damn well it can," said Flandry, "be-

cause Warouw has been promised the cage if
Biocontrol does sabotage the Central prematurely. He'll cooperate! Also, remember what slobs
the Guard Corps are. A half-witted horse could
cheat them at pinochle. Bandang and the other
governors shouldn't be hard to diddle either, with
their own trusted Nias Warouw assuring them
everything is lovely."

"When will you come back?" she asked.

"I don't know. Not for a good many days. We'll
take along enough scientific material for the antitoxin to be synthesized, of course . . . and
enough other stuff to convince the Imperial entrepreneurs that Unan Besar is worth their attention. A large supply of pills will have to be made
ready, ships and ships full. Because naturally
Biocontrol Central will be destroyed when they
arrive, by some idiot like Genseng. But the merchant fleet will know where all the dispensaries
are, and be ready to supply each one instantly. It
will all take a while to prepare, though."

Flandry sought yellow Spica in the sky, which
was now quickening with stars. Here they called
Spica the Golden Lotus, doutbless very poetic and
so on. But he felt his own depression and tiredness slide away as he thought of its colony planet,
bright lights, smooth powerful machines, sky-
high towers—his kind of world! And afterward
there would be Home. . . .

Luang sensed it in him. She gripped his arm
and said almost in terror: "You will come back,
will you not? You will not just leave everything to
those merchants?"

"What?" He came startled out of his reverie.
"Oh. I see. Well, honestly, darling, you've noth-

ing to be afraid of. The transition may be a little violent here and there. But you're welcome to remain at Ranau, where things will stay peaceful, until you feel like a triumphal return to Kompong Timur. Or like getting passage to the Imperial planets—"

"I don't care about that!" she cried. "I want your oath you will return with the fleet."

"Well—" He capitulated. "All right. I'll come back for a while."

"And afterward?"

"Look here," he said, alarmed, "I'm as mossless a stone as you'll find in a universe of rolling. I mean, well, if I tried to stay put anywhere, I'd be eating my fingernails in thirty days and eating the carpet in half a year. And, uh, my work isn't such that any, well, any untrained person could—"

"Oh, never mind." She let his arm go. Her voice was flat among the leaves. "It doesn't matter. You need not return at all, Dominic."

"I said I'd do that much," he protested rather feebly.

"It doesn't matter," she repeated. "I never asked for more than a man could give."

She left him. He stared after her. It was hard to tell in the dimness, but he thought she bore her head high. Almost, he followed, but as she vanished among leaves and shadows he decided it was best not to. He stood for a time under the stars, breathing the night wind. Then faintly across ten kilometers, he heard the crash and saw the flare of guns.

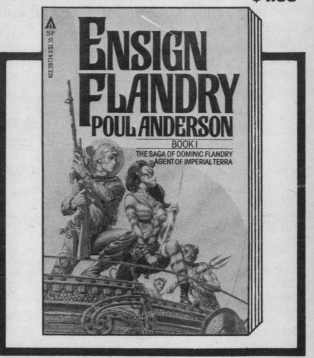

POUL ANDERSON

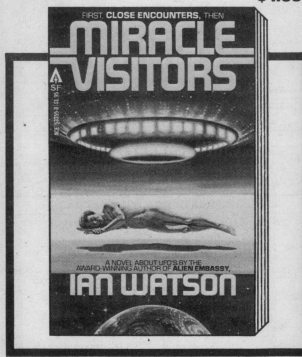